THE MAGIC RING
And Other Tales

Félix Fernández-Madrid

Publisher Information

EBook Bakery www.ebookbakery.com

Email: fMadrid@med.wayne.edu

ISBN - 978-1-953080-41-7

This book is a work of fiction. Names, characters, places and incidents are the product of the author's imagination and are fictionalized. Any resemblance to actual persons, living or dead, business establishments, events, or locales is coincidental.

Dedication

To my beloved Anita, my life's inspiration,
and to my children
Rosemarie, Félix Esteban, Ana María, and Iván Jorge,
who have given us so much

Contents

Forward

These stories are about contemporary or past men and women, about a few non-human beings, and even about a few inanimate objects that come to life in my imagination; the action takes place on a global stage. While globalization is an economic concept, my stories are not intended to judge globalization or evaluate the phenomena as either good or bad. Rather, I am interested in its impact on people, be they in Argentina, Indonesia, Japan, the United States, Europe, or elsewhere on the planet. Technology is an integral aspect of globalization, and it colors our culture in ways that can not be underestimated. Technology has appeared and taken hold in our time as a powerful leveling force that transforms us gradually, almost imperceptibly.

Technology's influence is universal and cannot be ignored. Moreover, to ignore it would be tantamount to foolish suicide. Instant communication, even in the most remote corners of the globe, is undoubtedly wonderful. Every day science discovers new secrets about nature. Many things that might have been relegated to the realm of magic in the past, are now accepted as rational, even commonplace. Hyper-communications have shrunk our world.

While diversity is unlimited in our time, the media has a certain homogenizing effect as it reaches even the most remote places. It tends to make everyone similar somehow, at least superficially.

We've shifted from the printed word to flashing screens with insufficient time to digest what media exposes us to, we are forced to analyze instantly and determine whether there is any truth behind the pre-digested and rapidly changing images on our screens. What we see is almost imperceptibly absorbed by our senses.

Millions of neurons and nerve connections are progressively invaded by trivial information which threatens to impoverish us. A new kind of lonely man is being forged who increasingly lives in a world of virtual reality and interacts with computers and television screens, but increasingly less with fellow human beings in real life. The number of men and women who make cyber loneliness a way of life is likely to increase geometrically, further propelled by the COVID-19 pandemic's isolating impact. And the advent of robotics and AI may have a further distancing affect on the human species.

Individuals who believe themselves to be sophisticated, imitate like monkeys. As if compelled to follow every fashion, they see and parrot the way of life of the most powerful countries. This is nothing new, of course, and is not completely negative. We easily recognize the phenomenon across history from primitive man to current civilizations – all of which have left their mark and contribute to what we have become. But let's not confuse culture's civilizing influence with the negative impact of globalization.

One of the most chilling aspects of globalization is the speed at which a homogenization of the masses is occurring, which the philosopher Ortega y Gasset so poignantly described. Some of that force is unifying and healthy and indicates progress. But a large part of it leads us inadvertently towards intellectual and moral regression. In truth, I am wrong to mention morals, for nowadays this word is not only taboo, but worse, it's outdated. So don't think the stories that follow are intended to moralize, although some do focus on issues we should at least occasionally consider. But in most of them, I merely present the problem and leave the reader the freedom to find solutions.

I believe that different cultures have much to contribute to the germinative plasma that will forge the men of the future, and we must therefore preserve our traditions, our language, and particularly how we experience life. For example, Latin American countries have a strong bond and sense of family that, regardless of age, is itself a civilizing influence. The economics of the wealthier nations also have a powerful influence, but it's often a factor that separates rather than unifies.

As we continue to interact with the rest of the world, let's analyze critically, and adopt those novelties we deem to be good for us, but let us not be embarrassed to respect our own culture. It might help us avoid being absorbed into a global, homogenized, dehumanized humanity and become a mere number.

In 1999 I published a collection of short stories titled *Grey and Pink Tales* which quickly sold out. In this current collection, I included a few of those stories that I think may be especially relevant to the issue of preserving the best in our culture.

Anita, my lifelong companion, encouraged me, reading, rereading, and correcting each story, her valuable contribution can be found in each one. Marcela Fittipaldi gave constructive criticism and convinced me that my stories might have broad appeal. Sylvia Pellizari, Martin Preusche, Alex Wand, Don Jones and my daughters Ana Jones Madrid and Rosemarie Sullivan offered valuable suggestions. Matías Fernández Madrid provided the photographs that were the basis for the book's cover. I assume responsibility for the translation of the quotes preceding the stories, in some cases they may not be entirely accurate.

This collection of stories would never have been published in Spanish or in English were it not for the contribution of my editor, I. Michael Grossman His infinite patience and infectious humor transformed a tedious process into a pleasant experience. We are grateful as well for the skillful translation from Spanish to English by Denise Cikolta.

My thanks to them all.
Félix Fernández Madrid, July 2023

Introduction

Scientific Thinking, Medicine, and Fantasy

Those who don't know me may find it strange to read this collection of stories, written by someone who has spent most of his professional life in the realm of scientific research. I suppose many will think it's unexpected for a researcher to plunge into such an untethered field as fiction because there is no obvious link between the creative process that gives birth to a novel or short story and the rigor and discipline demanded by scientific research. I repeat that although the relationship between scientific thinking and the complex creative process that creates fiction is not immediately evident, and might even at first glance suggest incompatibility, I find the issue a fascinating subject to which I've devoted my attention for years.

If a scientist delves occasionally into the world of fantasy, his reputation would suffer. If he invents results based on forged data, we speak of scientific fraud. Spreading false information facilitates the proliferation of castles built on air, and often results in huge, expensive quantities of sterile research. A writer of fiction on the other hand also expresses truth perceived through a unique lens, with an intent to convincingly convey an imagined reality, though not to deceive the reader. And I don't believe the process has anything in common with the thinking of a scientist that lives in the world of fantasy. However, in my opinion, there are important points of contact between fantastic ideation and scientific thinking that are often overlooked.

Fiction is a wonderful mosaic that, like science, demands rigor and discipline. Writers develop an idea probably born from their own or others' experiences, which moves further and further away from the real world as they create a virtual reality. They shape characters and name them. They invent human or supernatural relationships, and if they're good at their craft, they weave the threads of a story with the power to persuade us.

The scientist develops an idea based on knowledge and personal experience, but while the fiction writer enjoys greater freedom in choosing and developing his subject matter, the scientist's options are necessarily more limited. The scientist's limitations depend on factors such as existing prior studies that cannot and should not be ignored. The first limitation for the scientist in developing a research project comes from his or her field of interest. Thus, a celebrated writer might expound on the astrological meaning of the Orion constellation, write an entertaining comedy, a horror novel, or use metaphors to describe man's daily endeavors, but it is unlikely that a nuclear physicist would publish a study on phylloxera, or that a pediatrician would produce an authoritative dissertation on the habits of the platypus.

I don't suggest that the writer's freedom is unrestrained, but I do feel that they have an immensely broader choice of themes at their disposal than the scientist. They face fewer limitations related to subject, although most certainly their freedom of choice is narrowed by both their own breadth of experiences and their convictions.

The scientist's freedom of choice is restricted like a horse with blinders. Individuals dedicated to science identify an unsolved problem in the field of knowledge they consider important, and then they delve into their limited field of choice. Big and small have different meaning for the writer of fiction and the scientist. For the latter, the field of choice is relatively small of necessity, and if they attempt to broaden the scope, it will often be said that the scientist lacks focus. This can stain the scientist's reputation for in the realm of research it is generally accepted that to be successful in research, one must keep a project's objective focused. Furthermore, the scientist often encounters preconceived, generally accepted ideas within their restricted field of choice. Dogma is usually based on compatible direct or indirect experimental results and supported by the opinions of established investigators. It is approved by the leaders in their field who are the powers who channel research funding or who head up the editorial boards that consider works for publication.

How similar is the creation of scientific truth from fictional truth? The latter is an altered vision of reality that springs from an author's imagination and then is embellished, diminished or changed in some way. While the limits of relativity are narrower than those of fantasy, still scientific truth is far from absolute. It should not surprise anyone that scientific truth is fluid and may be altered in time. Few ancient dogmas have withstood the onslaught of time. The history of science teaches us that scientific truth evolves and many ideas dominant a few centuries ago now seem mere sorcery. Moreover, reading serious works published only decades ago by prominent scientists reveal erroneous conclusions that are now obsolete.

Knowing this leads to an awareness that today's dogmas will be scrutinized in the future, and some of them will give way to newer thinking. Alternately, the opposite can be true. There have been highly qualified scientists whose prophecies were dismissed by the science of their times only to be resurrected after decades. An example was the study authored by Rudolph Virchow, who proposed that the irritation of tissues produced by chronic inflammation can be one cause of cancer. While the study was rejected at the time, the relationship between chronic inflammation and cancer is widely accepted today.

Another noteworthy example is the effect described by Otto Warburg who observed at the beginning of the last century that cancerous cells tend to favor metabolizing glucose to produce energy instead of favoring oxidative phosphorylation in mitochondria, preferred by most normal cells. Although the Warburg effect was eventually confirmed in many labs, its cause continues to be a subject of research.

In general, dogma impedes the evolution of thought, and it often holds back science's progress. At first glance, dogma is like a huge giant terrorizing the novice researcher who attempts to pose questions in areas thrashed out by established researchers before him. The fiction writer, of course, also finds stereotypes that the society of the time either accepts or rejects. So, the scientist and the author of fiction may have similarities that were not initially apparent. The creations of both may clash with preconceived ideas.

In his worthy study on the meaning of writing fiction, Vargas Llosa states that rebelliousness is the starting gate of a writer's vocation. By creating fictitious characters and imaginary events, the writer reveals a rejection of life as manifested in the real world and expresses the desire to substitute a life that the imagination manufactures. I have no doubt that a similar rebelliousness is a facet of scientific thinking, and that it is common ground between the fiction writer and the scientist. A researcher delving into a scientific area for the first time often finds that dogma is treated as if it borders on infallibility because it is so firmly upheld by renowned researchers. In searching through bibliography, it is possible that the young investigators will discover findings that can't be explained by the dogma, and if they are enterprising and daring, they might attempt to formulate an alternative hypothesis that explains known facts.

This is the point - rebelliousness - where the minds of the fiction writer and the scientist resonate at the same wavelength. Scientists might find it difficult to accept that they use elements of fantastic thinking in the process of formulating hypotheses. A scientific hypothesis can be tested by experimentation which offers a chance to obtain evidence in support of or against it. While scientists revere evidence, the relativity of scientific fact usually goes unrecognized. Even experiments that seem to offer conclusive proof can later be interpreted differently as the result of discoveries made in parallel fields. Anyone who has worked in a laboratory knows that many experiments yield negative results, and that discoveries are not made every day. We can't know the magnitude of erroneous scientific hypotheses because the negative results are almost never published.

It is healthy to adopt scientific truth as a starting point and guide to research. But often the fact that scientific truth is relative is ignored both by the general public and by those members of the scientific community who elevate science to the level of religion - one where the dogma is never questioned.

The fiction writer doesn't need to test their fantasy through experimentation, but they also have difficult obstacles to overcome. The tale they invent must be coherent and persuasive, which might explain why, given the enormous mass of fantasy written across the centuries, only a select minority has been strong enough to resist oblivion. Here too we find a parallel between the scientist and the author of fiction since many scientific works are never accepted for publication, and many volumes of fiction that are published, never receive public acclaim.

While the author of fiction must create convincing scenes and characters to be persuasive, the writer will not be impeded by dogma. Peer review is an important aspect of scientific investigation. However the scientist who highlights new observations and sparks the interest of the scientific community will sometimes face reviewers who do not perceive its importance. This is especially true in the case of an original work if their judgment is enslaved by dogma and their minds are closed to new ideas. They may lack the proper background to appreciate the meaning of a unique discovery.

A good fiction writer can appeal to a broad audience. However, while a good scientist's work may be transcendent and cited in hundreds of publications, sometimes the scientist may write for a narrower circle. To be clear, imagination is a desirable, and probably essential prerequisite for a researcher aspiring to contribute to science's advancement. One's methodological prowess, and theoretical or even encyclopedic knowledge, while important, are, without imagination, the attributes of a mediocre investigator. A leading scientist adds imaginative thinking to these essential conditions and exhibits a talent to link seemingly unrelated facts.

We often wonder about the origin of the narratives written by fiction writers. In fiction, an original creation produced in a vacuum and without precedence is extremely rare. Fantasy usually takes shape from facts, circumstances, or people who have left a mark on the writer's mind and set the creative juices flowing. The creator of fiction begins with a naked idea and gradually dresses it in imaginary clothes to the point where it is almost impossible to recognize the fantasy's origins. Vargas Llosa compares this fantastic thought process to an inverted striptease.

But where do the ideas that lead to a scientific discovery come from? Applying Vargas Llosa's metaphor in reverse, we see that scientific thinking is like an actual striptease. Scientific truth is shrouded in layers, and one by one the researcher sheds heretofore unimagined garments until his experiments finally reveal a naked truth. Truth can turn out to be as the researcher imagined it, thus confirming his hypothesis, or perhaps it may take him along untraveled paths to a novel discovery. Even when the naked truth is not as expected, it is still worth finding.

We can't overlook the background that Cervantes himself provides when evoking Don Quixote's virtual struggles with Malambruno and his fantastic journey with Sancho on the back of a wooden horse, or the exploits of Pegasus, Bucephalus, Brilladero, and other famous horses, including the one at Troy. Therefore, Cervantes' ingenious idea, and others that seem to spring out of nowhere in fiction, cannot be considered completely original inventions. Nor can we conceive of a totally original creation in contemporary scientific ideation. A scientific hypothesis must take into account known facts that usually arise in a field where there has been profuse thinking and experimentation, regardless of how unique the researcher's approach might be. Even the most inventive idea generally has a foundation in knowledge that has been painstakingly acquired by the scientific community.

However, there are intangible forces that influence both the scientist's and the fiction writer's ideation. These forces resonate with the mental process that originates a pristine idea that has no obvious antecedent in either fantasy or science. García Lorca was interested in the basic elements of the creative process that give birth to fiction in general and poetry specifically. García Lorca speaks of man's intellectual growth as a process that leads almost unfailingly to a learned ignorance that gradually decreases his creative potential. Here García Lorca was referring to the inhibiting influence of preconceived ideas - including the dogma that prevents both writer and scientist from creating. The poet spoke of intuition or inspiration, or an elfin effect, not unlike the innate wisdom found in children. I would add, without religious intent, that some poets such as García Lorca seem also to have been touched by a "divine hand." In that creative moment, the artist sees the person or object with an inspired uniqueness, a freshness that has never been seen before. One returns from such inspiration like one returns from abroad, says García Lorca, and the poem is the narrative of the journey.

To further dissect that creative moment in science as well as in fiction, I turn to Horatio Walpole, the eighteenth-century English politician. Walpole distinguished himself as a writer and settled in the village of Strawberry Hill on the banks of the Thames. There he had a press on which he printed the first edition of most of his works. Walpole was considered the best letter writer in the English language, and among his many noteworthy works is *The Castle of Otranto*, the first Gothic novel and one that greatly influenced generations of authors. I mention him because in a letter written in 1754, one of his over three thousand letters, he addresses the issue we are discussing - the relationship between fantasy and a scientific hypothesis.

In his letter, Walpole mentions a discovery attributed to "serendipity". In creating that word, Walpole was inspired by Ceylon's ancient name, Serendip, and the word itself came from a title, *The Three Princes of Serendip*. The tale chronicles three princes who, during their travels, make accidental discoveries of unsought facts with great sagacity. So "serendipity" has two main attributes: the chance of discovery and an observer's attentiveness and openness to discovery. In addition, a shrewdness is essential to correctly interpret the meaning of the accidental discovery. One might say that serendipity leads to a fortuitous discovery captured by a receptive observer.

For serendipity to have consequence in science, the researcher must possess imagination that allows him or her enter unexplored territory. For example, a technician makes an accidental mistake that changes the experimental conditions, achieving an unexpected result. In such a case, one's initial thought is that the result is merely a technical error, and this is usually correct. But sometimes it is an original and repeatable outcome that the qualified researcher will recognize as having special significance.

Pasteur, possibly the most brilliant scientist of all time, knew the value of serendipity. For example, when researching tartaric acid, he accidentally discovered crystals that deflect polarized light in the opposite direction, forming mirror images, which ultimately led him to define a new class of substances, isomers.

Another classic example of serendipity involves Argentine scientist Bernardo Houssay, who as a young researcher noticed that his diabetic dog, who had been flooding its cage with a sea of urine every day prior to its surgery, was no longer doing so. This extraordinary phenomenon was related to a pituitary gland resection just performed on the dog. Houssay imagined that the gland could be linked to regulating the metabolism of carbohydrates, and focused his research on the physiology of the pituitary gland. Serendipity placed before young Houssay's eyes an unexpected fact and the alert researcher let his imagination fly. His experiments led him to remarkable discoveries that eventually earned him a Nobel Prize.

Serendipity can play an often-unrecognized role in fiction. Perhaps the writer of fantasy is convinced that his creation is original. Unsought tangents, however, surprising encounters that suggest a character, or ideas that come to mind when taking one street or another, or because we missed a train and witnessed by chance an unexpected scene, are facts that may influence the imaginative processes, and are interpreted in the context of a story and become unrecognizable once they take shape in fiction.

The character in a novel, initially a mere sketch, gradually acquires a personality in the writers' mind with brushstrokes whose origins they can't always pinpoint. I would say that with the sketch as a starting point, a fictional character seems to create itself, and serendipity is hidden in many of the brushstrokes that add to that initial mental drawing that brings a character to life. It is a process similar to spontaneous generation which may occur in fiction but doesn't happen in science and was disproved by Pasteur and Spallanzani.

Both a writer's authenticity and his or her independence are issues that have attracted the attention of literary critics. Those who even subtly use plagiarism as an instrument are not, of course, independent, nor perhaps are those who copy an author's style, though in this case there may be exceptions. Scientific authenticity is not as evident to the lay public who might be dazzled by unpronounceable pseudoscientific terms. A scientist's lack of authenticity, however, is easily detected by the scientific community. While as a rule a fiction writer is the sole author of the work, the complexity of modern research often requires the collaboration of scientists who come together to participate in the publication. The author whose name appears first may be the principal researcher or the one responsible for a critical aspect of the study, but the one appearing last on the list is often the project leader or the scientist with the original idea. A researcher's participation in a publication with multiple authors does not necessarily negate their authenticity since contemporary research requires a convergence of disciplines.

A clear example of when a scientist appears to bring an authentic contribution but does not, is provided by the scientist who participates effectively in numerous quality publications as part of an established team, but disappears into obscurity when no longer in the protective orbit of the institution. When judging them, consider the categories of the journals that publish their work. How thoroughly have they researched their topic during their career? Or have they jumped from multiple, unrelated themes and thus reveal their lack of focus?

Diversity of subject - considered a positive attribute for the fiction writer which underscores his or her imagination and versatility - is usually a negative factor for the scientist. The well-read reader might rightly remind me that this statement is contradicted by the publications of Louis Pasteur, whose extraordinary contributions range across different fields, some apparently quite removed from a chemist's interests. The French genius left an indelible mark in areas as distant from each other as the study of isomeric molecules, his work on fermentation which revolutionized the wine and beer industries, his demolition of the theory of spontaneous generation, his research into silkworm diseases that were ruining the silk industry in France, or into the prevention of fowl cholera, anthrax, and rabies through vaccines, named as such by Pasteur in honor of Jenner. Moving comfortably between varied fields of study, Pasteur behaved much as a fiction writer would, addressing a diverse variety of subjects with impressive authority. In addition to the scientific rigor with which he approached these questions, Pasteur possessed a fertile imagination. While a writer's reputation can sometimes be created by one or two successful novels, a scientist's contribution must often be judged only by considering an entire career.

The last point of contact between fantasy and science concerns the writer's style and the scientist's methods. A novelist's or a poet's style must be convincing. A good example is *100 Años de Soledad* by García Marquez. While in fiction or poetry it may not be critical whether one uses a semicolon or other grammatical expression, what is essential is that the author's style be persuasive. On the other hand, a scientist's methodology must be exact. It is unthinkable for a serious researcher to commit methodological abuses. The effectiveness of a scientific work depends on the internal coherence of the experimental data as well as its repeatability. A scientific work lives on or dies based on its reproducibility independent of its creators. It endures to stimulate other researchers to take the baton and continue the endless search.

While in fiction the written word is practically everything, in a scientific work the written word is only one of many elements that contribute to a meaningful contribution. Good scientific prose is uniformly concrete, sober, avoids redundancy, and does not abound in adjectives. It conveys a concise and clear message. The researcher reports the data and describes what the results have suggested, then relates the experimental findings to previous works, some compatible and others perhaps conflicting. He or she may speculate within limits set by prior knowledge in the field.

There are examples of excellent writers whose scientific career doubtless influenced their literary style. Among those, Voltaire stands out as a prolific writer with a solid scientific background who was also a historian and philosopher. During his exile in England, Voltaire was influenced by the work of Isaac Newton. But it took Voltaire with his characteristically clear and convincing literary style as shown in his book *The Elements of Sir Isaac Newton's Philosophy,* to clarify Newton's ideas and make them accessible to the general public. Voltaire's style, ironic and without exaggeration, and his smooth and simple use of language might be a model for scientific prose.

Writers of fiction invent words or situations that are the fruit of an imagination stimulated by either actual events or by an inner "magic." Likewise, scientists invent words that attempt to metaphorically describe an abstract underworld, a new protein, or a hitherto unknown function. The microscopic world and the dancing of molecules inside a cell are often described metaphorically. As with the fiction writer, such abstraction takes shape in the mind of the scientist who invents a new and elitist language, a true scientific Esperanto, easily understood by a Spanish, English, French, or Chinese scientist while it may be as enigmatic as ancient Sanskrit to the general public.

I believe the parallel between fiction and science occur more frequently than one might think, and that there are fascinating similarities between fantastic ideation and scientific thinking which are noteworthy.

1

The Mansion on Fifth Avenue

1961

To reach the port of heaven,
we must sail sometimes with the wind
and sometimes against it –
but we must sail,
and not drift, nor lie at anchor.

-Oliver Wendell Holmes,
The Autocrat of the Breakfast Table

BLURRY RECOLLECTIONS from my idyllic childhood occasionally take shape and come into focus, nudging me to keep moving forward. I was filled with memories: like playing hopscotch and marbles on the hard-packed dirt of our grade school playground; pickup football games in vacant lots, especially the time I scored one amazing goal and the time I refused to dance the Argentinian pericón because I was too shy on the holiday commemorating when we broke ties with Spain. There were others: having to stay after class for not knowing my lessons; the face of my first-grade teacher, with whom I was hopelessly in love; the girl with a cute little snub nose and dark braids who sat at the desk near mine, routinely ignoring me.

I remember my mother's unhappy features and try hard to forget my father's wandering. Later on I recall my endless engagement to Elena, mercifully brought to an end when she tired of waiting and married another. And the crowning achievement of my youth: my failed studies.

It was such a huge disappointment for after burning the midnight oil for so long, I finally got my degree and hung it proudly on the wall of my bachelor pad. It turned out to be about as useful as a one-way ticket to the moon. It would certainly be easy to lay my failings on the country's situation, but in reality I have only myself to blame.

As a child I loved to climb trees. Behind our house there was an enormous oak tree with leafy, twisted branches which we all climbed daily. This tree was a powerful magnet for our small gang of friends.

As we climbed across the branches, decisions had to be made. There were thick, sturdy branches, and thinner, more challenging ones to choose. Some kids climbed higher than others, and the reward for any who reached the topmost branches was a spectacular view of the rooftop next door, where our beautiful blonde young neighbor frequently sunbathed in topless splendor. I only heard about it, because I never could reach the highest branches.

Now in the twilight of my life, I often think about that tree of decisions where I learned so much, albeit too late. In those days life was like the oak tree, whenever we reached the branching of two limbs, we had to choose one and the decision either led us somewhere, or nowhere at all. Sometimes, faced with two branches, I was unable to opt for one or the other, and I now understand that failing to decide was the worst thing I could do. In those days I did not know how to interpret my indecision. Today I think about stagnation or even worse, of complacency. So it was that I could only imagine my beautiful neighbor, while a few in my gang enjoyed the view from the highest branches. Just as I was incapable of seeing my neighbor's curves from the top of the oak, I never progressed beyond my diploma which still hangs on the wall.

There came a day when I realized I was no longer a kid and I found myself at a loss with how to proceed and if I was spending my time fruitfully: the bohemian lifestyle of endless nights spent with friends at the corner café, solving the political and economic problems not only of Argentina but of the whole world; playing billiards with friends or sitting across from them at a mesmerizing chessboard; the Saturday night dances at the neighborhood clubs; all of it was sprinkled with abundant sweat during the many daily miles racked up in my unauthorized gypsy cab. This was the sum of my existence.

The country that I observed while driving my cab was quite different from what politicians saw when searching for their next business opportunity, or what rich young men viewed through their rose-colored glasses, or what foreigners experienced as they pass through town, or even the world as experienced by the profiteering investors and hard-hearted IMF bankers who carried on about austerity measures. I could write an entire book, or maybe several, based on my experience as a cab driver.

On one Sunday evening after dropping off a passenger in Barrancas de Belgrano, I was on my way home, tired and hungry. I had to slow down as I neared the River Plate football stadium for a crowd of reckless fans leaving after the game and crossing the avenue while weaving dangerously through traffic. Not wanting to hit anyone, I drove slowly. Almost at a standstill, I suddenly noticed a group of guys surrounding someone in a threatening manner. I don't know why I did it, but I immediately swung the steering wheel towards the sidewalk and shone the cab's headlights on the scene.

As if touched by a magic wand the thugs vanished and only a young man remained in the spotlight, looking like a wet chick, soaked in sweat and with an infinite relief on his face from being freed of the siege. His turned-out empty pockets were evidence of the abuse.

He approached the cab and said in clear Spanish that I identified as being from somewhere in Latin America, "Thank you! Thank you. Can you take me downtown?"

I wasn't planning on picking up any more fares, but as it was on my way I said, "Hop in."

"Thanks again for saving me. You've changed my opinion of Buenos Aires cab drivers."

"Why is that? Have you had a bad experience with one of my colleagues?"

"Nothing overly upsetting. My day began in a cab and ended in a cab. I flew in from Miami this morning, and as I didn't have any change, I determined the cost of the ride with the cabdriver beforehand, as I always do, and when we arrived, he gave me my change in dollars. I went to see the game carrying only the change from the cabdriver, leaving he rest of my money in my hotel room."

"Say no more, I can imagine what happened."

"Yes, exactly what you're thinking. When I went to the ticket counter, they stared at my money for a long time. I asked if there was a problem. 'Don't you accept dollars?'

"He said, 'Of course we do, but only real ones. The only thing these bills have in common with real ones is that they are green,' and he handed them back to me.

"I put them in my pocket and walked away, discouraged.

"I was resigned to not seeing the game when I was approached by a scalper who offered me a ticket at "a special, low price", which was actually much higher than the published ticket price. I didn't think twice, stuck my hand in my pocket, pulled out one of the green bills and smiled, saying it was all I had. That was true, but it wasn't the whole truth. The guy snatched the bills from my hand, handed over the ticket, and vanished.

"The game was excellent, but as I walked along near where you found me, six or seven guys came up to me. At first, they walked on either side of me and spoke gruffly, asking whether I was a foreigner. I told them I was Colombian and visiting Buenos Aires. They asked whether I was a fan of River or Boca, and I assured them I was neither so nobody would feel insulted. But my indefinite reply didn't work. They told me I should know that it's dangerous to walk around in Buenos Aires with money. I said I was aware of that, which is when they surrounded me and their leader demanded all my money!

"They grabbed the rest of the fake dollars, checking all my pockets. Just when the thugs were patting down every nook on my body, your cab lights illuminated the sidewalk and they vanished.

"Just imagine how the gang must have cursed me when they tried to spend that money and discovered the fake dollars. I do feel a bit sorry for the ticket scalper because he was only trying to make a living."

We were nearing the end of the ride and my passenger hurried to say, "Please wait while I run up to get your money for the fare."

"Don't worry about it," I said, "I was done for the day." I laughed, adding, "I don't accept dollars because I can't tell the fake ones from the real ones!"

When I look back, the memory of the tall tree in my backyard comes to my mind. I wonder if it's possible to find a branch that leads us to our destiny without breaking off. Too often I chose a weak branch that couldn't hold my weight. I've fallen so many times though my stumbles had no more physical consequences than a scrape or two. Occasionally, before the branch gave way, I would realize that it was about to crack, and I would inch back to avoid a fall. I would try to climb on to another branch that I had previously forgone.

The oak taught me that seizing the right moment is essential when making decisions. Time is an abstract dimension that we have difficulty comprehending, and when we are young, we waste it because we think we have so much of it.

My friends used to tell me that with all my abilities I would go far. I wouldn't respond, and although their arguments were not convincing, and after much pondering, feeling there was nothing to lose, I decided to seek new horizons. With a few pesos I got by selling my rickety cab and some cash my uncle Venancio gave me - God bless him - I headed out with the hope of a new life. Many, many moons have passed since then. How many? I can't remember but a great deal of time did pass.

I woke up late this morning and left my enchanted mansion as I do every day, with the hope of conquering the world. It had snowed all night but the sun shone brightly on the city.

I walked several blocks and arrived at one of my favorite corners, where there is a lot of student traffic and a low marble wall where I often set up headquarters. I brushed off the dry snow with a newspaper I had picked up off the sidewalk and set up my chessboard, pulling from my pocket my usual sign that is now almost illegible since the white background is so faded: *"One game, 50¢."*

At noon students would swarm from their classes and frequently one would take my bait. Sometimes I would earn enough to get something to eat.

My first victim that day was a beautiful Asian woman who appeared on my radar, her books in a backpack. Smiling broadly, she asked, "Why are you selling yourself so cheaply?"

With a strained smile I eyed my tattered sign and replied, "It's not that I'm selling myself cheaply. That was the price when I began to use my sign a long time ago. I guess inertia has impeded me from changing it."

We played rapid chess, and after only a few moves I knew this girl was a wolf in sheep's clothing. I won in a pawn endgame, having thoroughly enjoyed the tough match. It isn't every day that I find someone who challenges me.

The young woman unnerved me so that I lost the second match, unable to counter a surprise attack on my king's flank. When later in the stillness of my enchanted mansion I analyzed the game, I set aside my cheap excuses. But the defeat hurt my pride. I had fallen for her ploy like a novice player. The woman's smile showed her perfect white teeth and her lively eyes seemed to impishly say, "*Gotcha!*"

I tipped my king over, shook my opponent's hand and while she paid me, I suggested a rematch to avenge my defeat.

"Play another?" I asked, unable to hide my eagerness. The girl stated she hardly had any time left, but not wanting to deny me a chance to get even, she relented.

I got the white pieces and used an English Opening that I thought she wouldn't know. This time I focused and poured onto the board everything I had learned from master Jacob so many years before, but the woman seemed possessed and anticipated my most brilliant combinations. It soon became clear that we'd reached a stalemate, and we called it a draw.

She opened her purse to pay me but I refused. I had asked for a rematch and it was a matter of principle even if I could have used the money. Maybe I stupidly thought that ethics were more important than hunger.

The day turned inclement; thick dark clouds hid the sun and very small snowflakes drifted about. The cold was freezing my rear which rested on the marble and after a while, seeing as no other prey was forthcoming, I gathered up the pieces, tucked the board under my arm and walked away whistling softly to myself. The match with the young student had my blood running, and my earnings enabled me to buy two fresh buns and a chunk of soft *brie* at a special place I know.

One of the stores on Fifth Avenue had hot air fans at the doorway and I stopped under one to thaw out my frozen bones. I slowly ate the cheese sandwich that I made using one of the buns and put away the other one in my pocket for later that evening.

While I finished my meal, I looked at the store window. There were all styles of clothes, from fancy to bizarre. The mannequins depicted young and old, black, white, and yellow, most of them were dressed elegantly and artistically arranged. But suddenly an especially strange one caught my eye, and I thought, *That one's in poor taste!*

In the window I saw a mannequin dressed as an old bald man with a white beard and unfocused eyes that looked like hard-boiled eggs. His torn, faded coat, ragged pants and old sneakers with holes had seen better days. I pondered on the window-dressers' stupidity. *Why use worn, second-hand clothing?* At that moment a uniformed man stepped into the window scene and placed his hand on the mannequin's shoulder as a polite voice instructed me firmly, "Please move along, sir."

I wandered aimlessly for a long while, following my instinct, sometimes changing my direction whenever I brushed against pedestrians.

Night fell quickly and I found myself walking slowly down Fifth Avenue, the snow thick on my shoulders as I sung a sad tango about love and loss.

After a while, I thought it was time to find somewhere to spend the night and spotted a round snow-covered "igloo" shape. I wiped off the soft snow, revealing the pale, blue plastic beneath. The "igloo" seemed ideal. I shook the blue plastic sides preparing to enter when I heard a growl from inside – sounding not unlike a bear.

Annoyed, I thought, *Too bad. It's taken.*

I continued walking until I saw another large "igloo". A potential competitor was walking quickly toward it from the opposite direction. I quickened my pace and arrived before my rival who glanced at me disdainfully, walking on when he realized I had already staked my claim on the fine lodging. Infused now with the peace of mind of one who has arrived at his destination, I brushed off the dry snow covering the plastic and found that it was pink, a color that has become my favorite in the latter years of my life. I carefully undid the string that held one end of the "igloo" closed, releasing from inside a warm, pervasive, and very promising smell of aged Limburger.

There is much life here! I cheerfully thought.

Opening the edge of the plastic bag, I inserted my feet and made my way through the tangle of precious objects. Once inside I found that my chamber was quite spacious, and I closed it up from within, having acquired a special skill to that effect over the years. The streetlight shone through the pink plastic dimly illuminating the furnishings in my handsome dwelling, bringing life to the wonders surrounding me.

As I settled into my mansion, my hand brushed against a warm, sticky mass that trembled on my palm and which I immediately recognized. I was hungry as I hadn't had a thing to eat since the cheese at noon, and remembered I still had a bun in my pocket. Happily, I found that it was still fresh, and tore it in half. Sinking my hand into the seething mass I pulled out a fistful of long thin little noodles that wiggled around in an infernal dance, tickling my palm. I covered one half of the bun with the delicacy until it overflowed, and placed the other half on top.

So delicious!

Still tasting my delightful dinner, I fell asleep, lulled by the warmth within my lair, plunging once more into nocturnal bliss.

That night I was visited by the young student who I had been unable to defeat despite my best efforts. I was immobilized by her ease, her confidence, her enchanting smile that showed beautiful, ivory teeth. The spell finally broke and I woke up. I tried to dream of her again, to find her again and play the definitive match, but she did not return that night.

At dawn I decided to leave the warmth of my enchanted mansion. I untied the end of the bag and slowly exited the "igloo", returning the luxurious furnishings to their proper place. Then I closed it – always being thoughtful of others – and left it exactly as I had found it the night before.

The freezing morning air was invigorating. Snow fell softly on my bare head. I shook happily like a wet dog, and with my chessboard under my arm and Neruda's *The Captain's Verses* in my pocket, I left my enchanted mansion and strolled along the streets whistling my favorite tango, "La Cumparsita", ready once again to conquer the world.

2

A Masterful Caricature

1995

Art is the magic mirror you make
to reflect your invisible dreams...

-**George Bernard Shaw,**
Back to Methuselah

I -IDYLLIC SILESIA

MY EARLIEST recollection of Silesia is of the imposing Rauenstein Castle, rising in the mountains of Saxony near the border with Czechoslovakia where my father was a gamekeeper. The castle, built around 900 AD when most of the population was Slavic, had changed hands many times over the centuries. After the vandalism that swept the region during the Tartar invasion, the ravaged town of Breslau was rebuilt as a German city.

Once a year, a group of richly-garbed lords would come to hunt in the forests surrounding the castle and to stay in the castle chambers for a few days. After the hunt, during a great feast, their shouts and loud guffaws disturbed the peace of the castle late into the night. The castle was empty except for our family and a few caretakers and servants, and as a child I had the run of the place and knew all its nooks like the back of my hand. Except during the dreadful yearly hunts, I thought that the castle belonged to me.

As we gathered near the burning logs of the fireplace on winter evenings, my father would regale us with memorable legends of the bloody struggles between Bohemian, Polish, Austrian, and German princes. The great castle door still bore several gaps, evidence of the damage inflicted upon it by Prince Otto's troops during the previous century.

In the middle of the castle's large flagstone patio, whose high walls were bordered with suits of armor, there was a beautiful fountain with tiles studded with reddish spots. According to the legend, it was here that, one by one, Prince Charles of Bohemia, his wife Princess Charlotte, and their six children were beheaded.

One of my favorite games was to roam the castle's darkest corners and chat with the ghosts of those who had lived there in the past. This amusing pastime was brought to an abrupt end when, just when it was getting interesting, Mother happened to witness my romantic tête-à-tête with Caroline, one of Princess Charlotte's daughters. At the time, I felt Mother's categorical ban was quite arbitrary.

During a childhood devoid of siblings or friends, I developed a passionate interest in nature. I loved to roam the wildflowers and the mysterious forests teeming with birds and wildlife, and the mountains and meandering streams rushing down from the snowy peaks. Wandering joyfully through the woods, I would not encounter a single soul for miles. I loved to be alone with nature. In time I understood that the quiet was not silence, but rather a symphony of leaves fluttering in the breeze, rain falling on the forest, and the birdsong I knew so well. It was as if the large and small animals and even the tiniest insects played their instruments like musicians in a celestial orchestra performing exclusively for me.

My memories of the harsh winters in my earliest years are very clear. From the castle on the mountain, I would ski downhill and arrive one hour later at the tiny school on the outskirts of Breslau. Mr. Schmidt, the schoolteacher, had students of all ages. Some, like me, could already read and write, while others were just learning. The amazing Mr. Schmidt was the heart of the school. He maintained rigid discipline and the older students helped him. Equipped only with an old blackboard, some chalk, and one eraser, we took turns reading from a limited number of books.

I was eight in 1918 when the Armistice silenced the cannons. This time the quarrel between Poles and Germans over ownership of Silesia hadn't reached Rauenstein Castle, but I recall that my parents traveled down to the city to vote in the plebiscite that would divide Silesia. As good Saxons, my parents were usually very phlegmatic, but this time they were quite agitated. As a result of the voting, the castle where we lived was now located in German Silesia.

This unforgettable bucolic period of my life unfolded amid untamed nature and the dozens of books that I would devour with great pleasure. I had time to think about a world I dreamed of seeing.

As the years passed, I came increasingly to look like my father. During summers I would help him chop wood, stacking it next to our house before the first snows of autumn.

One summer afternoon, during one of my explorations in the thickest part of the forest, I came upon a mountain river lined with pines, a feast for the eyes. Here I encountered a simply-dressed young woman sitting quietly on a stool and painting the view on a canvas set on an easel. I approached her slowly, her painting pulling me like a magnet. Noticing me, with a friendly smile the artist invited me to come closer.

I greeted her, saying "May I watch you work? I promise not to bother you."

"You are no bother at all," she replied as she wiped her paintbrush clean, choosing another blend of colors.

Two hours or so passed as I watched in awe until she had finished her work for the day. We chatted and I told her I would like to paint like her someday.

"If you are interested in learning you can come here every afternoon this week, and we shall see what you are capable of," said the artist.

My heart was pounding that evening when I returned to the castle. I knew that meeting would change my life. I returned every afternoon to observe the painter, who introduced me to a world I never suspected existed.

On the day she left to return to her home in Berlin she said to me, "You are practically still a child, but I see that you have a talent for painting. Maybe one day you will be a famous artist and remember me."

Often during my life, I thought about my providential encounter with the painter. At the little school in Breslau, I put all my efforts into our art classes and started painting on my own with my scant beginner's equipment. Imagine my surprise when almost a year later I received a letter postmarked from Berlin. That well-known artist had not forgotten me and had recommended me for a summer scholarship at a fine arts school in Berlin.

II -BERLIN, A PRESSURE-COOKER

The Berlin scholarship opened the doors to a new world for me. The pastoral, contemplative tone of my early years in Silesia vanished and my life became a whirlwind. The contrast between my rural upbringing in Silesia and the sophistication of my life in Berlin was noteworthy, but both stages of my life made a permanent impressions on my personality. Although I worked hard and adapted to the maelstrom that was Berlin, I also continued to enjoy solitude and meditation.

During the last half of the 19th century and the beginning of the 20th, Germany had undergone an industrial revolution and became a world power. That was lost, however, when the Great War crushed it. Millions of men died in combat, morale was poor, and Germany's national pride had been mortally wounded.

Despite the country's precarious post-war economic situation, by the 1930s Berlin once again became an important center of industry and commerce.

I was 18 when I arrived in Berlin for my studies. The economy had improved somewhat but was still weak and unstable. Inflation had reached astronomic levels, there was rampant unemployment and the economic burdens tied to reparations from war damages made the lives of Germans very difficult. The collapse of the New York Stock Exchange in October of 1929 echoed throughout Germany where the economic crisis worsened. Though I was in the midst of this economic disaster, as a scholarship student I was temporarily sheltered from it.

A little over three years later, after having received only about 800,000 votes in the 1928 elections, the National Socialist party carried Adolph Hitler to power. He came at a critical moment for the country and succeeded by offering an attractive political and economic platform that promised glory and jobs. The citizenry idolized Hitler and young people bubbled with enthusiasm, viewing him as an engine for German recovery after the humiliating defeat of the First World War.

My life hurdled along and I had little time to think about anything but my art which flourished within me. Yet I was concerned about the country's political and social situation and particularly anxious about Hitler's rabble-rousing speeches and his thinly veiled racism that later turned to blatant anti-antisemitism. It was hard to stay out of political issues, but I managed to do so by concentrating on my studies and focusing my efforts on my career. I stayed focused on my art despite the fact that several times I was emphatically urged to participate in activities organized by the National Socialist Youth.

My studies at the art school were not in vain and by the time I finished, I felt self-assured and envisioned my future with optimism.

After graduating from the Fine Arts Academy, I was employed at a Babelsberg Film Studio. It was the golden age of film worldwide, culminating in the development of the first films with sound in 1927 which did not come to Germany until late 1929. Artists were in great demand to paint all types of backdrops and advertising posters. Nothing was routine at Babelsberg. Every day was different and time seemed to fly. I frequently worked at the studio until very late, and when I could no longer stay awake, I would sleep in one of the "Star" dressing rooms. One morning I overslept and was startled awake when someone shook my legs.

"Wake up, you lazy bum. I must change my outfit," a familiar voice said laughingly. Sitting at the foot of the comfortable couch where I had spent the night was the Blue Angel herself, Marlene Dietrich. She began her daily routine and I hurried out of her dressing room.

Babelsberg vigorously attempted to compete with Hollywood. The studio benefited from the mark's devaluation which lowered production costs and taxes, and made it attractive to export films abroad. But the battle between Hollywood and Babelsberg was short-lived. Soon Marlene and other stars, and the best producers and specialized technicians were absorbed by Hollywood. Nevertheless in my tiny, youthful artistic world, I felt like I was living a dream, painting backdrops for many of the best films of that era.

It was then that I met Hans, who worked in the studio's laboratory. An industrial chemist, Hans had been hired because of his photographic expertise. It was not uncommon to find him working in his lab at all hours, surrounded by developer trays, silver halides, and dark purple permanganate crystals. We became good friends and frequently went out together in Babelsberg to dine, drink beer and have a good time.

Hans had a strong political convictions and no doubts about the Führer's political intentions. We agreed that the persecution of Jews was not only obvious but that the Hitler's supporters suppressed much of the opposition, labeling them as treasonous. The meetings of the Social Democratic Party, to which we both belonged, were often violently interrupted, its speakers assaulted, and its press releases suppressed.

One day Hans did not show up at the studio for work, and it was said that he had been "volunteered" into the army. All my efforts to discover his whereabouts were in vain. World War II broke out shortly thereafter.

III - SILESIA TURNS GRIM

The Führer proclaimed that German Jews were responsible for Germany's ills. Between 1933 and 1938, with a series of laws, seizures, and pogroms, Hitler eroded the political and economic foundations of German Judaism. Jews were successively stripped of their German nationality, their synagogues, and their assets, and were transported in rail cars to concentration camps where they were systematically exterminated.

During the century's second world war, Germans established a concentration camp called Auschwitz-Birkenau near Oświęcim. The camp was situated in southern Poland, in Kraków province, near the confluence of the Vistula and Soła rivers, an area which had been incorporated to Silesia in the 12th century. Hans had not only been inducted into the army like most Germans of the same age, he had been assigned to a post at Auschwitz that tortured his soul. The first Jews arrived at Auschwitz in July of 1940.

The emaciated prisoners were transported in rail cars and were already half dead from hunger and thirst upon arrival. Seeing gas chambers, and mass graves leveled with tractors was routine at Auschwitz and Hans could not bear what he witnessed. Finally he refused to continue being one more cog in the terror machine that surrounded him. He frequently vomited, and the nausea never left him. His gaunt face turned even more pasty, and he lost so much weight that his uniform hung from his frame. He reported to the camp's infirmary, but the military doctor determined that Hans was healthy and able to continue performing his duties.

IV -HANS' LEGACY

After the Führer's downfall, the German army scattered, and predator became prey. In a small village in northern Czechoslovakia, just when the town was being overrun by the advancing Russian forces, I encountered Hans once again on a narrow street.

Hans and I along with others who survived the machine gun fire were quickly rounded up by Russian soldiers. Hans had deserted the army and left his camp shortly before and he was ordered into the prisoner truck with me, destination unknown. For a short while our destinies followed the same path, and Hans was again my companion. When we arrived at our destination, the Russian soldiers opened the truck doors. Hans felt it was a horrible nightmare. He had recently concentrated all his energy on escaping the camp where he had been stationed for four years. Now fate brought him back to that very camp, this time as a prisoner.

The infirmary of the concentration camp at Auschwitz was as similar to hell as one could imagine: a huge barracks with cold cement floors a single door guarded by a couple of soldiers. Dozens of cots were lined side-by-side in an open space in the middle where a few wooden tables were crammed. Shelves were lined with dirty jars and bandages stained with urine and blood. Anyone entering the barracks was bowled over by the fetid stink in the air though the poor souls inside had grown used to it. The infirmary could not keep up with the number of prisoners due to an epidemic of diarrhea that overwhelmed the concentration camp's sanitation facilities.

I had had explosive diarrhea for over a week, and I hovered between life and death in the infirmary for days. All around me dozens of dying men lay in puddles of their own excrement, adding to the desolate panorama. No one was ever released from the infirmary. Prisoners died soon after being admitted and were rapidly replaced by new patients in an equally dire condition.

Considerable time had passed since Hans' sudden disappearance in Babelsberg. Now Hans lay on a cot beside me, barely recognizable, exhausted from his diarrhea, dehydrated and bloated. In one of his last conscious moments on his deathbed, Hans pointed with a shaky hand towards a bucket filled with bluish liquid. I could barely see it, and at that moment I didn't have the strength to give the colored brew a second thought.

Hans drew his last breath during the night, and after a while a couple of guards took him away, taking Hans' body, wrapped in a faded burlap bag. I spent a troubled night, in and out of delirium, when I remembered my friend's ineffective attempt to try to tell me something important. But it wasn't until after his death that I was able to understand what he had been trying to show me.

With barely enough strength left to reach the nearby bucket, I moved it towards me. By the time the guards came back to ready the cot for the next candidate, Hans' bucket was mine. This was the only legacy that Hans left behind, a bucket filled with a colored liquid, standing next to my own deathbed. Treating the diarrhea epidemic at Auschwitz had depleted all hydrating liquids and medicines, and even water was scarce. I was so weak I could barely sit up.

I suddenly came to and again remembered Hans' bucket. I dipped my fingers in the bluish liquid and put them in my mouth to see what it was. It tasted horrible but I recognized it immediately: potassium permanganate.

Inspired by providence I lay face down on my cot and placing my lips on the edge of the bucket I drank deeply, consuming nearly half of it. As I drank, I felt a fire burning my insides. I fell into a restless sleep, waking often to the sounds of some poor dying soul wheezing, and the removal of the remains by the men assigned to that sad task. Each time I awoke, I sipped the remainder of the permanganate despite the burning sensation in my stomach.

The situation around me the next morning was macabre. Several cadavers remained, laying exactly where they had died since deaths in the infirmary happened so quickly the orderlies could not keep up. To my surprise, however, I felt much better. My tongue was no longer stuck to the roof of my mouth and I was easily able to stand next to my cot. My gut had finally settled down. Poor Hans had bequeathed to me the gift of life, but lost his own. The morning medical review confirmed my recovery, and I was quickly sent back to the regular detention barracks. I had lost a lot of weight and felt weak, but I slowly recovered with the daily rations and some water.

One afternoon shortly thereafter we were grouped together like cattle in front of the square – there were several hundred of us. We were told we would be split into two groups with no other explanation. We were herded like animals to the slaughterhouse – which was not too far from the truth. They sent us up the road and I could discern a cargo train at the top of the hill, its engine puffing. Two soldiers stood at the top and split the column of prisoners, sending some to either one side or the other. Their choice seemed random to me. I soon learned that prisoners still strong enough to work were kept alive, and those that seemed weaker and useless were sent to board the train to their final destination. As soon as I saw the train, for some unknown reason I knew I didn't want to get on it. When it was my turn and the soldier pointed me towards the tracks, after a few bumbling steps I changed direction and quickly joined the other column. My rapid move went unnoticed by the soldiers, who were busy directing traffic. My intuition once again saved my life, for none of my fellow prisoners who boarded the train were ever heard from again. It was said they were gassed to death.

My health continued to improve although I was very pale and looked like a skeleton. One afternoon we were in line for the weekly prisoner check when I noticed that someone had left some paper and a pencil on a nearby table. I instinctively picked up the pencil and without thinking began to draw a cartoon of the Russian officer in charge of the prisoners.

It was finished in a minute. I can still recall it: a grotesque face with very tiny eyes, thick eyebrows, and a small mustache under a ridiculously large nose. My companions in line could barely contain their snickers. Then, noticing unusual activity, the officer asked what the fuss was about. Though nobody said a word, their glances gave me away and I had no recourse but to lay my artwork on the table.

The officer stood stiffly and stepped back to better appreciate it. His severe face did not bode well for the caricaturist. It was very quiet for an instant though I felt the moment lasted forever. But finally the officer burst into laughter and slapped me on the back, almost tumbling me to the floor. He told me to see him the following day.

In all my career as an artist, the highest price I ever received for my work was what I was given for that caricature: a bath, with soap, clean overalls to wear, somewhat decent food, and an occasional cigarette.

In Auschwitz, this was an incalculable fortune.

3

The Enchanted Villa

1995

Ode to Pinot Noir

Peerless red wine,
...your body is always mysterious,
at times subtle and sensual,
or firm and harmonious
like a celestial dancer,
but at your utmost grandeur
you have the body of a god on Olympus
transfigured within the crystal

-Félix Fernández Madrid,
Calidoscopio

WE TRAVELED FROM Paris to Beaune searching for Saint Romain in the heart of Bourgogne, where we would meet Gaston and Marie. Although Saint Romain is a very small place that did not appear on any of our road maps, Gaston's instructions had been clear and we were sure we would find it easily.

Ten kilometers after Beaune heading south, a turn to the right and arriving at Auxey Duresses, we encountered Saint Romain, a jewel in Côte de Beaune with meandering streets climbing the steep hillside slopes. Gaston had said that if we did not find them home in their house in lower Saint Romain, we should head directly to the villa used for their frequent guests, to which we had also been given instructions – though not as clear.

Arriving in Saint Romain late in the afternoon, we found that they were not at home, so as instructed we went on to the villa where we were to spend the night. We drove uptown towards a small group of ancient houses built on the crest of the slope. Past the small plaza in front of the old church built in the 12th century, we easily recognized the house with the white gate and rang the bell. When nobody responded, we opened the gate and saw quite prominently displayed on the door a handwritten note that said: "Welcome, please make yourselves at home." The door was unlocked so we went inside the obviously empty house.

Sunsets are splendid in Bourgogne. Through a large back door, we stepped into a garden with a spectacular view of the Côte. We were surrounded by wonderful, natural beauty and were happy to have been welcomed so splendidly despite finding no one in the villa. We enjoyed the patio, exceptionally designed with abundant flowers and carefully tended. The heated swimming pool seemed to have been uncovered just for our enjoyment.

In the dining room the table had been beautifully set for two. A magnificent bouquet of fresh flowers as a centerpiece, a platter of assorted cheeses, a tray with cold pork, and a salad of fresh greens had been prepared by a benevolent fairy. We chose a large ground-floor bedroom with a view of the mountain, and settled down to await the arrival of our hosts.

We enjoyed a refreshing shower, a relaxing dive into the warm pool and chatted while enjoying the beauty of the Côte. As the sun set behind the mountain, it quickly got cooler, and we hurried to the warmth of the welcoming mansion. Our phone call was answered by an emotionless machine, and I left a brief message:

"Marie... Gaston... Hello... as Bourgogne has received us with minimal pomp, it will be less difficult to continue on our way tomorrow. But please call when you can."

We drank a glass of champagne in honor of our missing hosts, and ate the cold dinner, savoring a delicious *Pinot Noir* placed on the table for the occasion. Later, a snifter of Armagnac, a stroll under the stars, and we got ready for bed. We had not heard from Marie and Gaston.

My slightly sarcastic phone message contained an element of truth, for we really did have to continue on our way, and we left the lovely villa the following morning without ever having heard from our hosts. Before leaving higher Saint Romain, we wrote them an affectionate letter thanking them for their hospitality and suggesting that we get together someday soon.

Three weeks later our holiday had come to its end. Our minds were otherwise preoccupied, and we were no longer thinking about *Côte de Beaune* until on our return we found, amid the pile of mail waiting for us, a letter from our friends in Saint Romain.

> We regret that you were unable to enjoy a stay in our villa, which had been prepared for you. We had laid out a cold supper with a good *Pinot Noir*, and were very disappointed that you could not make it. We thought that you would find the villa easily with our directions. We hope you were comfortable wherever you spent the night

and that you pardon our inattention. We could not call you when we returned because you forgot to leave your phone number.

Until next time,
Marie and Gaston

We read the letter again, even reading the words aloud to each other, but uncertainty lingered like the scent of the fine *Pinot Noir* we had enjoyed and the enchanted villa we visited.

4

Monica and I

2001

"Why did millions of people kill one another when it has been known since the world began that it is physically and morally bad to do so? Because it was such an inevitable necessity that in doing it, men fulfilled the elemental zoological law…

One can give no other reply to that terrible question."

-Leo Tolstoy,
War and Peace

I -THE DESERTED TOWN

I BARELY REMEMBER FATHER. He would show up in our home every once in a while, and was very affectionate with Mother and me, but he always seemed nervous and hurried, as if he was eternally escaping from something.

I remember the time – I don't exactly know how long ago as I've lost all sense of time – that Father had just left the house when it was overrun loudly by a legion of menacing soldiers.

After turning the house inside out, they left the same way they had come in - like a tornado – not having found what they were looking for. Once they were gone, Mother kissed me and held me for a long time.

That night we huddled together in bed, keeping each other warm. Embraced in my mother's arms, I dreamt that I spread my wings and flew. From a great height I could see the soldiers storming into the city and into our home, while Father scurried away through the shadows out the back yard. I could see him leaping from one hiding place to another until he finally disappeared into the hills.

Before dawn Mother gathered together a few things and shook me awake, saying "Let's go!"

I stared at her, unable to decipher whether I was still dreaming or whether I had awoken.

As we left the house, we noticed unusual activity out in the street for such an early hour. It was as if all the villagers had agreed to run away at the same time. Mothers with nursing babies, barely dressed children, young and older women and the very old, had loaded everything they could carry on their backs and in their arms.

I can still see Mother's thin shape, with her bulky belly and her skirt flapping in the wind. She looked tired and her arms were filled with a bag full of clothes and a package tucked carefully under her arm. I held firmly to her skirt with one hand, holding my baby doll against my chest with the other.

The human column – old people, children, and women of all ages – crept slowly along on a mysterious course. Much later I learned that the young men had either perished in the struggle or were hiding in the hills. At that moment my own path was uncertain.

On the outskirts of the village the dirt road had become a human river, moving slowly, silently. In a flash, I thought of our empty house and the abandoned village while I held tightly to my mother's skirt.

The sun finally came up and the shadows acquired human forms. Familiar faces now wore expressions I had never seen before - such despair, anxiety, hopelessness. We followed the road with the others, and as time passed we were joined by new groups from neighboring villages. I knew only what my mother had told me before we left – probably without a hope that I would understand – that we had to go to a safer place where Father would be waiting for us.

I was unnerved by the scene. Nobody spoke and only the muted rumbling of thousands of feet trudging in the dirt, drenched by a sudden shower, could be heard.

II -BEYOND THE VILLAGE

Stanislaus came home furtively in the night. He was almost unrecognizable, his hair long and unkempt, his face bearded, his clothes in tatters. I was well aware of the imminent danger, hearing machine guns rattling and helicopters hovering near the village.

"This is crazy! Why have you come? Don't you know that the soldiers are closing in and will be here soon?" I exclaimed.

"I know," he replied holding me close. He approached the small bed where Michelle slept and kissed her forehead. Awake, she sat up in bed and watched her father rush out the back door. Stanislaus turned at the threshold and threw us a farewell kiss.

A few minutes later I heard a massive banging at the door and hurried to open it, standing quickly aside to avoid being run down by a group of soldiers. One of them, apparently in charge, asked me, "Where is he?"

"We're alone," I responded immediately, pointing to the little girl.

After checking every corner of the house, they ran out and were swallowed up by the night, continuing their search for the men of the village. I will never know if my obvious pregnancy protected me, but the truth is that, miraculously, they never touched me. I closed the door again and tried to comfort Michelle who watched me fearfully without understanding.

I took her to my bed and we slept, huddled closely together the rest of the night. I remember dreaming that I was happy and floating along on a river, sitting on the edge of a giant lotus blossom, my fingers trailing in the water. My white craft slowly meandered under the branches of huge trees that formed a bridge over the river. Little by little, the river widened and the banks seemed far away. The current shook the lotus blossom, spinning it wildly, and I could now hear the roar of a nearby waterfall. In an instant I felt myself falling down the roaring gorge, and was jolted awake.

It was still dark. It would be hours yet until the bulk of the troops took over the town. I gathered some ragged clothing, packed some bread and cheese and some ripe figs, and woke Michelle, saying, "Let's go."

She looked confused, her eyes open very wide, and didn't say a word. Shortly, we joined the human current that was escaping, me carrying my precious load in my womb and my little girl holding tight to my skirt.

III -A MOTHER'S DREAM

Mother was not waking up. After sunset, we stopped to rest and have some food. More than hunger, I felt terrible thirst. Suddenly, we heard loud bangs and the people around us scattered in every direction. I recalled having heard similar rattling noises for New Year's, but I didn't really know what was happening. I imagined it was nothing good because the people were running away in terror, and their faces showed their fear. I wasn't worried because Mother had laid down to rest with her head on a rock.

With Monica cradled in my arm, I lay my own head on her belly, which was moving like it usually did, and I also fell asleep.

I dreamt of Mother. She was happy, and so pretty. She was slender and proudly held a beautiful baby girl in her arms.

"It's your little sister," she said to me, tenderly placing her in my arms. She put her in the crib I had used when I was a baby, and together we sang her a lullaby so she would fall asleep. I awoke with the melody ringing in my head and for a moment I continued humming the lullaby, only now it was Monica and I singing to Mother who still slept peacefully. Poor thing, she was so tired.

Pale moonlight occasionally filtered between the clouds. I looked around as shadows stretched across the rocks, and placed Monica next to Mother while I stood watch over them.

After keeping careful vigil for a while, I decided to wake Monica. I suddenly noticed that one of the shadows was approaching, carefully avoiding stepping on the sleeping bodies. As she neared I recognized her face, a neighbor I had often seen in the village.

"What are you doing here all alone, little girl?" the old woman asked me.

"I'm waiting for my mother to wake up," I replied.

The old woman bent down to look at her closely and hugged us tightly, saying, "Your mother will never wake up from this sleep, dear. She's dead. Come with me."

IV -I LEARNED ABOUT DEATH TODAY

Until today I did not know about death. Mother had surrounded me with love, and I imagined that she would always be there - nearby, omnipotent, perhaps immortal. How I cried when I learned about death! I thought that maybe Monica also cried. Evangeline, the neighbor from our village, was quick to comfort me.

"There will be time enough for crying later," she said firmly, adding, "We must continue walking," and taking my hand she began to walk between the bodies lying across the rocks. I began to suspect that maybe they weren't sleeping but were dead like Mother, but I didn't think about it anymore.

We had only taken a few steps when, following an impulse, I let go of Evangeline's hand and ran back to Mother, who was waiting for me. I covered her face with kisses, placing my hand over her unmoving belly. I ran with Monica back to Evangeline, who had waited nearby.

We walked all night, but not along the road. Instead we made our way through the woods to avoid being seen by patrols. Evangeline would occasionally stop to listen carefully to the forest sounds. I remember that she would sometimes carry us when it was too difficult for us. But I could tell that the old woman could barely manage. It seemed Evangeline was familiar with the road, and at dawn we arrived at a military post where we were allowed through and taken to a huge tent with a red cross on it.

Two days with hardly any food and without water had taken their toll on Evangeline. She was practically dragging along. The last thing I remember about that day was that I held tightly to Monica so I wouldn't lose her, and it seemed that the tent's red cross got increasingly blurrier until it was completely gone.

I don't know how long I slept, but when I opened my eyes, I found myself tucked into a bed with cold, white sheets. I did not recognize the place, but was comforted by Monica's presence at my side.

V -A NEW WORLD

They took me in an ambulance from the tent to a hospital, where something very important happened. It was the first time that Mother was not at my side. But at least I was with Monica, and we spoke every night before we fell asleep.

"What is death?" I asked her. "What became of Mother? Where could she be? What happened to the little sister she promised me?"

Monica told me that no matter where they were, she was sure they'd be together, and that I shouldn't worry. But I couldn't stop thinking about Mother. I also asked her about Father. "What was he like? Do you remember him?" Monica remembered Father as being tall, strong, dark-skinned and with a deep, affectionate voice. I concurred so as not to contradict her, but the truth was that Father's image was so blurry that I couldn't bring it to memory. Little by little an image created by the two of us found a place in my mind.

I never saw Evangeline again, but I remember her fondly. I hoped she was well and had reunited with her son in a distant city. I knew she had been good to us, and had saved us.

After I got well in the hospital, I was taken to a city much larger than the tiny village. My new home was huge, with many rooms and halls, and a large, central patio. Most importantly, in that house there were many children like me. I knew then that it was a place of shelter for children who had become lost in the war. We had clean beds, gray-colored uniforms and enough to eat.

After all difficulties we had suffered, Monica thought that the shelter wasn't so bad. We spent most of the day in class where I learned to read.

Winter passed, then spring, and summer arrived. Although I was now quite accustomed to the routine at the shelter though the nights were long and lonely. They turned the lights off early, and then I was alone with Monica. Every night, we talked about Mother. I kept busy during the day, but during the long nights, I felt awfully alone.

One day the precept in charge came and spoke to me about adoption. He explained it was a way for some of the children to obtain a substitute mother and father. At first, I didn't like the idea of replacing Mother with some other woman. I wasn't as concerned about Father since I had barely known him.

The shelter held monthly meetings for war survivors who would visit in hopes of reuniting with their children. We weren't exactly on exhibit, but the children assembled in the patio to meet the visitors, and we all had a nice time. Among the many visitors I spoke with, I thought I recognized some faces from the village. But the tall, strong, wide-shouldered, dark-skinned man that Monica talked awbout never visited.

VI -THE FATHER DISCOVERS HIS DAUGHTER

Though they made a decent living and had a lovely home, married life for MAría and Stanislaus was anything but typical. María was a beautiful and intelligent woman, and they seemed very much in love. However, the country was going through a time of unbearable oppression, and a few months after they were married, Stanislaus had to leave his pregnant wife to join the guerrilla forces in the mountains. Thereafter, he became an occasional visitor to his own home.

The village where they lived was about to be overrun by troops and Stanislaus wanted to see María and Michelle before the village fell into enemy hands. Stanislaus' last brief visit was etched into his memory along with the steady roar of the tanks as they advanced up the road without encountering any resistance.

María was startled to see him and greeted him with, "Why have you come? It's much too dangerous. Just go!" They embraced fiercely, and Stanislaus kissed his wife and his daughter. Then without a word he went out the door to the patio. María pleaded, "Please be careful, love!"

The bloody fighting continued on the plains and in the mountains until the government quashed the guerrillas. Many sought shelter in the mountains. Others, like Stanislaus, chose exile.

On the few occasions when he could inquire about his family, the vague information he obtained was not encouraging. Nobody seemed to know anything about them. Two years earlier, the village where they had lived had been occupied by the military. He assumed that shortly after his last visit, María and Michelle – who would have been almost two – had fled towards the border.

Neither of them were registered on the refugee list periodically published by the Red Cross. Stanislaus refused to accept what his buddies had said: that most likely they had perished along the way because government forces shot those they encountered regardless of whether they were guerrillas, women, old people, or children. Stanislaus reasoned that a seven-month-pregnant woman would surely have been helped by the Red Cross or registered at regional hospitals. He had given María and their unborn daughter up for dead. But he still secretly held hope of finding Michelle.

Stanislaus' search eventually led him to a shelter for war orphans. He happened to visit on a day they had one of their monthly gatherings for parents who, hoping for a miracle, came to search among the lost children for their own child.

The children were happy, calm, and dressed impeccably in uniforms with new shoes, in stark contrast to the tattered appearance of the visitors. The children smiled happily, but the visitors' faces reflected the hardships they had endured and their anxiety about an uncertain future.

Suddenly Stanislaus' heart began to pound vigorously. In a corner of the room he saw a little girl. She looked to be about four and had Michelle's unmistakable features. Of course, after two years she had changed, but he was almost certain it was her. She had blond hair like his and María's features. He approached the director and asked for some information about the little girl, explaining that she looked familiar.

"We know almost nothing about Clara," the director replied. "She was brought by a woman who had fled one of the villages on the battlefront. She said she had found her in the middle of a field, standing with a rag doll in her arms next to her dead mother. The little girl had no documents, and the woman who found her was injured and died shortly afterwards. I recall that when the child arrived, she babbled only two words, 'Mother' and 'Monica' which she repeated endlessly. We later learned that 'Monica' was the name of her doll. We named the child 'Clara'. She is bright and very fortunate for a couple who are well off want to adopt her. Do you know anything about her?"

"I'm not sure," Stanislaus lied, "but I'd like to speak to Clara."

The director walked with him to where the little girl sat. The battle-hardened guerrilla soldier was overcome, and his legs were trembling, but he controlled his excitement. Smiling, he said, "Hello, little one. What's your name?"

"Good afternoon, Sir. My name is Clara."

"I wanted to speak to you because you resemble my daughter. Do you remember your mother?"

The little girl paused, looked at him with tearful eyes and said, "Yes, Mother was very good and loved me very much."

"And your father? Do you remember him?"

"No. Father was almost never home, and I hardly remember him."

"But, do you remember what he looked like?" asked Stanislaus.

Clara looked at her visitor for a long time, her eyes wide open, and thought about what Monica had told her in her dream. Finally, she answered tonelessly, "I don't remember."

Stanislaus took a good look at himself and realized for the first time that he had sacrificed his wife and had been a terrible father. Overcome, he was quickly losing control of his emotions and felt he might explode. He wanted to continue talking with Michelle, to tell her he was her father, to hold her and kiss her. But his decision was made.

He kissed her forehead and said, "Clara, I wish you every happiness."

Stanislaus turned to the director, who was watching them, and they walked to one side of the room. Alone there, the director asked whether he recognized anything about the little girl.

"No. Nothing. The similarity was a coincidence," he lied quietly.

The following morning Stanislaus left the city and headed for the mountains to join the decimated guerrilla forces.

VII -A PENITENT'S CONFESSION

Seeking to forget his heartache, Stanislaus diligently embraced the battle, even volunteering for the riskiest missions. At times he felt guilty for having left his pregnant wife and Michelle. But he told himself that he had performed his duty for the country he loved; that what had happened was regrettable but unavoidable.

Stanislaus had always excelled in school, and even before his marriage things had always proceeded according to plan. He possessed a strong personality, was an excellent athlete, and was rarely second in any competition. His motto was: *"Win at any price"*.

Stanislaus and María had lived together for only a few months before it was obvious to both that the marriage was a failed experiment. The realization left Stanislaus confused for the first time in his life, and he was unsure what to do. Years later, as he reviewed his past, and to further complicate his thoughts, his life had become empty and monotonous since the day he had said goodbye to María and Michelle. It left him with many sleepless nights, going over and over the same thoughts without finding relief for his guilt.

"Be careful, love," María had said to him the day he left. He remembered that he hadn't been able to find the words to say goodbye and had merely thrown them a kiss with his hand. His memory held on to the image of María with her swollen belly, and Michelle with her inseparable rag doll.

Stanislaus was not used to defeat. Though he tried to erase everything that had happened, he could not. From his observation post on the helicopter, he saw the rugged mountains that seemed to impede their passage and far off, the vastness of the ocean.

He was aware that the moment was approaching, and that in order to once again triumph, he had to reject the past and face the present lucidly. One by one, his comrades' turns came, and finally, almost unexpectedly, it was now his turn.

Aloft now in the air, Stanislaus felt infinite relief at being free from worldly confusion. The sky was blue, cloudless, liquid. The air was cold and invigorating. He left behind his earthly indecision, and in a flash saw the truth.

María had faced his decision to join the guerrillas with fortitude, and had said goodbye without complaint. In a flash of insight, Stanislaus saw that during his entire time with María, he had thought only of himself. But the clock could not be turned back.

The desolate ocean seemed far away now, and the mountain grew ever nearer. Stanislaus fleetingly realized that he had been motivated by egoism, and that even his love for country could not justify his behavior. He could no longer see the ocean, but only the mountain growing larger before him. His life plan had been decided. He would erase from his mind all traces of the past, and begin a new life. In that moment, his mind conjured the scenario that the orphanage director had described: Michelle guarding her mother's final rest, clutching Monica and standing beside María as she lay across a rock.

Stanislaus attempted to concentrate on what he could make of his life as he grasped the lifesaving ripcord that released his parachute. Moments later, he was swallowed up by the forest in order to complete his mission.

5

The Right to Life

1995

The fetus wished to live.

Stubbornly, sometimes astonishingly,

the fetus struggled to live.

But the power of its life - or its death-

had to reside with the mother.

No other alternative was possible.

-Joyce Carol Oates,
A Book of American Martyrs

I -FANTASY OF THE OVAL CHAMBER

HE DIDN'T KNOW HOW OR when it happened. He only remembered a primordial feeling that changed with each moment. Then the feeling acquired an uncommon vigor and the pace quickened. Simultaneously, he was surprised by sound, or rather by a polyphony arising all around him, buffered by an invisible barrier.

At the beginning of time, he became aware of an accelerated trembling in what his fingers recognized as his body. At first rhythmically diffuse, the trembling was concentrated in a tiny region of his chest. Eventually it was no longer perceived continuously and only returned to his consciousness occasionally as a rapid pulse in his temples. Multiple new stimuli repeatedly assaulted his senses. Although his chamber was dark and he was coming from eternal darkness, his effort to glimpse life was occasionally interrupted by fireworks. He learned to recognize the flashes when his head bounced painfully against the walls of his chamber. Other than that, absolute darkness was his only view. Immersed pleasurably in a warm syrup, he explored his oval chamber like a blind man. In time, his remaining senses were sharpened and developed quickly.

Rich, tactile sensations made him aware of his shape. He discovered he had arms and legs that not only floated aimlessly in the warm sea, but they responded to his demands as he learned to swim. He perfected a primitive breaststroke that let him reach the furthest limit of his chamber.

New discoveries were constantly made despite his restricted environment. He discovered that he was joined to his chamber by a thick, warm cord through which his minuscule fingers could feel that pulse he first perceived with his earliest memory as something diffuse. The cord was so long that it allowed him to swim freely from one end of his private sea to the other. The cord was his first and only toy. An essential part of his daily routine was playing jump rope and wrapping his legs or neck with the cord. Over time he gained a visceral understanding of the cord's importance. It was also obvious that his body was growing, and it seemed natural that his chamber grew as well.

He appreciated how spacious his chamber was and the benevolent effect of the liquid that surrounded him. He was initially surprised by a shaking that occasionally took place when his chamber moved from one place to another, sometimes gently but at other times rather violently. The tumbles shook him, and at some point he concluded that there was another world outside. This discovery led to a profound review of the situation.

Yet all was not movement. He gradually realized that with foreseeable regularity, his chamber felt suspended in space and for what seemed an interminable time, it remained almost completely still. He discovered that his travels from one end to the other of his oval chamber, the hours he spent swimming and his games with the cord, affected the chamber's position. It was wonderful to find that he could coordinate his activity with the movement of his chamber, and his sleep with its stillness.

As time passed, he learned to recognize new signals from that unknown outside world; they reached him through the walls of his windowless home. Though blind for the time, his imagination was blasted by overdeveloped senses that created images that became part of his existence. He imagined that the climate outside his chamber was tropical, warm like the liquid bathing of his skin during unchanging seasons.

He gradually concluded that the muffled sound he perceived had significance. Like the movement, the sound arrived in a predictable, foreseeable cadence. As his environment moved, many sounds furiously attacked his eardrums. He discerned a series of incomprehensible, high-pitched sounds and while most of them were variable and faded, sometimes disappearing completely, others grew louder. Strange little strident noises always accompanied him, and were completely foreseeable. He concluded his chamber was connected to those sounds which, while initially undecipherable, were unmistakably habitual. Like a tiny Champollion, he attempted to decipher the audible hieroglyphs. His developing cerebral computer associated sound stimuli, noted the circumstances, and linked them to other sounds and to resting and active times, until the sounds began to achieve a primitive meaning.

There was no doubt about it now. The being that bore his oval chamber was the source of the squeaky little voice that always accompanied him, using a strange language he tried to decipher. He discovered other high-pitched voices with considerable differences among them. The squeaky little voice was clearly distinguishable from other high-pitched voices and there were clear differences in tone. There was, however, a contrast between the high-pitched squeaky voices and other lower, stronger, sometimes louder voices. It seemed the voices belonged to essentially distinct beings.

Based on a careful, tactile exploration of his own anatomy, he imagined that the beings that occupied the space outside his oval were similar and might look like him. He sensed that the owner of the squeaky little voice was a beautiful being with a head almost as big as his body, a big belly and relatively short arms and legs, and with a flat face that had huge eyes set apart. He concluded that the belly was the only part of the being's body that could house his oval chamber.

After hearing the same sounds repeatedly, he began to determine the meaning of some words of the being's strange language. He realized that the squeaky little voice always responded to the word 'Mimi,' and concluded that Mimi was her name. In this manner he gained a rich vocabulary which he repeated in his mind like a parrot. But the words were without context and lacked meaning. He tried repeatedly to make his vocal cords vibrate to imitate the words but was unable to emit any sound. With practice he was able to produce a tickle, a muted gurgle, but nothing like what his ears heard.

He liked Mimi's voice and sensed they were somehow linked. That sometimes Mimi was happy was obvious from the tone of her voice and what he later learned was a chorus of laughter. On these occasions, something frequently happened that he didn't quite understand. He would suddenly fall into a lethargic state, and it seemed that the walls of his oval chamber moved crazily. He would lose all sense of distance and continually get tangled up in his vital cord. It left him irritated and made him kick furiously at the walls of the oval chamber, though he would gradually become quiet again.

On one occasion when he was ready for the restorative rest, something extraordinary happened. The invisible walls surrounding him, trembled, and his chamber suddenly flattened violently as if squeezed by a powerful weight. At the same time a battering ram pushed rhythmically against his shelter as if trying to penetrate his world with a violent force. All the while a spectrum of sounds reached him, varying from little shouts to deep moans of satisfaction.

Mimi was clearly playing with someone, and they were enjoying it greatly. While their diabolic dance lasted, he couldn't think. He was completely bewildered and found himself bounced in every direction. Finally the battering ram withdrew with spasmodic rhythm and the chamber quieted. Mimi and the battering ram with the deep voice continued speaking for a long time. As he listened, he felt frustrated at being unable to prevent the intrusion into his privacy. Mimi was saying words he couldn't understand: "I have a right to my own life, too, I do…"

As time passed and his daily routine continued, he found increasingly less space to move around in within his chamber. The apocalyptic game that Mimi played with her friend was often repeated, and over and again he heard the words, "I have a right to my own life, too."

He mentally mimicked the words without understanding the meaning: *I have a right to my own life too.*

Mimi's words seemed emotionally charged, and he sensed from her tone that she was going through a difficult time. There was a storm coming without a doubt.

One day, different from all the others, his oval chamber moved through a cloud of words. Initially a murmur, it soon became unexpectedly intense:

"Hail Mary, Mother of God... Our Father, who Art in Heaven... Forgive her Lord for her sins..."

The meaning of these words was a mystery. The murmur faded, finally disappeared and everything returned to normal.

But Mimi's voice didn't sound right and seemed distraught. Then a feeling overtook him similar to what he'd experienced when Mimi was happily having fun with her friends. He felt softened as if the room were spinning, and imagned Mimi was experiencing it too. Then, for the last time, they were flooded together. The ocean that had bathed him for as long as he could remember suddenly vanished. His world collapsed, destroyed by an invasive, frigid claw. His last experience was a blinding light and the blurry, unfocused vision of an unmoving figure beside him while shadows around them moved in a macabre dance. Afterwards, once again, there was only darkness. Silence.

II -FORGIVE HER, LORD

Mimi left the building and headed purposefully to the coffee shop where she usually met Carlos. Since she had started her new job as a secretary in a commercial firm, her life had changed considerably, the result of her long-awaited freedom from her parent's house.

At 23, Mimi was a beautiful, smart woman who had been carefully educated by a family that believed deeply in respecting their traditions. Education was important to her family and to Mimi who went to night classes to obtain a degree in economics. She was good at her job and had a plan for her future and strong ambition.

Mimi acknowledged that since having met Carlos, her studies were not going as well. Carlos was good looking and appealing to many women who tirelessly chased after him. So Mimi was thrilled that Carlos was attracted to her, and she enjoyed their relationship though like Eve in the Garden of Eden, she knew their relationship was not without potential danger.

One night Mimi told Carlos she was worried.

"I think I'm pregnant," she confessed.

Carlos didn't think her symptoms were convincing, and calmed her with his usual confidence.

"No, Mimi, I'm sure you're mistaken. You're just a little late. There's no reason to concern ourselves."

A few days later, Mimi began feeling sick in the morning, so she went to see her doctor who confirmed she was pregnant. That evening she told Carlos firmly that they should get married as soon as possible and begin their lives together. But Carlos wasn't about to give up his life as a bachelor. He liked Mimi but not enough to marry her, and surely not enough to sacrifice his independence and live with her. As for her pregnancy, he could care less.

The days passed, and Mimi's tears dampened the sheets, though her pleas were drowned out by their nightly enjoyment which neither was willing to give up. Mimi was as tormented as Carlos was unconcerned. She desperately tried to retain her lifestyle, going out with Carlos and a group of friends, dancing and drinking to forget her worries. At night, still under the influence of the Bacchus, they would surrender to passion and sleep deeply until the morning, when Mimi would wake up with her now prominent belly pounding violently.

By choosing her wardrobe carefully, Mimi was able to conceal her growing waistline. She realized she would have to make decisions on her own, for as far as Carlos was concerned, they should continue as they were for as long as they could.

Mimi finally decided that allowing the pregnancy to continue was not a viable option. It didn't seem fair to compromise her future, nor fair to a child who might grow up without a father. Her parents would never forgive her. She would not be able to keep her job, and she'd have to give up her studies.

Given her Christian upbringing and her natural maternal feelings, Mimi didn't think she was capable of terminating her pregnancy, especially as far along as she was. But in time her convictions wained.

"I have a right to a life of my own," she told Carlos who agreed.

She gathered the pertinent information, took her savings, and made an appointment at an abortion clinic located far from her home. On the day of her appointment, Mimi couldn't find Carlos anywhere, and bravely setting out with determination, she went to the clinic by herself. On arrival Mimi encountered a large group of men and women blocking the entrance to the building, some standing and others kneeling.

Seeing people who were obviously judging her was a huge shock to her tormented soul.

"Hail Mary, Mother of God... Our Father, who Art in Heaven... Forgive her Lord for her sins..."

Mimi shoved through the crowd of praying people, badly shaken by their condemnation. Inside the doctor's office she tuned them out and soon drifted away under the effects of anesthesia. A short while later, a beautiful fetus covered with blond fuzz lay between her legs, never having drawn breath. It was quickly placed in a plastic bag and Mimi, still woozy from the anesthesia, never saw it.

Mimi was physically recovered in a couple of days and took a short vacation, which did wonders to get her focused and find the strength to go on. Her disappointment over the end of her love affair, and her despair over the son she'd never know, had pitilessly battered her soul. But Mimi discovered that she had great powers of recovery.

As soon as possible, she went back to work, where she was greatly appreciated. She returned to night school and no longer frequented the coffee shop where she used to meet Carlos. She also stopped seeing some of the friends they had in common, and dedicated her efforts to forgetting him, wiping the slate clean and starting over.

After a couple of years, she finished her studies and set up a consulting business, greatly improving her finances and enabling a move to a spacious apartment in a chic neighborhood. Mimi had been able to get her life back on track. She was young, beautiful and successful professionally and financially, but she wasn't happy. She thought of Carlos often.

One evening on leaving her office, out of old habit she headed to the coffee shop they used to frequent. She sat at a table and ordered a cup of coffee, but Carlos did not appear. She didn't see him on that occasion or on any of the other times that she returned hoping to encounter him.

She had almost stopped thinking of him when, quite by chance, they met again. Carlos was more charming than ever. He was looking well and seemed to have money. She didn't tell him that she had searched for him like crazy. He told Mimi that he was busy with important matters and had no time for frivolous things - for her or their old friends. He told her about his business trips to Bogota.

Yet he soon found plenty of time for Mimi, visiting her often. He told her that he really liked her new apartment, and before long the two had resumed their previous life together.

Having thrown caution and precautions aside in the heat of their passionate reunion, Mimi once again became pregnant. But this time she resolved to settle things immediately. She and Carlos were both successful now. Maybe they could have a real relationship. Yet Carlos hesitated and wasn't willing to commit, and once again he vanished into the night. It was too much for Mimi.

Alone with her problem and her conscience, Mimi was again faced with a difficult choice. How would her family react? What would others say?

She made an appointment at the same clinic, and arrived alone with only her conscience for company. Again she faced the wall of battering words:

"Holy Mary, Mother of God, forgive her Lord for her sins..."

And again, she was greeted by a chorus of mumbled curses.

When she finally found herself alone in the waiting room, she wept in distress, reviewing everything that had happened. *"Forgive her Lord for her sins..."* echoed in her mind.

She felt alone as she sat in the waiting room. But this time when the moment of truth arrived, she wiped her tears, stood up, and left the clinic.

III -LIKE FATHER, LIKE SON

Carlitos was a handsome young man with a slender figure and blond hair just like his father who had disappeared from Mimi's life a long time before. She'd heard from old friends that Carlos had returned to Colombia, and she never saw him again.

Mimi's fears about her parent's reaction had fortunately been unfounded. Though their daughter's misstep had upset them, they were understanding and helped out while Carlitos was little.

Mimi was proud of Carlitos, and bought him everything she could, so he never wanted for anything. As she was a busy professional, Carlitos spent his day in daycare. Mimi would pick him up in late afternoon and shower him with affection. Mother and son spent the evenings together in the luxurious apartment, each with their own activity. Mimi had her work and Carlitos had every toy imaginable.

Mimi had married Antonio, a successful professional and a man several years her senior. Days were spent with her husband, her son, her friends, her exercise classes, budgets for her clients, and multiple other activities.

Though bright, Carlitos had problems in school. His teachers suggested that the child was bored in class, and noted that he made little effort to excel.

At sixteen, his parents bought him a sports car. Carlitos went from bad to worse, taking drugs and changing schools frequently. Mimi was disappointed and Antonio tried to convince her that she needed to be firmer with the boy. Mimi had a long, private conversation with Carlitos, but her son was as good looking and charming as his father, and she found herself incapable of putting her foot down with him.

Seeing Mimi's weakness, Antonio confronted Carlitos and asked him to leave their home. Carlitos happily agreed especially after receiving a large amount of money. He vanished for a while, then dramatically reappeared when he was arrested for drug trafficking.

Mimi cried when she visited him in jail, and the wayward sheep swore that it was all an accident. It would never happen again. She paid his bail and Carlitos was released, only to disappear again, this time for several years.

Mimi and Antonio lived their lives quietly until one night they received a surprise phone call. Carlitos invited himself to dinner, and he was as charming as Carlos had ever been. As his father had before, Carlitos told Mimi whatever she wanted to hear. Mimi was amazed at the similarities - the noble features, the eyes full of mischief, the deep melodious voice. It was déjà vu.

She enjoyed the lovely stories Carlitos told her. Having suffered from her son's poor choices, hearing of his improved circumstances was an unexpected gift for Mimi. Carlitos told them that he had partnered with a rich South American merchant, and had become a financial magnate. Antonio, not knowing the whole story, listened with mixed amazement and incredulity.

After dinner, they sat around the table for a longer time than either Mimi or Antonio could recall. After having coffee and cognac, Carlitos called his driver and affectionately said goodbye. After so many sleepless nights worrying about Carlitos, Mimi could finally relax, knowing her son had succeeded and, in a way, feeling that Carlitos' success was proof of her own redemption.

A moment after closing the door, Mimi and Antonio were shocked by the sound of machine gun bursts. A short silence followed, and then they heard police sirens. Opening the door, they found Carlitos lying face down in a pool of blood a few steps from their apartment door.

Mimi was devastated at Carlitos' funeral. Standing next to her son's body, she concentrated on her final farewell.

She closed her eyes, and reviewed her life, overcome by the thought of her past mistakes. Staring into the coffin, Mimi saw Carlos' face in her son's features, and wondered how growing up without a father had shaped his life.

Minutes passed as Mimi stood still as stone. Around the casket, she heard mourners weeping. Their prayers reopened old wounds:

"Hail Mary, Mother of God...
Our Father, who Art in Heaven..."

And in Mimi's mind she heard a faraway voice:

"Forgive her Lord for her sins."

Now the stone's features became those of a woman who wept inconsolably, pressing her lips together in a rictus of pain, murmuring bitter words of regret which nobody could hear.

6

The Cause

1998

We are all tattooed in our cradles
with the beliefs of our tribe;
the record may seem superficial,
but it is indelible.

-Oliver Wendell Holmes,
The Poet at the Breakfast Table

I -A PERSUASIVE EDUCATION

ADRIANO WAS EUPHORIC about his academic success and graduation. The auditorium was packed with students, professors and friends as diplomas and awards were about to be presented to the graduating students.

He had been an excellent student and found the classroom environment appealing. Adriano was especially attracted to young Father Carmelo's dynamic personality, and the Father in turn had exerted considerable influence over his students. His charismatic personality was felt beyond the schoolrooms as Father Carmelo was also the families' spiritual director, in particular for many of his students' mothers who echoed the Father's teachings.

The priest taught languages and philosophy, and excelled at both when debating complex issues or simply discussing practical life matters. A man of considerable intellect, the Father was at the same time down to earth and as likely to simply take off his robes and share a pickup game of football with his students in the schoolyard. There was no doubt that Father Carmelo was especially popular with the students.

At the graduation ceremony, Father Carmelo's star was at its zenith. At a certain point in the speech he made before handing out diplomas, he said, "Today we celebrate an exceptional group of graduates called to great destinies. You will gravitate to many different vocations. Some of you will be professionals – lawyers, doctors, or engineers. Others may follow a career in the armed forces, and yet others will go into business or other important occupations. But I know that no matter what activity you dedicate yourselves to, each one of you will hold a position of leadership in society.

"If you remember nothing else from today's ceremony, remember this message," said Father Carmelo pausing and raising his voice. "We have provided you with the weapons for your fight, and you must use them in any manner necessary to bring about the triumph of truth, of our truth - the only truth. Fight without reservation for you are the chosen ones, the owners of our truth, and you bear a huge responsibility. Society's salvation is in your hands."

The teacher's inspiring words uplifted the young men. They imagined themselves as bearing the torch of truth, the flame of the only truth as they walked along the road of life.

There were no flaws in Father Carmelo's thinking and no objections since the student body had been carefully selected and sheltered from opposing ideas. Father Carmelo spoke extensively and warned the young men about the dangers they would encounter in the future, and the difficulties they would face when attempting to impose the truth.

"Do not be daunted when you encounter disapproval; turn deaf ears to any twisted arguments that detract from our beliefs. It's is the only way for you to be sheltered from the many flawed ideologies that corrupt our society."

That night, Father Carmelo's words repeatedly resonated. Adriano was unable to fall asleep as the words echoed,

"...ensure the triumph of truth, of our truth,
of the only truth, at any price..."

II -THE FACELESS BLONDE

After a long sleep, Adriano opened his eyes but found himself in total darkness. He started to wake up, but his head was throbbing painfully. The pain was especially sharp in places where a sticky substance covered his head and had glued his hair to a hard, cold surface.

He tried to move his numb limbs, but found movement restricted by walls he could not see, but that surrounded him. His wrists were firmly tied behind his back. His feet also touched a hard surface that he couldn't see. Trying to move slightly forward, he bumped his head against another unyielding wall.

Confused, Adriano tried to recall how he got there. At first everything was a blur, but he slowly began to situate himself in the reduced space where only the most minimal movement was possible. The headache impeded his ability to think, and jumbled memories struggled for a place in his consciousness. A damp, warm gag muffled the sounds he tried to make, and it quickly became apparent that shouting would be in vain. His only entertainment was to chew incessantly on the rag covering his mouth. Initially the gag tasted of something sweet, but the flavor faded and then disappeared completely. Stale air made breathing difficult.

Adriano's muddled thoughts gave way to a blurry recollection. He'd left Nicolas's headquarters and was driving along a familiar road when a blonde girl stepped into the street, waving her hands frantically. He slammed on the brakes to avoid her and stopped by the side of the road. He lowered the window to swear at her, but the only thing he could recall following that was the sharp sound of a dry crack that echoed in his head before his world plunged into darkness.

As he struggled in the tiny chamber, Adriano began to understand that the faceless blonde had been a trap, and he had fallen for it like a fool. He tried to calm himself, noting that agitation only made his breathing harder, and that it was becoming ever more difficult to get air. Inside his narrow chamber, Adriano heard nothing but the sound of his labored breathing magnified in the small enclosure; no outside sounds penetrated - at least that's what he initially thought. As his senses sharpened in the dark, he realized he hadn't been abandoned in some deserted spot. He sensed another presence - that someone else was near.

Hours passed and he lost all sense of time. A warm liquid bathed over him repeatedly, and he detected the smell of urine. His tight belt restricted the flow of feces, though his clothing, absorbed the urine as it rose up his shirt until even his collar was soaked. His mouth was dry and though he wasn't hungry, he was intensely thirsty - a torment that lasted during the time he remained conscious. His tongue was dry and the gag turned stiff as cardboard.

The air Adriano breathed, rich with exhaled carbon dioxide, had a narcotic effect that made him sleepy. He floated in and out of reality and had a vision. He saw dozens of pigeons suddenly congregating in a plaza, and a long line of women, mourning for their lost sons and daughters, walked slowly, deliberately towards him. They raised their arms to the sky, drying tears on their scarves. One of the women approached him, menacingly, almost touching him and waving a photo of a baby-faced young man. The photo grew larger until it completely filled his horizon, before it turned into a blurry stain and finally disappeared.

The dream continued and Adriano found himself traveling on a huge silver bird whose beating, metallic wings made a deafening noise. Below he could see a mountain range, a bare silhouette in the mantle of night. They passed over a sleeping city, and a lake reflected in moonlight. The silver bird ejected foul smelling, oblong shapes that splashed the water, then rumbled on their way to the bottom. The bird suddenly deflated and Adriano's fell, rapidly descending into the void. Screams of pain penetrated as he fell through a thick cloud of cigarette smoke and the smell of burning flesh. The women from the plaza reappeared, the pigeons fluttering all around them.

The anguish the images provoked was temporarily calmed, however, by a vision of three small, blond angels dressed in white, running towards him after mass to kiss and embrace him lovingly.

Suddenly a hazy image of his graduation ceremony appeared taking him back to the indoctrination that shaped his actions for the rest of his life. Father Carmelo's figure appeared, and grew uncommonly large before him as the Father emphatically repeated:

"Enforce our truth at any price!
Enforce our truth at any price!"

Images of the blonde in the street appeared repeatedly. She was slender with long blond hair that hung to her shoulders, but he still could not make out her face. Adriano concentrated with all his energy, and after a while he made out almond-shaped eyes, a small nose and thin lips that twisted as she laughed sardonically.

A final, supreme effort brought the blurred images into focus as the blonde's features filled his horizon, only to fade again. Later, the dreaded plaza women reappeared, pigeons fluttering and encircling them, clamoring for their loved ones who had been devoured by violence of the times. Implacably came the faceless blonde, again and again.

III -A TRAPPED RAT

Knowing that the meeting at Nicolas' headquarters was almost over, we knew that Adriano would be the first to head down the rosewood-lined road, the guerrilla explained to his lieutenant. It was so easy. Beyond the sharp curve near the abandoned warehouse, the target slowed as his headlights illuminated Bertha's blonde hair as she crossed the road. The target slowed the vehicle almost to a full stop and lowered his window, probably to curse at her. It was the target's last conscious act.

Bertha and I stuffed him like a bale of hay into the back of my car, and I drove Adriano's car to a side street where it wouldn't be noticed. Then Bertha drove rapidly to our destination. I watched Adriano, completely unconscious, his face spattered with blood. We hated this guy, the hit man of the repression and had been trying to catch him for some time. When we finally had him, we decided not to kill him right away, hoping he might be more useful alive than dead.

We arrived at the house that Chulo had rented a month earlier as he carefully prepared to capture him. The place was perfect, remote and isolated. As long as we avoided suspicious activity, we hoped to be able to use it for a long time without being discovered. Bertha helped me drag Adriano to the living room, gag him and tie his hands behind his back.

That's when we discovered the masterpiece that Chulo had prepared so carefully. We found a small door practically hidden in a corner of the room which accessed a built-in chamber - a box as narrow as a coffin. We pushed the unconscious Adriano into it, feet first, until he was fully inside. I closed the access door, covered the area with wallpaper, then pushed a couch against it, not sure if I would ever see him again. That would depend on the circumstances. I felt no compassion whatsoever for our target.

The end justifies the means.
One life more, or one life less, is not important.

It was our unspoken rule, and it compelled us:

'To destroy the established order,
and create chaos to build a new order.

The only thing that matters is the cause!'

The entombment accomplished, Bertha quickly left without asking questions. From then on, I would try to maintain a semblance of normalcy at the house to avoid suspicion until I received my orders from command. I wasn't concerned about the target, because I knew, one way or the other, we would quickly decide his outcome. We would either use him, or he would die in his own shit. Either scenario was fine with me and neither warranted my concern.

However my prediction that the outcome would be quick was wrong. A whole week passed without news until suddenly a message arrived. It was not what I'd expected.

"Get out! Just leave him! Get out!" said a voice I knew.

IV -A TELLTALE SCENT

Nicolas was one of the repression's strongmen and top lieutenant. Adriano was his executioner. With a cherubic face and posture of proverbial righteousness, nobody would have suspected Adriano's brutal role.

Nicolas had imposed strict discipline on his men and seemed to have the situation under control until Adriano's kidnapping which took place in the very heart of the repression. The kidnapping was a severe and daring blow that took them all by surprise. Adriano's car, abandoned so close to general headquarters, had been found in minutes after the meeting, but the fugitives had enough time to disappear rapidly into the fog of night.

Nicolas assembled his team. Intelligence services had identified a few individuals who might be linked to the guerrillas and many others who had stayed neutral but disapproved of the repression's operations.

Since the kidnapping had left no trace of Adriano and no useful clues, Nicolas immediately ordered massive detentions that included both likely and unlikely guerrillas. Nicolas had no regrets about the detentions and or the repression's atrocities since the cause was just. He obeyed the dictates he'd been taught and held to deeply:

The end justifies the means.
One life more or one life less is not important.
No matter the cost, God's kingdom must be upheld.
Justice must reign, and family protected.
The only important thing is the cause!

Neighbors alerted police that there might be something unusual going on in the rented house. But when the police burst into Chulo's house, it was apparently empty. Yet it seemed obvious something unusual had occurred. It was also strange that there was no sign of the tenants who had apparently disappeared as if by magic.

Nicolas was with the agents when they entered the house the police suspected had sheltered the guerrillas. He was hugely disappointed to find it empty and without even a trace of Adriano!

As he picked up the telephone to make a call, Nicolas caught a whiff of a penetrating stench. He sniffed here and there like a hound dog until he located the strongest concentration of an ammonia-like smell in a corner of the room. He pulled away the couch, scratched at the wallpaper with his fingernails, and uncovered a small hidden door.

Shouting for his assistants to open it, hc watched, eyes watering, as they were overwhelmed by the intense smell of ammonia. They pulled Adriano from where he lay, in his funeral shroud of sewage.

7

Two Concurrent Worlds

1961

"I only know," Sancho said, "that while I sleep, I have no fear, or hope, or troubles, or glory; blessed be whoever invented sleep, the cloak that covers all human thought, the food that drives away hunger, the water that banishes thirst, fire that heats the cold, chill that moderates passion, and, finally, a universal currency that purchases all things, weight and balance that brings a shepherd and a king, a fool and a wise man, to the same level."

-Miguel de Cervantes,
Don Quijote de la Mancha

I -A BLOODBATH

THERE WAS LIGHT, and she went towards it stealthily. Like a magnet, the light attracted her ancestrally. When she began to move, the light suddenly went out and then came the calm of night. Her nocturnal quest continued relentlessly, spurred painfully by both uncontrolled hunger and ambition. Not a single corner of her world was left unexplored, yet she found nothing to satisfy her appetite.

She had learned to play her primitive flute as a youngster; now its monotonous, jarring melody broke the silence. Anyone hearing it would be terrified. She stopped moving and meditated on her miserable luck, her lonely, hungry journey. She thought about what she could not find but sensed was near, and felt the urgency of her quest.

She had not known parents or family - had no memory of a mother. As soon as life manifested in her, she set out into her narrow, dark world. Her expectant vigil was interrupted here and there by dreams of appetizing delicacies - universes to be discovered. But the hunger, initially painful, turned gradually to a vague, wretchedly nauseating sensation.

Aside from the nausea, in the midst of the total stillness that foretold her end, she became overcome by great discomfort, and then by a supreme hatred for all the unknowns she intuited. Her hatred gave way to bloodlust - an overwhelming thirst that would consume her to the end. It was a thirst for revenge for all the things she never had - for what she might have had. Deeper than some irrepressible irrational feeling, it was an ancestral manifestation on a visceral level.

She slept in a secluded corner of her world, safe from inquisitive eyes. Her night was slowly merging into eternity when, suddenly, there was a bright light. Opening her dazzled eyes, from her hiding place she fleetingly glimpsed a strange, gigantic creature. She had never seen anything like it. She couldn't see it clearly because the light was so blinding, but she heard water flowing, just as she had imagined it - a cold, crystal clear water, burbling as it fell between stones in a mountain river.

Soon, the water's lullaby was drowned out by the deafening noise of a storm. She imagined mountain peaks covered by threatening, black clouds, and thought she saw lightning strike with indescribable fury. Perhaps it was a divine warning given her excessive ambition and strange thoughts. Thunder followed torrential rain, as she imagined it might in the tropics. But unlike after a tropical downpour, there was no radiant sunshine - only a dark night unfolding again, without moon or stars.

Then silence again, but it was not absolute now. She imagined a soft, warm breeze filtering through the mountain peaks as it rhythmically caressed her dark hideout. In the black mantle of night, she could still see phosphorescent flashes like phantoms that streaked wildly across her horizon. Her agitated visions attenuated and become small, luminous spots that grew scarcer until finally, total night came. She slept and as did, she dreamed. She imagined herself torn from her parents - like an immigrant appealing for safety on a foreign shore, and she felt angry and betrayed.

Instinct helped her arise from her slumber, and she began to wander the night, searching for she knew not what. As she sleepwalked through the darkest corners of the area, she played her instrument tirelessly. She was soon able to distinguish shapes in her world of shadows. What her bedazzled eyes had perceived as a strange creature, reappeared, mirrored in a play of contrasts, laying inert at her mercy. This was an unexpected opportunity; her thirst for blood returned.

Uncontrollable inner forces pushed her to the target until she reached the elixir she dreamed of. Crazed by her infernal music, she plunged deep and drank her fill, but still it was not enough. Though she was delighted by her unexpected and improbable achievement, she was not quenched and went back for more and more. Though the rich feast temporarily numbed her hatred, she viciously renewed her attack, never knowing why. Suddenly, in the middle of the vengeful orgy… SLAP! A blanket of blood appeared. Fireworks with pointed lights followed but were extinguished one by one. Then there was only eternal night and this time it was forever.

II -A SUMMERTIME NIGHTMARE

I turned on the light, and Anita raced to open the tightly closed window. We leaned out in that moonless night to breathe the hot air. I quickly took off my wet clothes and rushed to the bathroom to cool off.

I often remember Hector, a good friend from my youth who – decades before Kevorkian – liked to talk about the minimum conditions required to justify continuing our existence.

"As long as we can enjoy the most primitive pleasures, living is completely justified," he would say.

The pleasure Hector talked about awakened a carefully secured sliver of memory, and I recall having heatedly disputed my friend's thesis. I took a refreshing shower and the benevolent torrent restored my tired body back to life. I dried off vigorously in front of the open window and turned off the light to sleep. I thought again about enjoying the basics in life. I stretched out full-length on the bed, and soon my hot skin was once again bathed in sweat. The beads gathered on my forehead, and the miniature rivulets coalesced to form tiny waterfalls and flowed towards my armpits.

I fell asleep instantly as if struck by lightning. My last conscious memory was of Anita's deep rhythmic breathing as she slept. And then, the dream.

I penetrated the world of shadows that I had traveled as a student, and revisited when our children were small. The road to Hades was as dark as I had imagined. The water of Styx was cold and unmoving, and seemed to offer no resistance to the strokes of the oars held by the gloomy boatman. My last death rattle barely expelled the gold coin that adorned my mouth, which Charon dismissively placed in his bottomless sack.

Recognizing the grove planted by Persephone, with its barren willows and black poplars, I found myself at the end of my earthly days. The world made the delicious fruits I had enjoyed available to everyone, but awarded them to only a few. I certainly counted myself among the chosen few. Through the mist that surrounded us, I glimpsed a multitude of the unchosen wandering erratically along the shore of the river Styx, unable to find their way.

All earthly fanfare was left behind. Mundane noise had given way to the supernatural silence of the lagoon. Charon had already left the sun-kissed sphere aboard his ship, with his double magic rod made of light and heat. I was surprised by the scene before me. Given my presumed earthly success, I was surprised that I had not been taken anywhere that resembled the heaven described in my childhood. At the same time, this was not Hades - the hell illuminated by eternal flames meant to purify our flesh. Instead, I had entered a cold and dark place.

Before my eyes a bird's-eye review of my life passed in a succession of images. As if rewinding a video of my existence, it captured my life in reverse - from death backwards to my birth. The rewinding of images gradually rejuvenated my aged face and my bald head was once again covered with hair. Wrinkles and gray hair magically disappeared.

I was soon surrounded by beings devoid of arms and legs who contorted rhythmically. I was barely able to glimpse the few humans near me since most of the creatures surrounding me were singing worms and they moved to the beat of a strange hum.

I could see that sometimes I had been brainwashed by the worms' chanting, and now I could see my own failings and know what I should have done - a truth which my fellow humans could not fathom. I was able to recap my achievements, but now, measuring with the cosmic scale of the Styx, my successes seemed greatly diminished. In image after image I saw myself basking in what I had presumed were my positions of power. Contemplating what I had seen as my apparent breadth of spirit, my false modesty, and my boasts of generosity, I could no longer deceive myself. I stood unmasked and saw myself as selfish, smug, petulant, and haughty.

When the rewinding arrived at my childhood, it held on an image I had forgotten - one that my first-grade teacher had related to my mother. On the first day of school, the teacher would ask the children what they planned to do with their lives. Legend has it that I replied that I wanted to be a good man. In truth, thc good man that my first-grade teacher had described had little in common with the clown surrounded by worms on that funereal procession.

When the rewinding arrived at the earliest images of my infancy, my sleeping consciousness registered the pressure of approaching the end of the journey. The silence was broken only by a flute dirge that was sharp and monotonous to my ears. The incessant hum, played by a spectral performer, gradually increased in tempo until it became deafening and terrifying.

An internal mechanism was activated and following the beat of the hellish music, and when the rewinding of my life reached the end, it paused, then reversed direction and played through again. This time it flashed from my earliest life to my death.

I judged my earthly adventure harshly. As I looked on at much of what I had experienced, I repeatedly questioned the decisions I'd made. It was distressing to consider each of my missteps when I lacked the ability to change anything.

Finally we approached the gate to the kingdom of Hades, jealously guarded by Cerberus. I was well aware that Charon had an unspoken agreement with the three-headed monster, and that my entry to Hades was assured. As the boat passed near the gate, the breath of Cerberus' flames scorched my skin. There would be no going back and upon arriving at my final destination, Charon and Cerberus vanished. Only emptiness and darkness surrounded me.

Then came the infernal flute again, humming cruelly with the monotonous melody that left me shuddering. Whatever madness the buzzing melody that penetrated my eardrums carried, the music quickly moved off again, giving me a brief respite. This hellish game driven by the master of Hades continued seemingly endlessly until it appeared that I had atoned for my worldly mistakes. I felt overwhelmingly anxious as I took what I believed would be my last breath before abandoning my earthly mask, when suddenly… SLAP!

I awoke, startled, bathed in sweat, my hand stained with blood.

8

The Secret Pact

1970

My days are in the yellow leaf;
The flowers and fruits of love are gone;
the worm - the canker, and the grief;
are mine alone.

-Lord George Gordon Byron
"On this day I complete my 36th year."

EULALIA AND RAÚL'S MARRIAGE had been a happy one. But shortly after joyously celebrating their twenty-fifth wedding anniversary with the entire family, Eulalia became ill and was diagnosed with cancer. The tumor was advanced, and it was evident to all including Eulalia that the end was near. The patient adamantly refused any type of invasive treatment except for narcotics to ease the pain. Yet despite morphine, Eulalia was undeniably suffering.

The couple spent their precious remaining time talking, revisiting the years they had spent together, and considering their satisfaction at having raised a family they were proud of. They chatted endlessly, murmuring words only they could hear. Clearly Raúl would have much to deal with once the pain of the task before him was complete.

Eulalia's face was a combination of pain and entreaty. After much discussion, Raúl agreed to his wife's pleading and with a shaking hand, he dissolved a yellowish powder in a glass of water. Eulalia drank it with relish. Raúl's kissed his wife's forehead for the last time and closed Eulalia's eyes which seemed to still gaze at him. The patient's death had been expected for the family doctor had told them it wouldn't be long. Nobody was surprised by her quick, benevolent demise. She was no longer in pain.

After Eulalia's death, Raúl's children and friends comforted him and tried to help him return to life as he'd know it. At fifty, Raúl was still young and vigorous, but his wife's death had not only changed him physically, it had altered his personality.

Unexpectedly, he announced his imminent retirement from the company he owned and managed, and he appointed a successor. Raúl met with his attorney to transfer the title of his home to his eldest son, and to settle other matters pertaining to his will. Ownership of any remaining properties would be transferred to his children. He wanted to leave nothing to chance.

Following Eulalia's death, Raúl spent many a sleepless night tortured by mixed feelings over having acquiesced to his beloved wife's wishes. Raúl lost weight. He didn't have the patience to cook and grew pinched and sickly. His tense face revealed anxiety. He rarely left the house and grew increasingly quiet, saying little. Friends saw a different person. Occasionally they would run into him on the street and were surprised to shake his hand and find it trembling, wet and cold.

Roberto, his eldest son, witnessed his father's rapid decline with concern and tried to be supportive. Although these days Raúl always had an excuse to avoid company, he accepted Roberto's offer to join him and visit Eulalia's grave on the following Friday, October 3.

They agreed to meet at the cemetery but unfortunately Roberto rear-ended another vehicle on the way. After the altercation on the street, and after giving the police his statement and then dealing with hellish rush-hour traffic, Roberto arrived at the cemetery nearly two hours late. Tired of waiting, his father had already left.

Roberto stood facing the grave that Raúl had covered with fresh flowers earlier. After a few minutes of painful meditation, his gaze was drawn to the marble headstone next to Eulalia's. He was surprised to find Raúl's name on it. Even more disconcerting were the dates engraved on it, August 25 1925 – October 4, 1975. Roberto read the date again, fearing he'd misread it. There was no doubt. The stone had been prepared to receive the new occupant on the following day, Sunday, October 4, 1975, the first anniversary of Eulalia's death.

Roberto rushed to his father's house. It was dark and closed. He rang the doorbell repeatedly, but there was no answer. He phoned, but got only the answering machine. Roberto saw his father's car parked inside the garage and had no doubt he was home.

Roberto left and returned home, arriving in a state of extreme agitation. On entering, he found a message from his father on his answering machine:

> "Dear Roberto, this is my good-bye to you and your siblings. Please leave me alone and don't try to change my mind. I love you all very much."

That evening the family held a turbulent meeting where many options were considered. Some wanted to call the police for help, others the fire department. They wanted to break into the house by force and dissuade him. But in the end they decided that Raúl had a right to make his own choices.

The next day the family gathered intending to hold an event reminiscent of a wake for Raúl - planned for what they assumed would be his last night. They talked about his life, his relationship with Eulalia and about things he had done and hadn't done. Gallons of coffee were consumed and forgotten, stories were recalled and shared again. Jokes were made about some funny episode, not of out disrespect but to celebrate Raúl's humanity.

Meanwhile at home, Raúl had put on a selection of his favorite baroque music and savored a glass of the wine that he and Eulalia had set aside for a special occasion. He meditated with his eyes half shut, mentally beginning to set himself free from terrestrial restraints. Soon he dozed and slipped into the world of shadows.

He dreamed and in the dream he and Eulalia chatted again at length. If by chance an observer hidden nearby could have observed them, he would not have been able to hear Eulalia's convincing words whispered to her lover. Eulalia's face, no longer reflecting pain, was bathed in peace and love. Raúl's face was hidden, buried in Eulalia's ample bosom. The two remained this way for some time with Eulalia whispering gently into Raúl's ear as Raul felt relief knowing his wife had found peace for all eternity.

A thin ray of sunlight peeked through the living room window when Raúl, sitting on his favorite sofa, finally opened his eyes. Looking around to get his bearings, he stood, had a last sip of the Barolo wine, and resolutely picked up his 45-caliber gun from the table. He carefully checked to confirm it was loaded, but then placed it back on the table. Calmly, like someone who had come to a definitive decision, he picked up the telephone and dialed.

"Hello. Is this the cemetery? This is Raúl Durán. There has been a change of plans. I would like to have the marble slab removed from plot 3624," he said, as he wrapped the gun in a square of flannel, and serenely put it away in a desk drawer.

9

Ménage À Trois

1998

Unlike us, the ant has the fortune
of being more sensitive to pleasure than to pain.
... The ant cannot be happy unless
it can provide happiness to those around her.

Maurice Maeterlinck,
The Life of the Ant

THE DAY OF MY EIGHTIETH BIRTHDAY dawned rainy and gray.

I had kept busy since my beloved Hildegard's death. Every summer was spent with Hilde's large family in Europe. Then I stayed in Arizona with friends for part of the winter - especially with my lady friends who took good care of me. Neither Hilde nor I would have suspected I'd enjoy life this much without her, for we had been so happy together. But my happiness faded when, as we had every year, I spent a few months in our old house in Michigan. The winter days turned long and boring.

The single highlight of my day was visiting the portraits I had painted who'd become my friends and hung in my private gallery. I hadn't painted much in recent years, but I still enjoyed looking at the old paintings marking various milestones of my life. Familiar landscapes, faraway places and the faces of dear friends paraded before me.

My imagination was set free, and I found myself delving into places I had known before and engaging in a conversation with the subject of my favorite painting, an old peasant that I'd revisited for years.

One morning a gentle rain imperceptibly turned into the first snowfall of the season, and absolute silence reigned in my pictorial museum. Sitting in my chair, I contemplated the face I'd painted of my old friend. His shoulders were sloped as if the centuries weighed heavily. He wore a straw hat above his noble face, his thick sideburns, white whiskers, and his short, graying beard. The portrait included his rustic jacket, the color of the earth tones typical of his region. Those who had seen the painting agreed that the expression on the peasant's face was its most captivating feature, and observing his image allowed me to rekindle many happy moments and to return to them frequently.

One morning I returned to spend a couple of hours among my paintings and memories, and as I gazed at my old friend, I thought I saw a new expression in his eyes. I often had lively discussions with the old man who seemed to hold my gaze with a mixture of compassion and severity. Hilde had loved this painting and often pointed out his changing expressions. But on the morning in question his eyes held an enigmatic look that I couldn't decipher.

I finished my coffee and walking past the dining room table, I was struck by something I would remember for the rest of my life. A tiny teardrop-sized bead of honey had inadvertently fallen on the table and attracted a black ant that was evidently enjoying the feast. As I approached the table, the ant was startled, but then possibly sensing my friendly attitude, it returned eagerly to the drop.

Careful not to make the slightest noise, I sat down to watch the tiny ant that came and circled the drop of honey for a long time. Sated, the ant continued exploring every inch of the table, repeatedly stopping in front of me as if trying to tell me something. At last the ant began her descent down one of the table legs, heading resolutely towards the wall and past the painting of my friend. It was as if my friend was watching her intently also.

The little ant climbed the wall and spent a while circling my peasant friend. I was thrilled with her arrival and couldn't take my eyes off her until out of the corner of my eye, I thought I caught a smile on my old friend's face. There was a mysterious familiarity to her that I couldn't quite place. The ant finally decided to seek new horizons, and I remained absolutely still so as not to disturb her. I watched until she disappeared and attempted to engage my peasant friend in conversation, but he resumed his usual expression as if nothing in this world could surprise him.

That night it was difficult to fall asleep. I couldn't clear my thoughts of my six-legged guest, and during my sleeplessness I tried to decipher the meaning of my peasant friend's unfathomable gaze. Evidently he was amused by the scenario. Finally a restful sleep came and momentarily erased the events of the previous day.

The following morning I was back enjoying my steaming cup of coffee and a greeting from the wall from my peasant friend. Without thinking, after breakfast I carefully wiped the table so not even a tiny drop of honey remained, and I became engrossed in the book I was reading.

But after a while I became aware of a black spot floating at the edge of my vision. I blinked several times to clear my eyes of the particle until I noticed that the particle was the black ant which had returned. Although I suppose all black ants look alike to us, I had no doubt that the ant walking back and forth across the table was the same one that visited the day before.

I glanced at the painting and noticed that my friend's gaze had turned to a mix of amusement and expectation. Apparently we both had no doubt that the ant was searching for the drop of honey, unable to find it since I had wiped the table clean. I went to the kitchen for the honey jar, and laid a tiny drop on the table, somewhat surprised that I did so almost automatically. Meanwhile my old friend watched, pleased to see that the ant did not take long to find the honey. The two of us were completely enthralled in the scene and watched for quite some time until the ant descended from the table and, after a second lengthy visit with my friend, she disappeared through a crack in the floor.

The following morning after my usual breakfast, I left a drop of honey on the table and continued my daily routine. I told myself the ant's visit had been a mere coincidence, and that I shouldn't expect anything. But I had not fooled my friend who smiled at me mockingly.

It was almost noon when the little ant made a triumphant return. Apparently the three of us enjoyed the visit equally as she appeared quite comfortable in our presence. Since then, I've gotten used to leaving a drop of honey on the table every day as we knew that no matter what, the ant would come to visit.

As winter came to an end, one day she did not return. My old friend's changing expression was particularly notable that day. Early in the morning, his face reflected what I had often observed before, a placid expression that perhaps foreshadowed death. Hours passed, and as the little ant did not return, my friend's face changed repeatedly, successively revealing impatience, anxiety, and restlessness.

The little ant never returned, and I missed the curious familiarity I felt when she was near. The old peasant and I waited in vain day after day, and sometimes when we thought that our beloved absentee had returned, I would catch a glimpse, a spark of life in my old friend's eternal gaze.

10

The Revealing Flood

1988

As soon as he first realized he was forgetting,
he found a remedy…
Those without memories, create paper ones.
It was an ephemeral illusion, however,
for it had gotten so bad
that he forgot what the reminders meant,
those notes he stuffed in his pockets;
he searched the house for the eyeglasses he was wearing,
turned the key again after having locked the doors,
and lost the thread of what he read
because he forgot the plot's premises
or the characters' allegiances.

-Gabriel García Márquez,
Love in Times of Cholera

AFTER MANY YEARS of faithful service, I was at last given a job of high importance of which I am very proud. In truth, it is a very difficult job, with huge responsibilities requiring a person one could trust without hesitation.

My daily routine to ensure that all is in order begins before dawn. I don't have a fixed schedule because my activities depend on what is occurring at my job in the moment and that's not up to me. I might have refused the promotion, but why would I? I'd have given up better pay and a position that requires maturity and common sense, attributes I apparently possess and which are greatly valued in my new position.

Failure to accept my promotion would have meant squandering a unique opportunity to be where the most important global problems are resolved, where the hottest issues of the day are discussed, where I rub shoulders with the world's most celebrated political figures, and where I am lucky enough to be in close proximity to our beloved President.

My position requires a professional demeanor - especially the ability to listen and be discrete. What takes place at my place of employment is strictly confidential, and I am never to discuss it with anyone. The topics covered within these walls are classified, and I do not mention them, not even to my family. I only write about them in my diary which I keep in a secure place, and I often reread my entries - although only in the privacy of my room.

Today began like most others, with one exception. During the morning a series of delegations from Arab countries filed through the building. There was apparently a great deal of concern about the oil issue. The President welcomed the Arabs courteously and assured them that he would defend their interests as if they were his own. I believe that was his intention.

While the Arab emirs were with the President, a delegation of Israelis also visited, waiting in another room. When it was their turn, they also expressed concern about the situation in the Middle East, but the President calmed them, assuring that he would defend Israeli interests as if they were his own.

I don't know much about politics or the economy, but I believe the interests of the Arabs are rather different from Jewish interests. If they have something in common, I'm not aware of it which made me in further awe of the President's ability to mediate factions at loggerheads, clearly one of the many reasons we elected him.

After the last member of the Jewish delegation left the elliptical office, a serious problem arose. Photographers and reporters from the International Press had come to interview the President about his upcoming reelection campaign. However the tribulations of the morning, first with the Arabs and then with the Jews, had exhausted the poor man and left him totally spent. Our beloved President collapsed on the sofa, but in moments the office was overrun by staff ready for that eventuality who arrived to remedy the situation. Their prompt response reminded me of racing cars at their pit stop; tanks are filled with gas, tires get changed, and a hundred tasks are performed in seconds so the cars are back on the track, good as new.

The crew practically carried our exhausted President to an adjacent room, where he was helped to undress and assisted into a hot bath with rainbow-colored bubbles. The bath was followed by a massage performed by a Japanese woman who patted him dry with an enormous towel and effortlessly laid him back on a flat table to vigorously rub his feet. I'm told foot massage is very good for the brain, and it was easy to see it worked wonders on our President. The Japanese masseuse completed her task by walking on the President's back, barefoot with her tiny feet, while terrified aides watched in fear.

Next came a crew who arrived to beautify and rejuvenate the President's tired, worn face. They smoothed his wrinkles and applied potions with surprising results. They brushed his teeth, sprayed his mouth and put magical drops in his eyes to dilate his pupils which made them shine youthfully. His barber made a triumphant entrance shaving him and styling his hair with dyes and creams that made it look fuller. Lastly, they helped him dress in a new outfit carefully chosen for the occasion.

The result of all these ministrations, which took exactly twenty-two and a half minutes as I timed it, might have seemed extraordinary had it been the first time I'd witnessed it. But since it happened daily - sometimes twice daily - it didn't surprise me at all. A few minutes later, the President looked splendid and youthful, ready to welcome the journalists with grace and aplomb as was duly reported in the news.

The message for the electorate was that this was a mature, yet still young president, full of vitality, in complete command, and with much yet to offer his fellow citizens.

Once the pack of reporters left, the President sat at his desk where one by one various government bureaucrats presented projects for his approval and legislation for his signature.

I admired our President's profound intelligence, his ability to resolve a diverse range of problems with a pen stroke. For example, with a wave of his pen he ordered the bombing of Karnuk as an exemplary punishment to a belligerent autocrat unwilling to accept the economic terms imposed by our President's administration. I don't know the specifics, but they say that showing strength and determination – such as ordering a bombing or declaring a small war – helps to enhance popularity, especially right before an election.

With the stroke of his pen, the President ordered economic aid for the government of Transpartania, which I found baffling. I'd thought of Transpartania as another corrupt dictatorship. The President of course knew something I don't and told reporters that Transpartania was one of our most valued allies.

Next on his busy schedule, our President received a visit from a congressional investigative committee regarding a matter so delicate I dare not reveal it even in my diary. But after an exhausting session during which they peppered him with questions, they were unable to wrest a single compromising declaration from his mouth.

His favorite reply – "I can't recall" – categorically underscored his innocence, which is surely why he repeated the phrase so often. I don't really believe he couldn't recall a thing, but I think it's a great answer as it ended the matter. Defeated, the members of the investigative committee withdrew, knowing they had met their match.

But the most noteworthy part of the day, or actually the night for it took place in the wee hours, was a discussion with the highest military leaders and the most important members of the ruling class. At issue was the preferred strategy in the event of an imminent nuclear war. This was truly important. The question dealt with how to proceed in the event of a nuclear attack that in minutes could eliminate half the world's population.

The lengthy discussion became heated with few solutions offered, and in the end all eyes turned to the President. He held the direct line to the military high command, and he alone had command of the magic presidential button. Pressed by his confident finger, it would unleash a massive attack, an effective defense that would relentlessly exterminate our enemies, though it could provoke a rapid nuclear response with cataclysmic consequences for the planet. That such a weapon of defense was in the possession of a single person sent a chill up my spine. But I was comforted by the fact that our beloved President was a man of visionary intelligence and quick impulses. Without question we are in good hands.

When everyone left after the meeting, the President went into his private bathroom to freshen up. The office was a mess, and of course it was my job to attend to it.

The President was in the bathroom for a long time, and he surely deserved some relief after a tiring day. Finally he came out and greeted us with his celebrity smile before retiring to his rooms.

My team was now hard at work, and as always, I personally took care of the President's bathroom. Opening the door, I went directly to the sink. As I did, I noticed that my feet were splashing in a dark yellow liquid that foamed when it came in contact with my shoes. I tried to see where the flood was coming from and saw that the toilet was spotless. It didn't seem to have been touched all day. In the corner, however, the waste basket was seeped in urine which covered most of the floor around it.

When I get home after a long day of work, I take a hot shower and go to bed. I usually fall asleep instantly. But that night, while wiping the soles of my stinking shoes, I recalled the ocean of urine flooding the President's bathroom floor and I couldn't fall asleep.

11

Vendetta

1970

I believe that order is better than chaos,
creation better than destruction.
I prefer gentleness to violence,
forgiveness to vendetta.

-Leon Tolstoy,
War and Peace

AS I WALKED WITH my fists clenched towards Pancho Gimenez's house – the stronghold of our bitter enemies – opaque memories of my childhood and turbulent youth reverberated through my mind. I savored the bittersweet taste of my coming vendetta - my brain riddled with images of what I'd just found - my wife's torn body, my slaughtered mother, and my dead daughters.

I couldn't tolerate the hot, stifling air and ripped off my shirt, as I walked. The scars showing plainly on my naked chest and arms were silent testimony to my countless, bloody fights in the slums. I had often prevailed, so I knew Pancho and his crew carried their own scars.

The endemic state of war with the Gimenez gang calmed somewhat when we moved to a small house in a different neighborhood. We weren't completely free of the gang, but moving gave us breathing room although we would often see one of Pancho's seven children prowling our new neighborhood looking for trouble.

The slaughter of my family reminded me of the time that we found Uncle Rosendo's body in his kitchen - another bloodbath. Though the police had no clues, we always suspected the Gimenez gang - sure it had been a revenge killing since they didn't even take the money in his pockets. We knew that Rosendo had been up to his old tricks, and they had sworn to get him.

When we moved away, the Gimenez family mocked us endlessly. "Chickens!" the children called at us, cackling noisily as they ran in circles around the old moving van in hopes of provoking one last clash. The gang considered it a partial victory that we were leaving the neighborhood, but not a total victory, of course, because we were still alive, and they resented that. Now after the slaughter, I think they believed they had achieved the definitive triumph. How wrong they were.

I kept replaying the scene I'd found on arriving home after work - my loved ones: María and the three girls, butchered, lay scattered about the room. A few steps beyond, my mother was stretched out in a pool of blood. There was so much blood that the five of them seemed to float on a red ocean.

The pain I felt on finding their bodies became a pressure that still takes my breath away. Crazed, I kissed them and, stained with their blood, took a Colt 45 revolver from a drawer - a gun that had its own history in my battles with the gang. I had absolutely no proof, but also no doubt about the murderers' identity. It was obvious that Pancho and his bunch had done it. The massacre had their unmistakable bloody signature, and I left determined to take justice with my own hands.

I rejoiced thinking that the remainder of my family would finally be able to live in peace once I erased the gang from the face of the earth. I stroked the gun's handle with pleasure but paused when I reached the ditch from where, filled with rage, I saw the house of my enemies. I became confused as a maelstrom of hellish thoughts clouded my mind.

Soon the cooling night air brought a sense of calm as I continued to reflect on my plan. We may be savages, I thought, but we live in a civilized country. We have a judicial system, and according to the law, people accused of crimes must be investigated, prosecuted, and tried in a court of law. In a moment of clear-headedness, I knew that even the Gimenez gang had the right to a defense, and that sometimes the way things initially appear are not the way they happened. It occurred to me that in a civilized country like ours, victims should not act as police, prosecutor, judge and executioner.

Wrapped in my somber thoughts, I slowly returned home. When I arrived, I again saw the scene that remains forever engraved in my memory. I tenderly kissed the beloved bodies of my family, placed the revolver in the drawer, and called the police.

12

Puppets of Kobe

1995

Japan's puppet tradition, Ningyö Jöruri,
developed as a dramatic form,
generally known as Bunraku, and
enabled the introduction of Japanese culture in a broad sense.
Jane Marie Law focuses our attention
on a small island near Kobe, Awaji,
the center of puppeteering since the sixteenth century.

-Jane Marie Law,
Puppets of Nostalgia

A TIMID MAN of few words, Masao studied electronics, easily passing every subject for he was a good student. After graduating, he had no problem leaving Osaka, the city of his birth where his parents and brother lived.

Masao was autistic, and so reclusive that when he began working as a technician in a computer factory in Kobe, nobody other than his family noticed he'd even left Osaka. Likewise in his new job, nobody in Kobe knew he existed since he rarely communicated. Yet his direct supervisor valued him highly because he was effective and could work well independently.

Masao's life continued in Kobe, and time drifted on with the repetitive monotony of the autistic. The months and seasons passed with no apparent changes. He lived in the privacy of the labyrinths of his mind, a world more complex than even the intricate network within his computers. Though he frequently tested the electronic circuitry of his computers, he never used them to communicate with the outside world.

Masao had lost touch with his family, and had no friends. He never dared approach a woman, and if a young woman ever wanted to enter his impenetrable world, Masao ignored her until she took the hint and sought other company.

In his modest apartment, his favorite pastime was to watch televised puppet performances which he did with such intense concentration that his expression would never change.

One January morning an earthquake shook Kobe, and millions of cracks spread across the ground. In seconds the earthquake destroyed or swallowed hundreds of homes. Many lost their lives and there were food shortages and potable water was scarce. Kobe was the picture of desolation.

A sepulchral silence followed the terrifying crash of falling walls. After the earth's deadly heave, Kobe was covered by a cloud of dust that slowly settled over the city. Hints of ghostly shapes appeared to rise from the rubble.

Still home about to leave for work when the quake hit, Masao found himself instantly covered under crushed stone. Had anyone been able to see his inexpressive face, they would never have imagined it was a moment of crisis. He was surrounded by rocks as if in a stone coffin. Mercifully, the rocks had piled around a fallen beam, forming a roof-like support that saved him from being crushed.

But the darkness was absolute. Masao found that his head occupied a space of unknown dimensions while his arms were trapped by the rubble, and he couldn't move them. He could move one leg, but it felt numb. His burial chamber was narrow, and the air was stale.

After several hours of silence and immobility, Masao noticed that the stones near his neck began to move slightly. He felt something soft and furry brush his cheek before feeling a sharp sting in his back. A sticky, warm liquid flowed while vicious teeth tore a wound.

For hours, Masao endured this torture without a whimper, until an aftershock shook the earth shook again. When the rubble surrounding him finally settled, Masao felt a gust of fresh air coming through a small opening, and he took a deep breath. His visitor, thirst sated and belly full, scurried away to the outside world. The tremor had put an end to its feast, and allowed a ray of light through the tiny opening.

As the hours passed, the sun went down and the light faded, leaving only darkness. Before long, Masao heard the disturbing noises of a hungry herd coming through the rubble. His guest from the previous night returned, but this time he was not alone.

Masao's only defense against the murderous assault by his voracious visitors was a limited movement of his head. He barely survived a long night of pain and flickering shadows until morning when a tiny ray of light again filtered through the opening. For the first time since being trapped, he heard noises from outside. His visitors sunk their teeth in one last time, then quickly left.

When the rescuers finally located him, Masao was in pain, hungry, and his mouth was as dry as an autumn leaf. A multitude of bites still oozed the blood that covered his skin. Freed at last, he tried to move but his limbs wouldn't respond.

They rushed Masao to a hospital for emergency care where he received intravenous saline solutions and healthy food. He appeared to improve and gradually recovered the use of his limbs. After several days, the nurses tenderly washed his badly bruised body, dressed him in clean clothes and he was released. Masao looked almost as he had before the quake since the injuries on his back and neck were not visible, although adhesive bandages covered the bite marks on his face.

He was alive and able to leave the hospital, but his state of mind was such that it was doubtful that Masao was luckier than the thousands who had been crushed in the rubble. He was confused, did not know where to go, and aimlessly wandered Kobe's devastated streets. Only ruins remained of his apartment house, and there was nothing left of the factory where he worked.

After days of homeless wandering, Masao finally found space in an emergency shelter. He was provided with a sparsely furnished room included a reed mat on which he slept and a rickety TV set offering blurry images. But at least he had electricity and a place to stay before the coming cold of the Kobe winter.

Day after day, Masao looked for work. He had no references and without family or friends every door he tried was closed. Overnight, jobs for highly skilled specialists like Masao had vanished. The city focused its efforts on rebuilding, and did not require his technical computer skills.

Masao had miraculously survived the earthquake. He was still young, strong and could walk, see, hear, and was in control of his physiological functions. But as far as society was concerned, he didn't exist.

Masao spent long hours sitting quietly in the lotus position in front of the small TV screen in the company of his beloved puppets, watching them and dozing, lulled by sips of warm sake and the musical sounds of the samisen. He had no visitors and had anyone seen him, they wouldn't have known whether he was asleep, awake, or dead.

While Masao vegetated, Kobe rebuilt. Spring arrived with a breath of life, and then summer, followed again by fall. There was a hint of frost in the cold Kobe mornings.

As one of the shelter administrators, I arrived at Masao's room for a routine inspection. We knocked discreetly on his door, hearing an animated conversation and the slow cadence of samisen background music. The voices continued, ignoring our arrival. We knocked again, and as nobody answered, we entered.

There was Masao in the lotus position, wearing his heavy winter coat, his back propped against the wall, staring inexpressively at the TV screen which showed a dramatically narrated puppet tragedy. His face was inscrutable as it had always been.

The autopsy revealed that Masao had died many months earlier, probably during the previous winter. We found an unopened letter from his brother on top of the television. It invited Masao to return to Osaka, where it might have been easier to find work.

Meanwhile, in the background the TV continued to offer the monotonous dialog of the puppets to the sound of the samisen strings.

13

The Submerged Colossus

1981

I think about what our great capitals might someday be.

-André Maurois

LEGEND HAS it that others before us explored these oceans and discovered distant lands beyond the horizon where the sun rises. If there had been any truth to the fantasies the elders related, it would have been lost in time since more than 12,000 moons passed since the great universal flood marked the beginning of our civilization.

The fantasy of the elders tells that survivors of the great flood occupied a region at a high elevation called Bod. When the waters rose and covered most of the land, the survivors took refuge on the top of a mountain – the only piece of habitable land remaining.

We are accustomed to enjoying hot weather and the tropical vegetation which extends to the very edge of our temperate beaches. So for us the legend is hard to believe - that our Kathmandu was once a city in a desolate, inhospitable region on a high mountain cloaked with a strange, white mantle. Today there are only a few hills around us, and they are always covered in lush greenery. We cannot imagine that our village was blanketed in a cold, white carpet, but that belief is part of the legend of the origin of Kathmandu.

There are hills on the island populated by palm trees and inhabited by capuchin monkeys that argue with the toucans over branches. The book of the unnamed prophet states that the legendary Himalayas had once been a chain of high peaks that only a chosen few could reach. The road to higher ground was dangerous, but the only chance to survive the encroaching waters was to reach the top. The summit was the reward for those who could reach it, and according to the scriptures, we are the descendants of the chosen few who did.

Stories passed from parents to children for generations describe mankind before the great flood as the spawn of evil. It is said that men plundered the earth, extracting its most precious riches by means of monstrous mosquitoes with giant, tireless suckers until the dry, depleted soil gave way under the weight of man's cities.

In their insatiable greed, the men of the ancient legend poisoned the oceans, decimating the marine life that sought refuge in the furthest, deepest waters. Men depleted the sources of drinking water and fouled the air with the stinking gases released by infernal machines. Disappearing beneath the waters after thousands of moons, the scriptures speak of a civilization consisting of millions of men - with skins of many shades and round eyes rather than almond-shaped like ours. They spoke many languages, and it's said they could fly like birds.

After leaving their planet a dunghill, the elders say that men even dared to defy God in space. The Almighty bitterly reproached himself before the council of gods for having begotten a stupid being that could not control its self-destructive tendencies and greed, despite that it had everything it might need to be happy. The scriptures describe that in that fateful time the earth, enraged by mankind's idiocy, swallowed entire cities in craters and buried an advanced civilization that perished.

The polar icecaps and the glaciers melted, and mountains sunk into the oceans. This caused the waters to rise relentlessly and erase all traces of man's existence - an antiquity we never knew. Men, women, and children tried desperately to climb the mountains before the seas rose, but most perished from hunger, thirst and cold.

In the wake of that exodus, forced by nature's irascible forces, came what the prophet calls the original sin of our race: the insatiable appetite for human flesh driven by hunger. As millions climbed for higher ground, meat became abundant because the weak, dying in scores, became food for the rest. When on occasion the feast did not exhaust every bit of the meat, the strongest survivors stored what remained in cold cavern, safe from hungry marauders.

All the signs indicate that extinction was fast and gory. As meat grew increasingly scarce, the strongest attacked the weakest until the strongest, now defenseless themselves, became nourishment for the few who were left.

The elderly disappeared first, of course. Besides being weaker, they were vulnerable to rampant epidemics, and they were unable to adapt to violent weather extremes. Though their meat was tough, its taste was sought after, and thus the old rapidly diminished in numbers. Children were also coveted morsels. When hunger was such that death seemed near, even the most devoted parents gave in to their instinct to survive. When the supply of old people and children was exhausted, women were next to be thrown into the pot to feed the men. A man would sacrifice his neighbor's wife to alleviate his hunger, and would only think of his own wife as an appetizing delicacy if his own situation became life-threatening.

Not even the flood could eliminate sexual desire, and the men often desired another man's wife to satisfy primitive carnal pleasures.

The legend tells that it wasn't long before every vestige of this self destructive civilization disappeared until only one man and one woman remained - the beginning of what is now Kathmandu. They were the origin of our race although many believe that the prophet's tale is only fantasy - the product of our tropical imagination.

In the many moons that have passed since that time, we have made great progress. But we have also paid a high price for our civilization. Kathmandu is small and while in the beginning there was plenty of room for the descendants of the original couple, as the population gradually increased, life became ever more difficult.

The island is rich with hardwood trees and wild cane, so it was natural that we built boats to fish and return home daily with food for our families. For generations we lived on the fruits of the sea. From earlier civilizations we inherited fire and the wheel, but we owe the distillation of cane alcohol to our own tribal genius. We use the alcohol for fuel to light our homes and as a source of energy. Someone used it in a small three-wheeled vehicle, and now there are so many such vehicles no one can walk safely anywhere on the island.

Kathmandu's concentration of people became so dense that the only option was to control the birth rate. Every child born in Kathmandu after the firstborn belongs to the community, and is sacrificed within seven days of its birth - no matter how painful it is to the child's parents. As a result, we no longer have large families. Thanks to the drastic regulations which limited the number of young adults, the elderly soon dominated once again and established a dictatorship.

~

Today, many moons later, I sail the ocean as the member of a crew. According to my calculations, it has been three weeks since we sailed from Kathmandu, and we haven't seen a hint of land. The day dawned cloudy making it even more difficult for the lookout to make out features on the horizon.

Our decision to sail for new horizons had been a difficult one. Although our motives for departing were clear, our relatives didn't approve of an adventure they called our youthful madness, and friends tried to dissuade us. Since the great flood, nobody dared travel out of sight of our island.

We were required to obtain permission from the Council of Ancients to travel, which they reluctantly granted. Nothing is done on Kathmandu without their permission. In a debate lasting days, we made our case to council that there could be other inhabitable lands beyond the horizon. Council accepted that while there were valid reasons to attempt the reckless adventure we proposed, the chances for success were remote.

What nobody at the Council dared admit, clearly we were suffocating on an island that was no longer a paradise; that with a bit of luck perhaps we could discover land for a new settlement. The ancients quizzed each of us thoroughly and made clear that while they might grant permission, they would not endorse our plan. We had to agree that the voyage and all preparations including the construction of the ship would be our own responsibility.

We built the *Marigalante* in twelve moons. It was the largest ship ever seen in Kathmandu, propelled by two lines of 25 rowers and a square sail on a mast attached to the boom. In a favorable wind, we could hoist a triangular sail attached to the mast, the latest breakthrough in islander nautical design.

There were no objections to my participation in the expedition, for I had no ties to anyone, and no one to support. We knew that this might be a one-way trip; that our final destination might be the bottom of the sea or the stomach of a shark. Or, we might encounter nothing but endless ocean, sky and more sky, and perhaps nothing else. Or, we might find success - another land - perhaps a small island like Kathmandu that would allow us to take a full, rich breath and expand our people's prospects.

Soon after our departure, Kathmandu became a tiny dot on the horizon, and then finally disappeared. The oppressive controls of our people faded, and for the first time we knew freedom. It wasn't absolute freedom, for it was limited by the edges of our ship, by the disciplines we accepted as our norms, the rules of navigation outlined by Namri, our captain, and by the immensity of the ocean surrounding us. I wondered if we had exchanged one oppression for another as I anticipated the hardships ahead and the proximity of death. But I clung to the hope of a possible change of fortune.

Captain Namri had a huge disagreement with Gampo regarding our route. Namri, a stubborn man, ignored him seeing no reason to head southwest as Gampo suggested.

In a few days an exceptional event occurred. To starboard, a short distance from the ship, we saw two birds flying that might be swallows. I was amused by Gampo's humor when he dared ask the captain, "Did you notice they are flying towards the southwest?"

I pretended I hadn't heard them as the captain was known as a fastidious man without a sense of humor. I kept looking at the birds without expression until they disappeared in the distance.

The scriptures prophesied that one day a son of our race would discover a lost continent. Some say that when Namri was meditating on the shores of Namtso, he saw himself on the surface of the sacred lake where mirages acquire prophetic meaning. He pictured himself standing on the bridge of a great vessel. In this vision, the vessel moved swiftly under full sail, further propelled by the strength of fifty rowers.

That vision convinced Namri that divine forces had chosen him to carry out this mission, so he accepted no advice. He would not consider Gampo's suggestion that the swallows might be an omen or that the land we sought might not be far. The birds were a sure indication of the proximity of land. Could we be near the fabulous lost continent that the ancients spoke of? They'd repeated ad nauseam the legend of our uncertain origin and of the time when our ancestors survived the great flood.

Sails unfurled by a tailwind and rowers thrusting, our vessel skimmed along swiftly during the day. At dusk, Namri ordered the sails lowered, and let the rowers sleep. He mistrusted the dark in the distance, fearful of getting too close to a coast and endangering the boat.

That night the vessel was ruthlessly battered by waves and winds so fierce that we began to miss even the monotonous life of Kathmandu. But after a harrowing night, the day dawned without a cloud. Namri ordered the sails hoisted and the rowers began their daily work. The wind that had whipped at us all night had subsided, and the wrinkled sails fluttered lazily. At mid-morning, the lookout scouting from the bow startled us with an unexpected shrill shout, "Land ho!"

The men released the oars and Namri ran ahead to see the land we had discovered. Our scout reported a small irregular spot which appeared on the horizon, and when we squinted it was as if the ocean had blemishes. The rowers returned to their task, and slowly the blemishes became increasingly prominent. As we drew near, they looked like hundreds of unmoving little soldiers, as if lined and ready for battle. We were soon able to admire the unusual landscape before us.

The soldiers, some gigantic and others comparatively dwarfish, took the shape of geometric blocks - cubes or rectangles - adorned with dark little horizontal and vertical dots. The blocks were peculiarly aligned as if to form streets or large avenues.

The vessel advanced slowly because the rowers didn't want to miss anything. The crew seemed in a trance, under the magnetic influence of this fabulous vision.

The lookout, vigilant at the bow, broke the moment's charm with a sharp cry, alerting us to a strange object ahead in the vessel's path. Namri ordered the helmsman to avoid it and lower the sails. While we scrambled to follow his orders, we heard a great noise to port side. The vessel shook and listed dangerously to starboard. It was obvious that the *Marigalante's* hull had collided with some obstacle. The vessel righted itself and Namri verified that fortunately the damage wasn't serious - seeing with relief that the small tear in the hull was only seeping a little water.

Namri gave orders to the crew, restoring calm and relieving two of the rowers, assigning them to repair work. We moved on slowly, unable to make out the rock we had collided with.

Slowly we approached the geometric blocks. We suspected they were the remnants of a monumental abode belonging to a vanished race. The black dots we had seen from afar became square or rectangular holes in a definite alignment.

Those giants, their feet submerged in the sea, watched with sleepy eyes from idle centuries as the *Marigalante* traveled along streets and avenues. No one dared disturb the sacred silence as Namri ordered the helmsman towards one of the most imposing blocks that resembled an artifact from ancient times.

Soon the *Marigalante* quietly approached the edge of a large opening, possibly once a window. Namri ordered Gampo and me to follow him, and once our vessel had been moored, we went cautiously to inspect the interior. We verified with a probe that the water in the room was only knee-deep. Sunlight filtering through the window fully illuminated the space. Further in we found a passageway that led to a very dark place. An alcohol lamp that Gampo carried provided light. We found a stairwell, steps leading down into the submerged part of the building, and up to higher floors that the water hadn't reached.

In my memory, I still see Namri climbing the stairs, thrilled with the discovery. The floor of the rooms closest to the water was covered by a shapeless, grayish, irregularly distributed material. We couldn't determine its origin. As if possessed by a restless spirit, Namri tirelessly climbed, going in and out of the rooms, observing and taking notes. As we moved further from the water where the *Marigalante* remained, we found the structure to be in better shape. We recognized the remains of what we imagined had been furniture. I think the most eerie find was piles of parched bones, bleached by the sun that had inexorably caressed them through the cracks in the walls and the broken windows during centuries of abandonment.

We found no life, not even rats. On the floors closest to sea level, we made our way past mounds of bones, piled up as if the bodies had fallen simultaneously from some plague. Curiously, as we climbed to the higher floors, we found fewer bones. After several hours wandering this vast vertical cemetery, we reached the highest level.

Inside a huge, almost empty room and near the window we found bones still resembling a skeleton. Gampo pointed out that while the bones we had seen so far had been scattered, this was the only skeleton left intact. Namri observed that it had undoubtedly belonged to a tall person – considerably taller than average for our race. We looked at one another silently trying to reconstruct a scenario forgotten by time.

Dizziness from the height overcame us when we leaned out the window to look out over the gigantic city that had been conquered by the sea. A landscape nobody had ever imagined revealed rows of grey, empty buildings lining streets and avenues. Below, moored alongside the building where two civilizations met, the *Marigalante* awaited our return.

For three days we explored the enormous, deserted city over thoroughfares now canals. Forays into other buildings revealed similar scenes. There were millions of bones, undoubtedly human, and a multitude of objects whose function was not evident to us - the remains of a flourishing civilization that had perished quickly under catastrophic circumstances.

Although the *Marigalante* had little left in the way of available storage space, we found room for the intact skeleton taken from the topmost floor, and for several objects of unknown materials. They would be the object of future study.

At dawn on the fourth day, Namri gave the order to sail. The tear in the hull had been repaired, and the *Marigalante* was at sea again. The tide was low, and the lookout noticed that the object that had damaged the ship was visible again, fully lit by the sun. We approached it carefully for a better view.

What we'd assumed was a rock was an enormous head lacking discernible features because it was covered with a creamy, green mold that appeared just above the surface of the water. I imagined that the head had been covered by a cap, and that next to it, an arm emerged, revealing something it was holding. I suspected the statue had significance for the ancient society that had placed it there.

Gampo had another disagreement with Namri. The captain wished to return home as soon as possible. In his mind the expedition had been a failure as we hadn't discovered inhabitable lands. But he believed the discovery of the submerged colossus would interest our people, and he was excited to share it with the Council of Ancients.

Although we hadn't found life in the submerged city, Gampo argued that the few birds we had seen flying on those last days had to live somewhere. But our supplies of food and drinking water were low, and it was prudent to head back. Namri paid him no mind, but it's possible Gampo might have been right.

14

The Candidate's Speech

1989

Democracy is the art of running
the circus from the monkey cage.

-H. L. Mencken
Dreyfuss newsletter, *Letter from the Lion*

AS CAMPAIGNING NEARED an end, the final address of the People's party's presidential candidate's generated enormous expectations, and it was expected that the speech would be viewed by the entire nation. Electoral guidelines limited the televised speech to 15 minutes. To win voter support, speeches had to project the candidate's charismatic personality and condense his quintessential political plan in that short time-frame.

The candidate's limousine stopped at the entrance to the television studio amid a passionate throng of supporters carrying drums, noisemakers, and flags. Uniformed policemen surrounded his limo as the door opened with deliberate slowness. TV screens filled with a close-up on a face lit by a wide smile that spread optimism. Fake tan, abundant hair, and splendid sideburns framed rows of gleaming, ivory teeth.

Dressed elegantly in a perfectly tailored Giorgio Armani suit, the candidate oozed self-confidence. He comfortably and artfully faced the several dozen microphones and cameras that crisscrossed his podium from every angle. It was obvious to all in the studio, to his millions of hopeful supporters, to his political adversaries and to anyone avidly watching the broadcast, that they were looking at the future president of the Republic of Serpentina.

The candidate held out his arms to greet an invisible crowd, and, after a prolonged pause, began to speak.

"My fellow citizens, my message is for both the poor and the rich, the young and the old - for every woman and man in our country.

"If I am elected president of the Serpentines in this crucial election, I promise to govern equally for all citizens. Remember the words of the distinguished party founder, our beloved General Obregón: 'Our greatest asset is our people!'"

"I solemnly promise that I will govern for the people - for the suffering citizens who have heard so many lies and broken promises - who no longer believe anyone, least of all a politician. This time the people's candidate won't let you down. I will fight to consolidate the social victories achieved by President Obregón, and I will refine them during my term in office.

"Today, I ask you to give me your most precious asset in a democracy: your vote.

"I am the direct successor of President Obregón whom you elected. If you vote for me now, you will see his dream become a reality. It is my hope that one day my presidency will be described as the fulfillment of Obregón's vision.

"Year after year, one government after another, our people have been plagued by administrative corruption and brazen bribery. Can there be no honest leaders among Serpentines today? Must all become enamored of the mighty dollar after they win positions of dominance? Must all capitulate without a struggle when they hear the sirens' song for riches?

"I promise the people that the corruption that has dominated the political scene in our country for so long will disappear forever. I assure you, on my honor, that my administration shall be incorruptible, a model of honesty.

"Like Obregón during his presidency, during my term one of the main concerns will be to ensure the future of our children. I will spare no effort, nor will I curtail funding to improve education for young people - including children from poor families - so that everyone in Serpentina will acquire the tools needed to compete in a global economy.

"'Global' is a buzzword politicians overuse to deceive constituents, and I want it to be perfectly clear about it. When I say 'global' I mean that in our country workers will have the opportunity to work for salaries that are competitive on a worldwide scale. Workers will be protected by social legislation that preserves our country's most important resource – you, the citizens of Serpentina. Our workers will not be underpaid like the laborers in China who work in sub-human conditions.

"Our country will flourish under my leadership and our workers will be adequately compensated so they enjoy the fruits of their labor.

"Following in the steps of President Obregón's leadership, I too promise that the oil, hydroelectric power, and the natural riches of the soil will belong to the future generations of Serpentines. With your mandate, I will become a zealous caretaker of our country's natural resources, and if necessary, I will protect them with my life.

"When the sacred moment arrives at the polls and you decide who will be the future president of this country, remember that 'global' does not mean working from sunrise to sunset for a pittance while executives get rich. 'Global' does not mean giving away state-owned companies for pennies to benefit only middlemen.

"Following in President Obregón's footsteps, I say, 'Serpentina for Serpentines!' This in no way means that Serpentina will adopt an isolationist policy towards the world. Rather, we shall claim our rightful place in the concert of free nations and will ignore economic pressure from international financiers who do not hold the people's interests paramount.

"And I will also spare no effort to provide our elderly with the dignified retirement they deserve after having worked hard their entire lives. I vow to ensure that retirees enjoy their proper place in society.

"Today I offer my service to the people, as our beloved President Obregón did with his revered wife at his side. I will defend our sacred Constitution and assure you that under my leadership, the Constitution will never be altered in any way.

"During my presidency, inflation will disappear forever, and the dollar will remain stable, no matter what and at any cost!

"The country could undoubtedly experience a short period when people will have to make sacrifices - sacrifices that of course will be endured as well by those of us who govern. I cannot predict how long this brief period will last, but in the end, we will prosper and reap the benefits of a greatly improved country; a country many may not recognize for it will have been so greatly transformed.

"I have great faith in the Serpentine people's resilience and perseverance. They will never be beaten down by unemployment, hunger, poverty, or a lack of opportunities. But I assure you the hard times that may come will not last forever.

"I am well aware that there is skepticism among a few voters, and I understand there may be some who might not believe my well-intentioned declarations. That said, since I am nearing the time limit for my speech, let me simply give you these truths you can hold absolute.

"The sun will come out after the storm, shining on our destiny with rays of hope, even though there could be less to call our own. We will be happy to be among the leading nations of the world, something, fellow citizens, that we Serpentinians have not been able to say since our forefathers pushed back the conquerors from our land.

"For all these reasons, as President Obregón's direct political heir, I ask you to think about all that my program will bring to our country. Cast your vote for me!"

The professional hand-clappers in the studio cheered while the candidate again raised his arms towards the heavens, gazing upward as if receiving divine approval. Glued to their TVs, millions of Serpentines were exhilarated by the candidate's speech, each one delirious in one way or another.

Popular reaction to the candidates' words was mixed.

"What a presence!"

"Yes, he's a straight shooter."

"At least this one is willing to make changes! So different from the previous crooks!"

"Don't forget he's Obregón's disciple."

"Obregón! Obregón! Obregón!

"It's so great. At last the Yanks will treat us as equals!"

"They'll surely support us, and we can regain Malvonas as our territory."

"Did you hear him? Serpentina will be a world power!"

Of course, there were those who were less enthusiastic to his speech:

"Do they believe everything he said?"

"What balls! He lied through his teeth! But we will surely gain from his election."

"That line about the peso being aligned with the dollar should not be misconstrued; it's not as if the dollar will be aligned with the peso."

"This will be the first time ever that we're voting for the Populist party, but it'll be worth it."

"If anyone finds out, my family will be vilified; but nobody will ever know how I voted. Votes are secret, after all. This is a democracy, isn't it?"

"It'll be in everyone's best interest. We're the only ones who know what this country needs."

"My crystal ball tells me this will create a wave of confidence about us in Washington, my dear."

"The stock market will soar."

"We must buy stock immediately!"

Relaxing the grand persona he'd put on, the candidate stepped away from the microphones, smiling. The television cameras still followed him as he walked slowly to the exit. His personal entourage kept him from supporters who strained deliriously to touch him, as if he were the mystical Savior trudging to Calvary.

15

Aurelia, Benigno's Sidekick

1993

Only ants among insects
have organized armies
and undertake offensive wars

Maurice Maeterlinck,
The Life of the Ant

EVERYTHING BEGAN in summer when the ant colony produced a few males and some potential queens. Benigno, one of the young males, had his eye set on one of the attractive, winged virgins waiting for nuptial bliss. He timidly approached the lovely maiden, aware that the price for his connubial desire was nothing less than his life.

His shyness led to his loss, or maybe to his salvation, however one wishes to interpret it. A rival male, faster and more daring than Benigno, beat him and leaped with great agility to mount the virgin queen. The entire colony cheered as the royal couple rose rapidly above the ants who stood, spellbound watching their passionate flight.

While the lovers continued their erotic flight, Benigno quickly took the opportunity to distance himself from the community and moved away to shelter in the nearby weeds.

He knew that once the queen was impregnated, the males, of no further use to the community, would be unceremoniously sacrificed, and he would be terminated along with the others. Benigno realized that as soon as the ants came out of the moment's revelry, they would exterminate every male as they had done for millions of years. Benigno wasn't ready to face death without having savored life to the fullest.

From his hiding place, Benigno witnessed the fertile queen's return and the slaughter of the colony's males. In the days that followed, Benigno's metamorphosis occurred. First he lost his wings, and then his shape changed, becoming similar to the other ants though not enough to fool them were he discovered.

Meanwhile, the queen had chosen her palace and had begun to lay eggs in abundance. The larvae were nourished by nutrients found in the queen's deteriorating wing structures.

One day a spy discovered Benigno in his hideout. Almost immediately a trial was held and, finding him guilty, the security forces dragged him to the gallows for his execution.

While Benigno meditated on this ancestral injustice and on how sex discrimination was about to cost him his life, the unexpected happened. Just as the security forces were about to carry out the sentence, the colony was suddenly surrounded by an army of "superior" ants, a race that habitually abused "inferior" races and subjected them to slavery, exploiting them for the benefit of their own governing class.

As the enemy queen and her army approached threateningly, workers from Benigno's colony tried bravely to oppose them. The invaders surrounded Benigno's queen and ruthlessly killed her as well as the workers who had rushed to her aid.

Distracted by their battle, the ants of Benigno's colony completely forgot their prisoner and his pending execution, and he stealthily withdrew to seek shelter in a cave far from the anthill.

In time the dead queen's eggs hatched, and her offspring grew under the foreigner's reign. The young ants accepted the invading queen as their own mother and obeyed all her dictates. Her indoctrination was effective. The young workers became her slaves, mere gears in the machine of her oppression, and Benigno watched them develop in a totalitarian society.

Once fully trained, the queen dispatched slave patrols to the most remote limits of the anthill instructing them to round up any remaining colony inhabitants they might find which would of course have included Benigno. The foreigner queen's savage ferocity convinced even the most reluctant ants they encountered that the only safe option was to comply with her authority.

Benigno was rounded up with the female workers. Though they knew he was a male, he was treated like any other slave if slightly stronger, perhaps, and a great laborer. In the slave community there was no sex discrimination against Benigno as long as he was obedient. They let him occupy his dwelling, and he had nothing to fear provided he achieved his assigned quota of the tiny leaves he was ordered to gather.

In time Benigno acquired a reputation within the queen's oppressive regime for being a faithful, hardworking slave, and it earned him a few privileges. His only entertainment - one of the limited privileges granted him - was that he liked to go hunting in the nearby jungles with his loyal sidekick, Aurelia, the companion always at his side in his dwelling. Benigno was invariably happy upon returning to his humble abode after spending a few days out hunting with Aurelia.

Benigno was well known to the dictatorship's overlords as they monitored the community's every activity. In their security files he was described as: "failed male, good worker, safe, not dangerous."

But his happiness did not last, and invariably he suffered under the ferocious, authoritarian queen's oppressive regime. Year after year, Benigno carried a cargo of leafs larger than his body on his strong back. He would stumble, fall, and pick himself up on the trail, load the huge pile back on his shoulders, and continue unsteadily, bumping into other slaves traveling the same road.

As a slave, Benigno lived in dignified poverty, honorably contributing his required quota of little leaves, while saving a tiny surplus. Like his fellow ants, he had been an innocent who believed that the ant universe was altruistic and generous. But after the enemy queen invaded and established her dictatorship, her tyranny became evident, and Benigno became disillusioned and depressed.

He would not participate in her military parades and was terrified to hear her speeches: the queen's imperialistic plan to extend her Empire and subdue neighboring colonies. Her unbearable reign of terror smothered free speech and crushed him. Benigno said nothing publicly, but in the solitude of his dwelling he engaged in revolutionary monologues.

He came to resent the queen's invasion and his slavery, and in his imagination he dwelled obsessively in a dreamland of freedom. He continued adding to his little surplus, bit by leaf bit, hoping to achieve his life's dream and find the freedom he yearned for.

After much labor and suffering, Benigno felt that the right moment had finally arrived. According to his calculations, the number of little leaves he had painstakingly accumulated was now sufficient for him to escape the totalitarian state. He hoped to find a new colony and be accepted as a political exile in a community more in line with his liberal ideals.

He carefully arranged the little leaves in bundles and when finished, exhausted, settled down with Aurelia by his side.

However, Benigno had underestimated the totalitarian machine's complete control. Regime spies discovered his accumulation of bundles of little leaves which represented considerable wealth, and they reported what they found to the queen. Her reaction was immediate, and upon returning from work, Benigno was surprised to find his home overrun by National Security agents and Finance Ministry employees who searched every corner.

The ant heading the investigating committee examined his bundles one by one, taking careful notes and skillfully interrogating Benigno.

The agents questioned him. "It appears that you've accumulated supplies belonging to the community."

"To what end were you appropriating such assets?"

"What was your purpose in hoarding supplies during a time of community shortage?"

"By what means did you accumulate such wealth?"

"What proof can you provide that these bundles are your property?"

Benigno explained that he had made all the community contributions the queen demanded, and that this accumulation was simply the result of frugality and his desire to save. Explanations that he had worked very hard, frequently doing double shifts while others slacked, that he had lived ascetically while the community embraced excess, that he had stolen from no one, fell on the investigating committee's deaf ears.

Aurelia was resting motionless in a corner while Benigno sweated profusely, unable to find the appropriate answers to so many unexpected questions. Of course, Benigno omitted his true motivation - his plan to escape from slavery with his modest capital and begin a new life.

The committee summarily decided to try him for hoarding, announcing that he would serve as an example and his wealth would immediately be confiscated as punishment and as fair reparation for the damages suffered by the community.

At a signal from the head of the committee, a squad of ants marched into Benigno's dwelling, and his small fortune vanished like magic. He was speechless when the chief ant presented a stack of papers filled with signatures and affidavits - clearly prefabricated - notifying him and justifying the expropriation. The papers also included an immediate summons to the queen's tribunal where he was expected to take responsibility for this criminal act. There would be no appeal, he was informed.

Without further ado, the chief ant, the rest of the committee, and the soldier ants withdrew leaving Benigno finally alone with Aurelia.

Benigno stared at Aurelia and without a word peeked out through a hole in his little abode. From this observation post, he could see the platoon leader directing the ants to deposit his precious, confiscated load.

Enraged, Benigno extended his trembling hand, comforted that his dear Aurelia was at his side. As always, she was willing to satisfy him, and his fingers reached and repeatedly squeezed her most sensitive part. He watched through his window as a few of the ants fell, while others abandoned their load and fled as leaves scattered across the hill.

Calmer now, Benigno grabbed his trusty Aurelia, still smoking and stormed out from his cave in search of the freedom he so longed for.

16

Land and Blood in the Middle East

I - THE WANDERING JEW

ASA'S FATHER WAS born and raised in Abbas on the Mediterranean coast. His most precious memories evoked his family's life in the tiny fishing town where his grandfather had set down roots after aimless wandering along inhospitable paths in Asia Minor.

At family gatherings his father would tell of Asa's Grandfather who talked about the twists of fate that led several generations beyond the edges of the desert, always through strange lands, to search for a piece of land they could call their own. His grandfather would often say that God had promised them a land of their own, yet they seemed destined to always live in foreign land.

Abbas was a small town of Palestinian fishermen with fresh air to breathe and the delights of a simple, peaceful life. Asa's father had learned the trade of building and repairing fishing boats from Asa's Grandfather who owned a thriving boatyard in Abbas. Mediterranean beaches blended with fig and olive trees, and life unfolded at a gentle pace.

Several generations of Palestinian and Jewish children were educated in the town's only school and over the years they developed bonds of mutual respect. "Despite religious differences and the burden of our people's ancestral hatred," Asa's father would say, "the few Jewish families of Abbas apparently lived with the Palestinians as our ancestors had done for centuries, if not millennia." That word, "apparently," might be important, but Asa's father never attempted to raise the issue.

At the end of World War II when the British announced that the land would be partitioned, there was a huge commotion in Abbas. For the family of the boat builder of Abbas, the land was an unexpected gift, and their happiness seemed complete.

"At last, after many centuries," Asa's grandfather said, "we have obtained the right to call a small piece of desert our own."

But tension soon replaced Grandfather's initial happiness. Life in the town became dangerous, and Asa, his father, and the rest of his family were forced to leave everything – their home, the small boatyard and all their belongings, in search of shelter in the Negev.

The Israeli army that was supposed to defend them flattened one village after another, blowing up homes so that neither Jews nor Palestinians were safe. In his grandfather's opinion, successive wars had forced the men to fight for a land that had taken thousands of years to obtain.

Asa's father recounted that when these struggles finally ended, he and his Grandfather had returned to the small boatyard in Abbas only to find a desolate scene. Houses, including their own, were in ruins. The walls of their home were demolished, and they found only charred, smoldering refuse. The Palestinians, once having been the majority in Abbas, now found that coexistence was difficult, and they emigrated in droves.

Abbas was now part of Israel, and Asa and his family worked with great determination to help build the new nation. Asa's father and grandfather toiled in the boatyard and helped improve the land they had dreamed of for centuries - Israel.

Asa's father told him that when the war was over, Prime Minister Ben Gurion had worked to improve living conditions in the Negev; to transform it into a habitable land. His goal was to convert the sand of the sterile desert into soil acceptable for an orchard. Fifty years later, Asa proudly felt that they had achieved the dream and had transformed much of Israel, if not the entire Negev.

Asa's father often spoke of gentle memories - of treasured moments shared with his dear childhood friend Ali, a Palestinian boy from a family of fishermen.

"We played football together," he recalled. "Before the war, I used to run off with the Palestinian boys during recess to an empty lot where we would use fig tree branches to mark goal posts. I got along well with everyone, and they treated me as one of them. Then came the war and everything changed. Ali grew quiet and surly. He married and his oldest son, Jawad, had to play secretly with Asa.

"Jawad's family remained in Abbas," said Asa, "and faced many hardships. It was obvious that doing so was difficult, and I was not surprised when they finally decided to leave."

Asa remembered his last encounter with Jawad in the small field where, before the war, their fathers had played so many football games. It was there that Asa learned Jawad's family intended to leave.

"But where will you go?" asked Asa.

"I don't know," Jawad replied. "We have nowhere to go, but life in Abbas has become too hard for us."

Asa sincerely wished him good fortune. They embraced and said goodbye.

After Jawad left, Asa often thought about his Palestinian friend, and Jawad certainly thought of his Jewish friend and their many fond, childhood moments. So it came as a pleasant surprise to both when they happened upon each other years later on a street in Tel Aviv.

Both were 20, and although their young lives had been very different, they had much to tell each another. Asa was an engineering student at the university. Jawad had abandoned his studies to search for work.

Asa, who only recently had left home, listened intently as Jawad described the ups and downs his family had experienced. Some of Jawad's family had spread throughout occupied territory while others moved to Jordan. Jawad had also tried to begin a new life there, but ended up wandering for some time in search of work. He'd looked first in the occupied West Bank and now sought a job in Tel Aviv.

It was clear to Asa that Jawad had a difficult life with few prospects for his future. Though they both had definite ideas about the problems facing Jews and Palestinians, on this occasion neither brought them up. They greeted each other effusively, and Asa again wished Jawad the best of luck, although he was aware that his empty words were not enough to improve Jawad's destiny.

Alone with his thoughts, Asa reflected that he shouldn't idealize his childhood friendship or ignore the reality of their differences. He would like to coexist with Palestinians but only under acceptable conditions.

Later, over coffee with his young Jewish friends, Asa discussed the issue of coexisting with Palestinians.

"We are blood brothers in a way, descended from Abraham, and we have been neighbors for many generations," Asa acknowledged. "But the Palestinians refuse to accept that this land is ours, and that we have a right to it. We are a peaceful people but cannot understand why suicide terrorists blow themselves up just to hurt us. It's true, however, that there are those among us who don't feel this way and want to cultivate the seeds of war.

"Two delicate issues must be addressed if our people are to live in peace with the Palestinians," Asa argued. "The most important one is the land that God promised to the Jews. It is essential that Palestinians recognize our right to our land and the existence of a Jewish state. At the same time I believe there can't be lasting peace until Palestinians also have a land they can call their own. For this to happen, we have to recognize that any land we obtained as the spoils of the war does not belong to us."

That said, however, Asa realized that for the millions like Jawad who had been displaced from their homes, having two sovereign states with separate land rights wasn't a viable solution. The unspoken thread of his consciousness continued. *Clearly a true Palestinian state can't exist unless we withdraw from the territory we occupied after the war, but that goes against our desire to take ownership of the land.*

The city of Jerusalem presents unique issues that are as important to us as how we deal with the actual land, thought Asa. *Old Jerusalem, only a small part of the city, holds the remains of the last Jewish temple as well many other places holy to us. Yet nearby there is a mosque that is sacred to Muslims and a church erected on the spot where Christ is believed to have been crucified.*

Asa felt that any conversation about peace had to focus on the right of both Jews and Palestinians to have a land they could each call their own. He also approved of the army's interventions to keep the population safe and put an end to terrorism and suicide bombings.

His recent encounter with his boyhood Palestinian friend was still fresh in his mind when, as he sipped his coffee, Asa saw Jawad walking by. Asa sprang up and took hold of Jawad's arm, saying, "Hello! What a nice surprise!"

II -THE WANDERING PALESTINIAN

Palestinian fishermen like Jawad's forefathers had fished the Mediterranean Sea for hundreds of years. Their way of life was to go to sea, fish, return to port, sell the fruits of the sea, live with their families, and return to the sea. As far back as any could remember, this was the cycle between earth and ocean that Jawad's ancestors had experienced for generations.

The family's most treasured memories were of Jawad's grandfather's fishing boat. As a child Jawad's father would accompany his own father to sea. When the grandfather became ill, Jawad's father took charge of the boat and of selling the fish.

His father would tell Jawad that even when World War II ended, the fishermen of Abbas seemed unaware of it for quite some time. After all, the rhythm of their lives hadn't changed. But following the war, things in the town suddenly did change. The British, who had governed Palestine for many years, announced an end to their mandate and partitioned the land between Jews and Palestinians.

"The British... the British..." his father repeated reproachfully in an endless litany. He would add, "but it's ancient history and can't be fixed. After partition came a bloody war which we lost. Then came a second war and they crushed us again."

Instead of childhood stories, Jawad's father would tell of the family's search for refuge in the desert. He described in vividly painful images how his people returned to devastated homes - pillaged by enemy troops. He told of the hardships of oppression and the humiliation the Palestinians suffered for years. Jawad learned from his father that the Jews had powerful friends in the United States who provided the military power to oppress the Palestinians.

"Long before partition," noted Jawad's father, "the immigration of Jewish settlers had increased gradually, unobtrusively. But after the war, Abbas and other fishing towns were overrun by thousands of settlers from all over the world who arrived to occupy the land."

It was inconceivable to Jawad and his family that after thousands of years Palestine could simply vanish. The Palestinians considered themselves peaceful people who'd become trapped in the clutches of an invading army. The army hindered them from working in their fields when all they wanted was to simply make a living for their families. A state of continuous war filled them with despair and uncertainty about the future.

As head of the family, Jawad's father, a pacifist who loved his land, urged them to stay in what had once been Abbas and to brave the military oppression.

Jawad's father told him that the best times of his childhood had been shared with Asa's father; that in school and on the football field they were a force to be reckoned with. But all that changed after the war, and the boys rarely saw one another. For a while Jawad attended the same school and played football in the same field that his father had played in for years. Asa was educated in a nearby Jewish village. When the situation in Abbas became unbearable, Jawad's family left with no set destination and finally settled in Jordan.

Jawad vividly remembered the moment when they departed from the family home, leaving the fishing boat behind on the beach that had taken his father to sea. They bid farewell to the sea which, like the land in Abbas, they believed belonged to them. They left on Jawad's tenth birthday and the boy remembered walking slowly away from the boat, looking back at it until it became a tiny dot that disappeared in the horizon.

The boy had witnessed the dispossession of a land that had belonged to his ancestors for millennia. Palestine had vanished like the fishing boat. Jawad felt oppressed and sad, but in time his feelings became a limitless hatred for those who usurped his land. He mourned the breakup of his family and saw some of his relatives emigrate to Gaza while others went to the West Bank. They found the living conditions inhuman in a land occupied by the enemies of their race.

When Jawad thought about the wars that followed, he wondered what motivated their leaders. If there hadn't been black gold in the Gulf, would there have been wars, and might Palestine still exist? After listening to the politicians and having believed their promises, Jawad finally concluded that the Arab leaders did not represent the interests of the people and had only their own interests in mind. Poverty and oppression overwhelmed his people and the hope that they would recover their land gradually vanished.

After many hardships, most of Jawad's family settled in Amman where his siblings were born. In Amman they learned that Jordan was another Arab dictatorship, and that it was certainly no Palestine.

Incredible deprivation followed, and Jawad was frustrated by his inability to improve his own or his loved ones' fates.

When Jawad turned 20, he felt the call of his old land and returned to occupied Palestine. Jawad possessed a tender spirit and his parents had taught him to respect his elders and love his neighbors. The teachings of Mohammed underscored forgiveness, kindness, smiling at your brothers and making each smile a gift. But each day it became harder for Jawad to smile. His father had taught him that not all Muslims practiced the teachings of the Prophet and urged him not to forget that the Jews had stolen their land.

One morning Jawad awoke early and felt the blood rushing through his veins. He changed his route several times to ensure no one followed. Turning a corner, a door opened, and Jawad quickly entered. Someone he did not know challenged him, and Jawad quietly gave the password.

"Allah is great," the person responded, and without another word he exchanged Jawad's backpack for another. In the blink of an eye Jawad was again walking down the narrow streets of Tel Aviv, mingling with the crowds on their way to work.

Jawad's mind filled with somber thoughts as he held the magical cord that would change his life. He'd been miserable, solemn, and dispossessed, but suddenly Jawad felt sure of himself, euphoric due to the power afforded him by the magical cord.

Reaching the square, Jawad saw a café full of people getting an early start to their busy day. He considered it ideal for his purposes and went inside resolutely, his index finger ready.

A firm hand patted his back, "Hello! What a nice surprise!" A warm voice greeted him, "This is great! I thought I had lost sight of you forever and now we've run into each other twice in a short time," Asa said with a smile. He added, "The last time we met I had many questions I wanted to ask, but there was no time. Today you won't get away so easily."

Asa had not changed. His kind smile automatically relaxed the tension in Jawad's index finger as he tried to smile back. The friends sat at a table and ordered coffee.

Asa was anxious to talk and began with his first question. "Jawad, I want to ask you something that I'm obsessed with because I can't find an answer. What do you think about the suicide bombers?"

Asa's question stunned Jawad. Did he suspect something? He couldn't say he was one of them or that they were about to be blown up together.

Jawad looked straight into Asa's eyes and said, "Frankly, Asa, as your friend I must tell you that whether it leaves a bad taste in our mouths or not, suicide bombing is the only choice the Palestinians have left. How else are we to recover what belongs to us?"

Asa had not expected this answer and replied, "I don't know what you mean by 'the only choice,' nor do I understand what you mean by recovering 'what belongs to you'."

"That it's our only option," said Jawad. "We believe winning the war does not give you the right to the land or to oppress the inhabitants. After over fifty years of listening to lies and unkept promises from our leaders, we have lost hope of ever returning to our homes, and we are tired of being slaves in our own land. Young people despair of ever finding work or having their own land.

"What I said about recovering what belongs to us is perfectly clear. You know well that we've been expelled from our land, and that Jewish funds continue to buy up what is rightfully our property. Groups of Jewish settlers expand across Israel and that denies us access to our own land."

"Don't you think that an agreement can be reached through negotiation without young suicide bombers having to sacrifice their lives and the lives of so many innocent people?" Asa interrupted.

Jawad eyes never left Asa's as he paused to think about an answer. "I don't believe so. Arab leaders cannot negotiate on our behalf. They are trapped by their own vested interests. Besides, your question ignores the fact that when there is so much inequality between the parties that there can be no negotiation. Israel is a military powerhouse thanks to the unconditional support of the Yanks, and we Palestinians are powerless. Do you understand that we can't defend ourselves?"

Asa tried to choose his words carefully. "That's true, but Jewish civilians shouldn't be a military target. Don't you think it's unacceptable that suicide bombers blow up innocent people to spread terror?"

Jawad was silent for a moment. His index finger tensed on the magical cord under his jacket. "What about Jewish terrorism at the hands of the Irgun, or the Haganah, or of the Stern Gang, or the bombing of Jerusalem's King David Hotel?"

"There have been excesses … it's true. But remember that we were fighting for our land," replied Asa.

"To call them 'excesses' is to wear blinders, Asa," stated Jawad. "Do you know how many innocent Palestinians have been massacred by Israeli violence; how many Palestinian homes have been flattened by the Jewish steamroller? Do you think these were military targets? Or is it a holocaust for the Palestinians?"

Asa seemed upset as he struggled for the right words. "Jawad, we believe it is in our own defense."

"How can you say such a thing! What you're saying amounts to anti-Semitism. Asa," Jawad continued. "Your people are not as innocent as you believe, and your lack of understanding contributes to the problem. Do you realize that more than fifty years have passed since you confiscated our land? The Jewish people have to take responsibility for their leaders. The people you say are innocent close their eyes as you do to avoid seeing the atrocities my people are subjected to."

For a while both were quiet and simply stared at each other.

Jawad finally added, "I repeat Asa that we Palestinians are at the mercy of leaders who don't represent us."

"What do you mean that they 'don't represent you?'" asked Asa abruptly.

"What I mean," explained Jawad, "is that most Arab leaders have huge conflicts of interest and are primarily interested in maintaining positions of power. You know very well that Arab oil gives them the power to moves continents. Riches from oil is like a claw that keeps us oppressed with our heads bowed."

"You exaggerate, Jawad," replied Asa. "You can't blame oil for everything that's happened. Besides, neither Israel nor Palestine have a single drop of oil."

"Yes, that's true. But there is a chain reaction linked to oil. Obviously the Yanks depend on oil from the Middle East. It's why they provide economic and political support to Israel and why Israel acts as their police state to protect Yank interests in the area. And don't forget the political weight of American Jews who provide much of the economic support Israel gets from the United States. Add to that all the money that fills the coffers of the Arab dictators who supply the oil. These factors together make democracy an unreachable mirage for Arabs," said Jawad.

"Those things have nothing to do with relations between Palestinians and Jews," added Asa, blinking nervously and immediately regretting he'd said it. He bit his lips until they bled.

"Look, Asa. Jews know what I say is true and they do nothing. What they haven't realized is that we Palestinians are out of patience." Jawad's right index finger again tensed on the magical cord, and a sense of serenity fell over him.

"Even if the extermination of Palestinians at the hands of the Israeli army continues, even if you build a wall between Israel and the rest of the world, there will always be those among us who continue to hear the call of the land and are willing to give up their lives for Palestine. You people will call it terrorism, but recruiters have no problem finding soldiers who wish to sacrifice their lives for the cause. Plenty of volunteers are ready to blow themselves up because a Palestine with true economic and political power does not exist," said Jawad.

"Then how come you rejected the Palestinian state the Americans proposed during mediation?" Asa interrupted.

"You're not listening, Asa. Their proposal would have created nothing more than a puppet state run by the Yanks. It was unacceptable. I've been talking about a sovereign state with real economic and political power; one that offers Palestinians a chance to coexist with Jewish neighbors and negotiate as equals."

"And if a such a Palestinian state is created, what do you think should happen to Jerusalem?" asked Asa, trying desperately to move past Jawad's ire.

Jawad sighed deeply. "It's premature to speak of how we deal with Jerusalem at this point. That's important of course, but there are many fundamental issues that have to be resolved first. The Jerusalem flag is always waved to avoid the core issue - which is restitution - not only of the land but of the Palestinian people's dignity."

"But suppose those issues were addressed satisfactorily," Asa insisted, "how then do you envision handling Jerusalem?"

"We know the Jewish people have sacred sites in Jerusalem, and we must respect that," said Jawad. "But Jews must acknowledge that we have equally sacred sites that also deserve to be respected. My father says that a fair division would be to make Jerusalem the capital both of Israel and Palestine. Both would have free access to sacred sites. That would be a positive approach to the conflicts between the two fraternal nations. For this to happen, we Palestinians, cannot deny the Jewish state's right to exist, and in turn Jews cannot deny the right of Palestinians to their own land. Were this to happen, there would be a rebirth of optimism among Palestinians who long ago lost hope. There would no longer be a reason for suicide terrorists to walk among us or for Jews like yourself to fear you won't make it through another morning. Maybe then we could live together in peace."

Looking exhausted, the two men stood and shared a long, warm embrace. Jawad broke the silence and implored, "I hope you understand now?"

Without another word, Asa left the café. He made his way towards a group of soldiers standing guard at the corner. Before Asa reached the military checkpoint, a tremendous explosion rocked the café behind him, spreading destruction, confusion, and terror.

Surrounded by pandemonium, Asa watched, mesmerized, looking at an enormous smoking hole where moments before the café had stood. He sorrowfully mumbled words he alone could hear.

17

Wartime Love Letters

2002

Life is bearable when you have someone to write,
and someone who writes you back.
Even if it's just one person.

-Eun-Jin Jang,
No One Writes Back

Berlin, August 12, 1936

Dear B;

I'm writing again to remind you I still exist, and that you are always on my mind. In a little over two years I will finish my studies at the university, and I would like us to think about several issues that will impact our future. You know I only have just enough means to finish my schooling. Under normal circumstances I would begin a practice after finishing my studies, but I don't know if that will be possible and not just because of my financial concerns.

Unfortunately the air in Berlin and all of Germany is increasingly stifling due to the political and social disturbances that you are well aware of. I needn't remind you that the new Reichstag meeting in Potsdam awarded dictatorial powers to the government. By leveraging the Hindenburg crash, Hitler and has taken control of the political scene and holds all the cards. That terrifies me because Hitler isn't hiding his intentions. Anyone merely scanning his *Mein Kampf* will discover his racism, focused on Jews but extended to many who are not native Germans.

Another conclusion I've come to after reading *Mein Kampf* is that we are embarked on a road that will lead to war, possibly even a world war. Hitler refers repeatedly to Germany's expansion, which can only mean he's intent on invading neighboring countries.

I'm bewildered by the people's overwhelming support of the Führer. I believe there are several reasons for this and one must sadly recognize that there are a good number of Germans who think as he does. Hitler has improved working conditions and then too the Führer's obvious charismatic personality can't be discounted. He has lifted German pride and the people's spirits after the disastrous World War I, and Goebbels' skillful use of propaganda boosts our egos even if it distorts the truth.

It's difficult to assess how many oppose Hitler because any opposition to the regime is mercilessly squashed. Dissidents keep silent fearing Himmler's security police who control every facet of civic expression.

You will note that I have omitted your name and leave my letters unsigned for fear they could end up in the hands of Himmler's minions. His network of spies is unbelievable. Nobody speaks freely for fear that friends or relatives will report them.

I am being this candid because I feel it is relevant to our future plans. I hate to drop this on you in a letter, but I don't think we should start a family under Germany's oppressive regime.

I am convinced it is simply a matter of time before Hitler takes the country into a suicidal war. I believe your parents think as I do, and I urge all of you to leave Germany. I don't know where to suggest that you go, because I think the coming war will involve all of Europe, maybe the entire world.

As for me, I will continue my studies and try to finish as quickly as I can, so you and I have a solid base on which to build when we find a safe place to make our home. I believe Hitler isn't quite ready yet to fully launch into war, so we find ourselves in a race against time.

Please tell me what you think.

Love,

S.

~

Weimar, September 16, 1936

Dear S:

I still have not recovered from the anxiety I'm left with after reading your letter. Here in the countryside, Germany's political reality may be less evident than it is near Berlin, but I see the same dangers you do.

Father, who travels frequently, agrees with your frightening assessment. Your letter's closing paragraph terrifies me. It is very difficult to think of leaving the land where our families have lived for centuries. Yet we agree with your suggestion even as we pray a relocation would be temporary and not last for the rest of our lives.

Our plan is to move to Denmark. Father has interests and friends there and we hope it's far enough from Germany. I think it will be relatively easy to emigrate now.

As for you dear S, I hope that you stay safe, and I pray that we win our race against time.

Kisses,

B.

~

Berlin, October 10, 1939

Dear B:

Here I am, stuck in Berlin with my now useless diploma, and I have no way to know if this letter will even reach you. I gave it to Lotte, a friend of the family with many contacts in Denmark, because she still travels to Copenhagen occasionally. The situation here is grim and likely to worsen soon. As you know the Führer's forces just invaded Poland, and only two days later Germany declared war against England and France. We have lost our race against time.

Everywhere I look, things are bad and becoming increasingly fascistic. Hitler has a natural ally in Italy's fascist leader. Mussolini's invasion of Ethiopia, defying the League of Nations, clearly indicates that the Rome-Berlin Axis has set its sights even beyond Europe. It has been three years since Hitler's troops invaded the demilitarized zone of the Rhine. The Spanish civil war has become a battleground in which the Axis forces support Franco's extreme right ambitions, while the Soviets support the Republican opposition. Ever since Japan invaded Manchuria several years ago, nobody can deny that the Japanese also have an expansionist agenda, making them potential allies for Hitler and Mussolini in what is becoming a worldwide conflict.

As for me, the worst has happened. As soon as I finished school, I tried to leave Germany but was denied authorization. A week ago I was conscripted into the army, and will be sent to a training camp near Stuttgart.

I must warn you that Denmark is no longer safe. It is almost certain that Hitler will take the war to Scandinavia. At least Denmark might be safer than other places in Europe only because it is defenseless and will offer little resistance.

I am trapped and don't know what will become of me. I abhor being another pawn in the Führer's relentless machine.

I pray for your safety and for your parents too. Take great care of yourself.

All my love,

S.

~

Dresden, February 12, 1945

Dear B:

I've written you so many letters! All without displaying my address or a signature. I hope you have received some of them. I know that you have been unable to reply, and the army keeps moving me across Europe. Fate finds me in Dresden since last week. I don't believe it's a definite posting, and I await orders that may never arrive given the chaotic state this army is in. I am desperate to see you, and can't wait until this terrible, useless war is over.

After the crushing defeat of our forces in Stalingrad, the die is cast. It is obvious that the Führer hasn't been able to bring England to heel, and that the Russians have dealt him a crushing blow. I thought that after last year's landing in Normandy, the Führer's mad adventure would end, and the outcome would be swift. I was mistaken. Though Germany has undoubtedly been defeated and our forces retreat on all fronts, Goebbels' propaganda machine continues full speed to spread lies and hide the reality of the Axis loss. I hope for everyone's sake that this madness ends soon for the longer it lasts the more we suffer. I pray that Hitler's and his henchmen's war crimes won't go unpunished, that justice will prevail.

I miss you and wish you were here with me in Dresden. It's comparatively safe here even if it is crammed with weary refugees who arrive day and night from all the war-torn corners of Europe. Few have lodging and despite the cold winter, thousands sleep on the sidewalks. It is a miserable sight, yet they still come hoping things will be better.

Dresden is a magnificent city, a jewel of Europe's culture for thousands of years and thankfully spared since there are no military targets here. It is a wonderful center with libraries, museums, auditoriums and places for scholars and artists to gather. I look forward to our reunion so we can finally start our new life together.

All my love,

S.

~

Copenhagen, May 12, 1946

Dear Siegfried:

It was a miracle, but after several months your letter of February 1945 reached me. I'd had no news regarding your whereabouts and feared for your life. I heard from Peter about the injuries you suffered during the bombing of Dresden, and what I care about most is that you're alive.

I agree with you that the German people share the responsibility for the war crimes Hitler and his goons committed. I know we won't be able to rid ourselves of the guilt, and that we will pay for these atrocities for many years to come. I am hearing about forthcoming trials in Nuremberg. Hopefully they will mete out justice, although there is no way to adequately atone for genocide or for the destruction perpetrated by the Führer's madness.

I am in dismay that no voice has been raised to protest the vicious bombing of Dresden. There were no military targets, and I can find no arguments to justify the annihilation of over 100,000 defenseless people during three terrifying days and nights of ruthless bombing. There is no justification for the indiscriminate death of thousands of refugees - burned to death, destroyed by bombs, or frozen by the brutal winter. Humanity has lost Dresden's priceless artistic and historic treasures forever - and for what? The allies had already won the war. The attack ought to be judged a war crime in the international courts. But I know that will never happen - for never have winners been known to find war criminals among their ranks.

I was with Liam last week. You remember him, don't you? I will tell you some other time how I ran into him because it's a long story. Liam participated in the Allied air attacks over Europe. He said that during the week of February of 1945, an airborne operation of almost 2,000 planes mercilessly bombed targets ranging from Emden to Berlin, Dresden, and Vienna to crush the German morale. He said he was one of the British pilots who flew over Dresden dropping destruction. I asked if he felt any remorse about Dresden, and after thinking for a moment, he said he did not. He told me he'd been in London in September of 1940 when the Luftwaffe relentlessly bombed the city. He recalled the night bombers spread death and destruction everywhere, and how devastating it had been for Londoners. After some silence, he added, *"la guerre c'est la guerre."* I was speechless.

Liam's words made me think how good it would be if future leaders could learn the lessons of the past.

Forgive me for rambling on about a war I wish to forget, but I cannot. I hope to see you soon.

Kisses,

Brunhilda

18

Night of Insomnia

1999

The metal tip of the pickax collides
With treasures of gold, carved rock,
While digging into the soil of the ancient city...
The strange life of extinguished tribes
Rises from the temporary mist;
The confusing legend is enlightened;
The mountain on which the ruins stand reveals its secrets.

-Ruben Darío,
Tutecotzimí

I COULDN'T FALL ASLEEP that night. I'm not sure why, but maybe it was that yerba mate tea I love to drink. At around three in the morning my wife decided to "invite" me to sleep in the guest room due to my tossing and turning, so she could finally get some rest. I turned on the bedside lamp and looked for something to read.

My eyes fell upon a book of short stories on the bedside table, and I began reading Cortázar's "Axolotl." I was astonished to discover that the protagonist, possibly the author, imagined himself embodied in an Axolotl, a Mexican amphibian with an inexpressive pink face. Cortázar's analysis of the imagined transformation could come up with no easy anthropomorphic analogy in the wee hours, and he could go no further than to focus on its triangular-shaped head and its tiny golden-colored eyes.

The author believed he could detect a metamorphosis in the axolotl that hinted at a mysterious prior humanity. Although he realized that the axolotl wasn't human, he'd never felt such a deeply personal relationship with a creature that wasn't human. He had a sense that throughout his life the axolotl had witnessed horrible tragedies.

With Cortázar's face glued to the aquarium's glass, and the axolotl's face immediately in front of him, the author attempted to unveil the mystery within eyes that had neither irises nor pupils. In a flash of insight, he understood and stepped away from the aquarium.

Though the story was nearing its denouement, sleep overcame me and I dreamed once more. In my dream, with my nose pressed against the glass again, hypnotized by his eyes, I stared mesmerized by the axolotl. As if looking in a mirror, I could identify a face in his eyes, undoubtedly my own, although it had a thick beard, something I had never grown.

The triangular, inexpressive face with sprouted eyebrows and thick lashes, began a transformation that changed the shape of his body. The tail suddenly disappeared, and its four extremities morphed into arms and legs. The aquarium glass dissolved, and the axolotl, transformed as a man, emerged with me standing face to face in Tenochtitlan, the heart of the ancient Aztec empire.

The Aztecs were fearsome warriors, known to crush their enemies aided by their warrior god, Huitzilopochtli. As such, they came to dominate a vast region, subjugating tribal enemies, including the Tlaxcaltecs with whom they battled viciously.

The Aztecs believed that their proclivity to battle assured their existence, and that their battles kept their god Huitzilopochtli strong and well fed. Though the Aztecs didn't need to justify how they battled, as Huitzilopochtli was a carnivore, they sacrificed their enemies in battle by cutting open their chests and tearing out the heart to offer it up to their Sun God. I asked myself whether this bloody practice might reflect the expression of implacable cruelty I saw in the axolotl's face through the glass.

As night wore on, in another nocturnal flashback, I recalled arriving in Tabasco with Hernán Cortés, and how we easily subdued the Aztecs. The natives offered little resistance, and we took possession of their women, considered the spoils of war. We were happy to find women since the Spanish women, of course, had refused to travel and face the rigors of conquest.

From Tabasco we sailed to Veracruz and marched to Tenochtitlan, the center of the great Aztec empire. To our astonishment the emperor, Moctezuma, welcomed us with great fanfare. The emperor believed that Cortés was the reincarnation of the god Quetzalcoatl which explained his unexpectedly friendly reception.

In Tenochtitlan I found myself face to face with an Aztec warrior I felt I'd seen through the aquarium glass in the tunnel of time during my night of insomnia. The Aztecs were a feudal society, and it occurred to me that my metamorphosed axolotl had an air of nobility about him. Although he did not speak our language, the Aztec warrior calmly tried to make me understand that he didn't want war. Instead, he pointed to a beautiful young woman with bronzed skin and a statuesque silhouette. Elated, I accepted her as if the gift was expected, and the Aztec prudently withdrew.

The beautiful young woman's name was Xochitl, a sweet name meaning *flower*, and henceforth she was under my care. Xochitl had a lovely triangular little face, black hair, and thick eyebrows. Her long, delicate fingers reminded me of the Xochimilcan lizards with their curiously human-like narrow toes with sharp nails.

In my dream, Xochitl and I spoke the same language. I don't know which one it was, but we understood each other perfectly. She was reserved at first and mistrustful, but gradually as we got to know each other, she lost her shyness and revealed that she was not Aztec but Texcocan, a people that had been allies of the Aztecs for generations until the Aztecs enslaved them.

Xochitl described the death of her brother to me, and her face twisted with pain. She told me the Aztecs sacrificed the child to ensure the prosperity of their people. They had not touched Xochitl, who became the property of the noble feudal lord I'd encountered. Obviously the Aztecs regarded women as possessions as we did.

During the dark Aztec nights when our bodies came together in bed, Xochitl's small eyes glittered like two suns. Looking into them I became lost in an immense, unknown world. Leaving the realm of her eyes I would move again in time, and find myself with my nose pressed against the glass of the aquarium, hypnotized by the penetrating stare of the axolotl.

As I watched, another small lizard moved lazily near the axolotl. Barely shifting his eyes from mine, the axolotl opened its mouth and in an instant devoured one of the little creature's front legs, as the tiny lizard slowly slid to the bottom of the aquarium, and remained motionless. I thought the creature was badly wounded and would die, and when I retired after my daily encounter with the axolotl, the little lizard had not moved.

The following evening when I returned, the cannibal axolotl was in his usual position as if waiting for me. But surprisingly, the tiny axolotl who had been left for dead, had all four limbs again. Its amputated leg had magically regenerated.

As the night wore on, I found myself drifting back to my time in Tenochtitlan. It didn't take long for the Aztecs to decide that Cortés was not the reincarnation of Quetzalcoatl, and the harmony that had reigned was broken. Yet, though known for their terrible ferocity, to our surprise the Aztecs behaved with an inexplicable timidity which made it easy for us to crush them. Many escaped, scattering in all directions while we pursued them relentlessly.

It was then that Xochitl confessed to me that the Texcocans and the others of her race hated the Aztecs who had oppressed them for over a century. After Tenochtitlan fell to them, the native communities surrendered to the invaders and soon lost their tribal identities.

As the Aztec's fled, legend has it that their god Huitzilopochtli, weakened by the lack of human sacrifices, attempted one last time to preserve the Aztec race before dying. Huitzilopochtli transformed those who fled and turned them into lizards. What genetic technology only attempts with fanfare in the 21st century, the Aztec's accomplished easily with magic and imagination.

Xochitl and I were happy and had many children, so many that I cannot count them. All were bronze-skinned with noble features, and they populated the areas surrounding Tenochtitlan for miles.

At this point I awoke once more and returned to reading Cortázar's "Axolotl". I became interested in the little axolotls that never leave the larval stage. Like the Aztecs in my dream, they are cannibals and survive by devouring other axolotls. Some metamorphose into a species of salamanders that lacks gills, perhaps reflecting a frustrated attempt to recover their humanity.

Shortly thereafter, I found myself again meditating behind the crystal of the aquarium, captivated as my eyes fixed on the axolotl only an inch from my nose. Remembering the original question that arose when I started reading Cortázar, I turned my head away. Only then did I understand.

Now I could fully relate to the mysterious world of the enslaved that the axolotl had inhabited. At last I understood that its deeply sad stare was not a reflection of cruelty. In my recurring dream, I'd seen tribes of oppressors and their oppressed. Every time I return to the aquarium, I look at those larvae with their triangular, inscrutable faces. Their tiny eyes like pinheads look at me with an unfathomable depth, and Xochitl comes to me, embodying a suppressed race that refuses to perish.

19

Pantaleon's Fate

1999

Isn't the useless rooster a brother bird of the poet?

No, it's just a rooster, and the world has no room for it.

-Jim Harrison,
Poetry Workshop

THE "COCK-A-DOODLE-DOO!" I heard at dawn interrupted my dreams as it had every day since my mother-in-law made us the gift of Pantaleon, and I've been getting less and less sleep ever since. His crowing wakes me at three a.m. with mathematical infallibility as he begins a cantata in which various neighborhood tenors, not wanting to be excluded, invariably participate enthusiastically.

Pantaleon filled an empty space in our lives. Our four free-ranging hens, not restricted by a coop, noisily ran around the whole yard at will to celebrate his arrival, The rooster conscientiously fulfilled his pluri-marital duties often, to the great rejoicing of the hens.

His debut into our family's bosom not only changed the chickens' love lives, but Pantaleon's arrival was a memorable event for the children as well. Peanut became especially attached to the newcomer, his best pal who followed the boy everywhere like a lapdog when the rooster wasn't attending to one chicken or another. The child would offer the rooster grains of corn from the palm of his hand while chatting animatedly in an unknown language. We had never witnessed such companionship.

The days passed without incidence to the children's joy and Pantaleon's satisfaction, until one day my mother-in-law visited again. This time she arrived with a surprise for the children.

"I've brought this chick for Stef and Peanut to play with. His name is Anastasios," she said, taking a small, ugly creature from her basket. It was only a few weeks old, sad looking and of an indefinite color.

Peanut looked at it with disgust, and little Stef with Olympic indifference. Anastasio reacted by hiding under a sofa in a corner of the living room. After that inauspicious beginning, and as Peanut and Anastasio never clicked, the chick found comfort in the company of the hens who literally took him under their wings.

Pantaleon ignored the intruder, and for a while acted as if the chick did not exist, sometimes glancing at him from the corner of his eye. However as Anastasio grew, Pantaleon paid increasingly more attention to him and stared at him with growing displeasure. Soon the little chick had become a young rooster and was beginning to court the hens, subtly at first, and then with uninhibited audacity. Pantaleon began to peck at him to keep him away from hens who were delighted by the interest they awoke in both suitors. But the hens' pleasure was short-lived as they could not keep up, ending each day exhausted from running around to avoid the implacable double harassment. Peanut became somewhat concerned about the roosters' rivalry since before the break of dawn, Pantaleon began with his cock-a-doodle-do, immediately followed by Anastasio's counterpoint, in turn echoed by all the neighborhood roosters. Nobody slept after that hour since the crowing was deafening and continuous, and the neighbors began to complain.

Anastasio had become a splendid rooster, acquiring the vigor to peck aggressively at Pantaleon's neck. The older bird feared his younger rival, and it was evident that Pantaleon no longer ruled the roost, though he still had the energy to happily perform his duties with the hens when Anastasio wasn't harassing him.

One week my mother-in-law came to visit and after dinner when the kids had gone to bed, we had a family conversation. After much deliberation, the decision was unanimous. There wasn't enough room for two roosters whose competition was too much for the hens, for us and for the neighborhood as well. Still, the final decision was difficult for we didn't want to hurt my mother-in-law's feelings. Though she accepted the wisdom of our position, she was ambivalent. It was argued that Pantaleon had seniority, as if he were a union member, and his behavior had been irreproachable, but he had been outpaced by the competition. His time had come.

As for Anastasio, he was vigorous with many years of service ahead, although he lacked Pantaleon's charisma. In the end we decided that keeping the younger rooster was better for the hens. After a quart of coffee and much animated discussion, Pantaleon's fate was decided: he was headed for the stewpot.

Saturday was the designated execution day. My mother-in-law, despite having taken part in the decision, announced at the last moment that she would not be coming to dinner.

"Chicken!" we accused her, as I set out to prepare our meal.

Annette decided that Stef and Peanut should not be witnesses to Pantaleon's demise, and took them to play at a nearby park. We would tell them a white lie later to avoid their sadness, and they would never suspect the presence of Pantaleon in my famously delicious, hearty puchero.

I chose the biggest pot we had in the kitchen. Then I put in vegetables – some potatoes, three ears of corn, the cloves of two heads of garlic, two spicy sausages, one Basque blood sausage, and a hearty chunk of bacon. After adding salt to the near boiling water, I headed resolutely to the backyard.

The only ingredient missing in the pot was Pantaleon who at that moment was chasing one of his favorite damsels. Not wanting to deprive him of a last satisfaction, I waited patiently for the lusty business to end. Once released, the hen took shelter under some bushes while Pantaleon batted his wings happily, fully content. I approached him slowly so as not to startle him and tossed him some kernels of corn, which he quickly gobbled up. Pantaleon looked at me expectantly as if to say, "Is this all you've got for me?"

I had the strange feeling that I was betraying him, but after a brief hesitation I tossed out a few more kernels and while Pantaleon avidly devoured them, I grabbed him by the legs and took him to the kitchen. During the short walk, Pantaleon crooked his neck to look at me, protesting this unaccustomed affront with a hoarse cackle. He was clearly expressing his discontent, "What's the meaning of this?"

The gallows was ready, and giving Pantaleon no time to be surprised, his head rolled across the cutting board and landed in a puddle of blood. As sorry as I was to do this to him, I rationalized that it had to be done, and proceeded to pluck his feathers.

At this point I witnessed an amazing event. The hens and Anastasio seemed to have mutinied, for they were gathered near the kitchen door, cackling with threatening insistence. I shooed them away with a shout that made them back off. But in short order Anastasio and the hens were back at the door, cackling in a tone that clearly resonated anger. Anastasio stretched his neck to see what was going on and flapped his wings with great agitation.

I had taken longer than expected to prepare the vegetables and execute Pantaleon, and had been distracted by the mourning chicken population. Just as I was finishing with the plucking of Pantaleon's feathers, a commotion arose that will be forever etched in my memory. While I was focused on my task, Peanut showed up at the kitchen door.

From a bird's eye view, I saw the scene that the astonished boy observed: a closeup of Pantaleon's head lying near the cutting board, seen through Peanut's eyes in gigantic proportions, its glassy eyes open and staring fixedly at the child. The half-plucked body, the huge murderous cleaver, and my bloody hands completed the horrific scenario.

I stupidly tried to smile as if it were all a joke, and picked up Pantaleon's head with his crest dangling like a trophy. Horrified, Peanut turned his head away. Tear-filled eyes expressed his reaction to the grim scene. His face evidenced grief, but his clenched teeth conveyed repressed fury. After what seemed like an interminable minute, Peanut slowly came out of shock, and, lifting his little head, he looked at me with infinite hatred and murmured so softly that I could barely hear him, "Dad, how could you?"

Not knowing how to respond, I tried to pick him up and comfort him, but he pushed me away, genuinely repulsed, and ran off as if he'd seen the devil.

Having noticed her big brother's unhappiness, a wailing Stef burst into the kitchen in tears. Annette, deeply moved by the kids' unexpected reaction, picked her up and disappeared. I stood alone, unsure of what to do.

In the end I returned to my unfinished task of plucking Pantaleon when Annette charged back into the kitchen, her voice muffled by sobs, and shouted, "Please, just stop. Can't you see how upset they are?"

Without a word, I scooped up Pantaleon's remains and placed them in a plastic bag, quickly storing it in the refrigerator. As I washed the cleaver, the cutting board and my hands, I noticed Peanut quietly crawling into the kitchen on all fours to pick up the feathers scattered on the floor. Gathering them carefully, he placed them gently in a small cardboard box which he clutched to his chest.

Annette wasn't speaking to me yet and was busy calming Stef, so I set out to finish my puchero without Pantaleon, substituting whatever I could find from the fridge. When the meal was ready, we all sat at the table. But though both Annette and I made an effort to smile and chat about anything at all, the children, huge dark circles under their eyes, acted as if they were at a wake. Peanut didn't eat a single bite of food and just looked at me as he held the box with Pantaleon's feathers, his big eyes no longer brimming with tears.

"Dad, why did you do it?" he asked again firmly as if expecting an answer.

My response was to explain, "He was old and weak, and was being pecked at by Anastasio."

"So, some day, when you're old and good for nothing, will I have to chop your neck off like you did to Pantaleon?" Peanut asked with a sad, faraway look on his face.

Annette interrupted, "Peanut, Pantaleon was a rooster and we're human beings. Besides, in a chicken coop there isn't room for two roosters. Anastasio is younger and stronger, while Pantaleon was just right for a tasty puchero."

Peanut sat quietly thinking, and wondered softly, almost to himself, "Is this how humans behave?" After a prolonged silence, his voice choked with emotion, he said, "Remember, Mom? A few days ago, you read me that story about cannibals.

How could I possibly eat Pantaleon? He used to eat corn from my hand, and we talked about all kinds of stuff. He was my friend. Eating puchero made with Pantaleon would make me feel like a savage!" Stef listened in fascination to her brother's words, babbling unintelligibly in baby language while she nodded and waved her tiny fists.

Nobody ate much that evening. Peanut's speech ended with a plea, "Promise you won't cook him?"

"Of course," replied Annette immediately. "We've changed our minds."

"Then can we bury him? Right now?" Peanut asked unexpectedly. After a brief moment, without waiting for an answer, he pressed on. "Now, Dad?"

Perplexed, Annette looked at me. Without a word, I took the plastic bag holding Pantaleon's remains from the refrigerator. Peanut tore it from my hands and headed resolutely for the backyard where the chickens had until now slept with the two roosters. I went silently for a shovel and then followed him.

Despite the hour, Anastasio and the four hens were there keeping vigil. The earth was dry and hardened by the summer heat, and it took some effort to dig a hole. Though I tried not to look at them, I knew Peanut, Anastasio, and the hens were watching me, keeping very still.

Annette and Stef arrived as I finished digging. Peanut approached and opened the plastic bag, gently laying Pantaleon's remains on the freshly turned earth.

The magic of the moment was shattered by Anastasio as he flapped his wings and shuddered. The hens' cackling sounded like a funeral dirge. Peanut looked at me, and I knew he wanted me to finish the ceremony. I picked up the shovel and silently filled the hole with dirt.

Stef held her mother's hand and Peanut walked back to the house alone. I followed at a distance at a deliberately slow pace.

Annette ushered the children to bed, finally putting an end to the dismal day. I kissed Stef's forehead. She fell asleep almost instantly. When I went to Peanut's bed, the boy turned his back to me, and I let him be. Later, I went to check that he was sleeping. He seemed restless in sleep. The cardboard box with Pantaleon's feathers sat on his pillow next to his head.

I didn't sleep well that night. Before dawn I heard Anastasio greeting the arrival of a new day, "Cock-a-doodle-do!"

20

Promises Broken

2002

Fidel Castro stated repeatedly:
"We are neither Communists nor Marxists" . . .
In a speech in January 1959, he promised Cubans
that there would be free and fair elections within 18 months. . .
However after 1961, Castro announced
that there would be no elections in Cuba.

-Félix Fernández Madrid,
Che Guevara and the Incurable Disease

VIVACIOUS, SENSITIVE, AND intelligent, Gladys fervently wished to dedicate her life to medicine. But after the second World War of the century, Cuba wasn't exactly a paradise for liberated women. There were female doctors in Cuba, but only a few.

Gladys' parents loved her, but they didn't take the ambitions of a girl seriously. At their insistence, Gladys sought guidance from her professors about a professional life. But the vocational advice they gave her was immensely disappointing.

"Medicine? Absolutely not. A proper lady must not be exposed to naked bodies. Can you imagine a more abominable work activity than to focus on a diseased, decrepit human body? Can you imagine yourself dealing every day with the pestilence of the flesh and the scourges of the spirit, with deformed, ugly beings, with the sum total of human misery, with painful agony, and death?" one of them asked Gladys.

"And even if you were able to endure such hardship, you must know that women don't instill confidence. A doctor must be like a priest. Can you imagine yourself listening to sins in the confessional? It's just as fortunate that you have not thought about entering a military academy. That would be the last straw. Medicine is a man's career!"

"Who has put these ideas in your head?" said another professor. "A girl must pursue a career that graces a woman, likc fine arts, painting, sculpture, music, languages, humanities, or possibly law. But she must never compete with men. Man has his place and woman has hers!"

"Naturally, you will want to marry at some point," said another, "and have children. We've known for centuries that even to have a bad husband is better than being left on the shelf as a spinster," said a guidance counselor.

Gladys pressed her lips together firmly so she wouldn't give those dinosaurs a piece of her mind. These were men who advocated a limited future for women. She exhaled deeply and, after thumbing carefully through the options left for her gender, she chose philosophy and literature. She received a solid education in humanities and obtained a doctorate. But despite her success, Gladys continued to feel unfulfilled because of her dream to become a physician.

She made many friends among her classmates at the university including a law student named Fidel and a medical student named Juan. Fidel was known among students and faculty for his activism in college politics. He was an egomaniac who loved to hear his own voice and not a day went by that Fidel didn't harangue classmates, lead a protest, or fly some banner.

Gladys began spending time with Juan and soon became his girlfriend. He was a brilliant young man who dazzled her with his erudition and clear intellect. After a few dates, Gladys and Juan decided there was no reason to wait, and they married before graduation.

Juan's and Gladys' personalities complemented each other perfectly. Juan was introverted, a man of few words who knew how to listen. He was reserved while she was extroverted - open and chatty. The young man loved medicine and soon distinguished himself at his profession. The couple enjoyed philosophy and in their free time they would delve into discussions and debate. Juan had a romantic if impractical temperament, while Gladys was intuitive, sharply focused, and objective in her reasoning. Consequently, she often had the last word regarding family decisions. The newlyweds' future seemed solid for they were intelligent, hard-working professionals.

But dark clouds of a coming storm threatened Cuba. Its troubled political climate grew more frighting with each passing day due to growing opposition to the U.S. backed president Fulgencio Batista's dictatorship. Having taken over the government twice by force, Batista increasingly curtailed the individual freedoms of Cubans. The situation in Havana grew unbearable as government led repression relentlessly crushed any opposition. Juan became more and more involved with a subversive movement that consumed him, robbing time from his professional and family life.

One morning the newspaper headlines were explosive. A group of rebels led by their friend Fidel Castro had disembarked on a beach in southeastern Cuba but had been completely annihilated by government forces in Alegria de Pio.

"Poor Fidel, he was always full of crazy ideas. Who else would try to invade the island with only eighty men?" said Gladys.

Newspapers described in minute detail how government forces had pulverized the insurgents. For several days, the invasion quelled by the army was the talk of Havana. Fidel's latest madness was quickly forgotten, and life on the island continued as always. Rumors made the rounds daily about some conspiracy or other that was crushed, or a friend who'd suddenly disappeared.

General unrest continued under an oppressive political climate until an important new rumor began to spread. It gained strength and one day it exploded. Gladys was astonished to learn that her good college friend, Fidel the rebel, had not only survived Alegria de Pio but had launched a guerrilla campaign in the Sierra Maestra. His invasion slapped the numbed Cuban people awake and stimulated a collective hope that they could become free of the dictator Batista. Yet Havana had become used to a flood of strange rumors, and neither Gladys nor Juan were convinced that this latest one was for real. Still ... they wondered if maybe this time...

At first the heavily censored Havana newspapers said nothing. However travelers arriving daily from abroad brought unconfirmed reports that Fidel and his band of insurgents had survived the slaughter at Alegria de Pio. In addition, rumors circulated that the upper echelons of the Batista government were nervous, and for the first time in years the stability of the dictatorship appeared threatened. The issue became so huge that the press was forced to publish an official version of the events:

> The rumors are totally unfounded. Fidel and his gang of murderers had been completely exterminated.' The news reported by the American press was lies, a fabrication aimed at weakening Batista's government.'

The official press proclaimed that there were no problems and urged Cuban's to dismiss the rumors as products of an international conspiracy against Batista.

As the days passed, however, the disarray within Batista's government and its contradictory explanations became evident, and they could no longer deny the facts. The American press branded Fidel as a Robin Hood, a nationalist with anti-imperialist, democratic ideas. Fidel, they wrote, fought to tear down the dictatorship and restore the Cuban Constitution which Batista had abandoned.

Herbert Matthews of the *New York Times* interviewed the bearded guerrillas in the Sierra Maestra, and their photographs arrived surreptitiously on the island and were passed from person to person.

On sleepless nights, Juan would tune in to the revolutionary radio station while Che Guevara transmitted from the hilltops. Mimeographed pamphlets began to circulate, written in inflammatory language, inviting Cubans to join the rebels in their fight against dictatorship.

It would not be an exaggeration to say that most Cubans hated Batista who remained in power by brute force and relentless repression. Batista had tyrannized Cuba during two separate periods with an interval of democracy between his dictatorial reigns. Two months before national elections, his latest military coup put on hold the voting procedures established by the republic's constitution. Life in Havana under the Batista regime became even more repressive as the dictator responded to Castro's Sierra Maestra campaign. Murder and torture were routine. His alleged political enemies and often mere suspects would suddenly disappear. The movement to oppose Batista had begun before the invasion by the guerrilla forces, but Castro brought new energy to their effort.

Opposition to Batista grew intense as independent groups with democracy as their ideology and elimination of the dictatorship as their goal, continued their support of the revolution. Castro, reading the climate in Havana, easily recruited followers, in time accepting thousands who joined his guerrilla force. Although he did not share their democratic dreams, Castro knew the time was ripe.

Like most Cubans at the time, Juan despised Batista and actively participated in the urban guerrilla movement. At dawn one morning, Gladys and Juan were startled awake by muted knocks at the front door. Juan opened it and saw that it was their close friend Alfredo, a lieutenant colonel in Batista's army. His brief, clandestine visit forever changed the young couple's lives.

"Juan, I've come to tell you that they have a file on you. You've been branded as a member of the opposition."

"How do you know?" Juan asked calmly.

"I saw your name on the blacklist, and I'm certain that your days are numbered. You don't have much time, maybe only hours. You're not the only one in danger. Your wife and children will suffer the same fate if you don't hurry. You know the routine. Leave immediately," Alfredo warned, and, after embracing them warmly, he left. They never saw Alfredo again, but they didn't forget that he'd risked his life for them.

Evening fell several hours after Alfredo delivered his message as the couple planned their next move. They made a rapid and definitive decision. Exile was the only viable option; they would leave Cuba, where it had become impossible to exist without constant fear. The following day, Gladys, Juan and their children emigrated to Spain, departing Cuba with only the clothes they wore.

In Spain, the deep wounds caused by Civil War were slowly healing. Life had become a bit easier. The food, water, gas, and electricity shortages that had been so acute in past decades had been mitigated by the time Gladys and Juan arrived in Barcelona in 1957. The Cuban exiles were warmly welcomed by their Spanish relatives and friends.

Though they had escaped Cuba's oppressive dictatorship, it was clear to the couple that Spain at that time was not exactly a shining example of democracy. But at least Spain's political climate was more benign than what they'd know during the Batista regime. In his old age, Generalissimo Francisco Franco had agreed that Prince Juan Carlos should return to be educated in Spain, and there was talk of restoring the monarchy. A year earlier Spain had returned to the worldwide family of nations by being readmitted into the United Nations. With the softening of Franco's dictatorship, the Cuban exiles found Spain less repressive although both continued to anxiously follow the news back home regarding advances by the guerrillas and the imminent defeat of the Cuban dictator.

Gladys and Juan decided to return to Cuba three months before Castro's victory. Juan profoundly believed that Fidel would bring democracy to Cuba. Upon arriving on the island, Juan wasted no time and joined the guerrilla forces in the hills where with the rank of captain, he took charge of the medical services. Although he had several hundred beds at his disposal, the medical facilities were primitive. Juan found only three or four obsolete surgical instruments and an old stethoscope, but these limitations were not enough to discourage him. He was glad to again be part of the struggle against dictatorship. But a few days after his return to Cuba, Juan suddenly disappeared, and Gladys had no news from her husband for three months.

Juan had fully supported the apparently democratic Sierra Maestra Manifesto signed by Fidel and other anti-Batista leaders with strong democratic ties. A critical analysis of the document only strengthened Juan's conviction that Castro would restore the country's democratic institutions. Gladys and Juan had witnessed Fidel's militant nationalism, and Juan was sure that their old friend desired only the welfare of Cubans. Hadn't Fidel promised to call for elections within 18 months so Cubans could decide their own destiny? That gave Juan the assurance that Cuba would have a brilliant future under Fidel's wise and fair direction.

"See, Gladys, Fidel is surrounding himself with the right kind of people," Juan would say. "Nobody would call Manuel Urrutia a Communist, and the new prime minister, Miró Cardona, has represented American interests. The new team in charge of finances is made up of men proven to be honest, impeccable, and openly anti-Communist. Fidel promised to end corruption, gambling, and prostitution."

Mistrustful by nature, Gladys would listen in silence. For a short while, things in Cuba did seem to improve. But soon the revolutionary honeymoon was over. After the triumphant arrival in Havana of Camilo Cienfuegos' and Che Guevara, subsequent events startled a lot of Cubans who had supported Fidel in good faith.

At first the guerrillas were cheered as heroes though the initial days of their regime were chaotic. The general confusion following Batista's removal was forgiven by most Cubans who were delirious that the dictatorship had fallen.

But rumors began to circulate. It was reported that shortly after capturing the city of Santiago, Fidel's brother Raul had personally ordered the execution of 70 captured soldiers. Raul had a trench dug, ordered the prisoners to be lined along the edge, and had them gunned down. A tractor piled them into the mass grave.

Though many applauded these acts as appropriate given the Batista regime's brutality, others were horrified by their excesses. The stuttering of machine guns could be heard daily through the walls of the fortress, La Cabaña. Executions were carried out after brief public trials in which the accused were undefended. There were few defense attorneys and the few that served were watched and considered potential opponents.

"The obsequious swine that tortured and murdered during the Batista regime are criminals, of course, and must be tried as such," said Gladys. "But the soldiers who were merely following orders do not deserve that treatment."

"The trials I've witnessed are a vulgar mockery," Juan would add.

More than a thousand political prisoners, some of whom had evidently participated in the abuses under Batista plus others who were simply suspects, were tried by a revolutionary tribunal euphemistically called the Purification Committee. It was common knowledge that Che Guevara was the high judge during these trials and his decision was final. There would be no appeals. For several months, hundreds of defendants were tried in this manner, and ended their days facing a firing squad. The daily rattle of machine guns no longer surprised anyone in the vicinity of La Cabaña. The defenders of democratic ideals that Juan had so admired, who had initially supported the guerrillas, were pushed aside.

It became obvious that Fidel was in full control, and his core group of guerrilla fighters assumed the key positions in the government. Eventually, the revolution acquired distinctly Marxist overtones that had not been evident to most Cubans before Fidel seized power.

Gladys had seen enough and decided that the family's only solution was a second exile. Her friendship with Fidel, which continued after his victory, did not prevent her from clearly seeing what was happening in Cuba.

Gladys had been pregnant when the guerrillas entered Havana, and Fidel visited them when the baby was born. Fidel spoke at length sitting on the side of the bed and before leaving he said, "I hope you name him after me because the boy has been born under the sign of the revolution." Juan assured him that it would be their honor to do so, but days passed, and Gladys never let it happen.

The dramatic events on the island unleashed a storm between Gladys and Juan which threatened the family's stability. The couple repeatedly argued and could not agree. Juan was convinced that Fidel's intentions were good and that in the end democracy would triumph.

Gladys didn't accept her husband's thinking, and he became ever more heated in his arguments. Juan insisted that the revolution was not intended to transform Cuba's social and economic structures; that the Constitution was sound and needed only to be vigorously followed.

"Fidel will at last be able to enforce the Constitution for the benefit of Cubans. As a nationalist leader he has the support of every Cuban sector," Juan explained.

"No," Gladys countered, "Fidel only wants power for power's sake, and he will change his tune whenever it suits him. He's surrounded by Communists. Just look at Raul and Che. They're not nationalists, they're Marxists!"

"You'll see," Juan replied. "Fidel will reinstate the constitution and eliminate the injustice and corruption that dragged Cuba down under Batista."

"Pure fantasy," argued Gladys, unconvinced.

They agreed that the revolution was not at its core a social conflict. They felt that it sprang from the Cuban people's deep conviction that they had to end the dictatorship by defeating Batista. Nor did they believe that Cuba's economic disparities justified a revolution. They were aware of pockets of poverty on the island. But that was also true in the United States and in many developed countries. But in fact, they agreed, the per capita income of the Cuban people was one of the highest on the American continent.

"Cuba's economy and its social factors," Juan argued, "do not justify a Marxist revolution. In the fight against Batista, Castro waved a democratic banner. He set out to oust a dictator, and succeeded. But Fidel also repeatedly assured that the next step would be to restore Cuba's 1940 Constitution, and he promised free elections in eighteen months."

The support of the Cuban people allowed Castro to overthrow Batista, Juan pointed out, and every democratic sector helped the revolution succeed under his command. But Gladys argued, Castro had abandoned the people and his dictatorial leanings soon led her to become a staunch enemy of his revolution. She disliked Fidel's demagoguery and his endless radio and television monologues, and she believed his political manipulations would lead Cuba to a Communist dictatorship.

The arguments Gladys and Juan had were echoed in many Cuban homes. Already a huge exodus began of professionals disenchanted with the new regime.

After being in complete control of Cuba for only a few months, Castro announced that his promised elections would not take place. Soon thereafter he declared he was Marxist. Some said that he had always been Marxist, while others argued that Fidel had conveniently called himself a Communist merely to hold political power and receive economic aid from the Soviet Union. The Soviets were eager to have a steppingstone near the giant to the north, if only to taunt the Americans.

After many nights of distressing arguments, Juan finally surrendered to the evidence, and the couple agreed to leave Cuba again, perhaps for good this time. They began planning the family's second exile, decidedly more difficult to accomplish than the first departure.

Fidel kept in touch with his old friend Gladys and considered himself close to Manolo, her 16 year old oldest son. When Cuba experienced huge financial difficulties and Cuban stores were devoid of many essential items, Fidel gave Manolo an extravagant gift - a bike imported from China since there were no bicycles available in Cuba.

Manolo was young, with a strong, healthy physique, and the teen excelled in school and sports. His parents and Fidel were proud of Manolo. Then one day to Gladys' and Juan's astonishment, they found the walls of Havana papered with posters of Manolo pictured face-to-face with Che Guevara. Underneath was a message for Cuban youth:

CHE, WE FOLLOW YOUR EXAMPLE

Manolo was pleased with the honor, but Gladys was not. A short time later Manolo, who'd gained renown as a sports star, was honored at a soccer stadium and introduced to the crowd as a shining example of Cuba's revolutionary youth. Standing in a jeep as it circled the track, he greeted the crowds in the stands with his arms raised while official announcements over the loudspeakers lauded the young man. For his revolutionary achievements, the announcer told the crowd, Manolo had been awarded a scholarship to study astrophysics in Moscow.

Gladys' stomach churned seeing Manolo cheered by frenzied crowds, and she was surprised and dumbfounded to learn of his scholarship. The announcer added that the scholarship opened the doors for Manolo to join the Soviet's extremely competitive space program.

"Now they want to make him an astronaut!" Gladys exclaimed in indignation. "I refuse to let him be brainwashed. Manolo will be the first of us to leave Cuba."

Gladys wasted no time. She hid her true objective and leveraged her friendship with Fidel and her acquaintance with his brother Raul to obtain permission for Manolo to travel to Spain. Manolo was allowed to leave before receiving his scholarship and before he would be drafted into military service.

The young man would never have imagined that the family's decision to exile him would shift his career from one in space to one in an operating room - a change he would never regret. Shortly thereafter, Juan and Gladys were able to get their younger child out as well and they joined Manolo in Spain.

Before leaving Cuba, Juan continued to work as a physician in the revolutionary forces, and towards the end of 1962, as the family was about to leave Cuba, he again disappeared as if he'd fallen into an abyss.

Something was up and rumors flew, but the press was silent until Fidel spoke interminably about a grave political moment that endangered the revolution. The Soviet missile crisis had led the USSR and United States to the brink of nuclear war, creating urgent needs in Castro's army. Without warning, Juan had been assigned to a subterranean military hospital that was preparing to receive wounded soldiers. The missiles with Soviet nuclear warheads were a threat to the Americans, and Fidel anticipated reprisals. The U.S. Navy completely blockaded the island, but at the last minute the Soviets capitulated and removed the missiles.

The crisis over, Juan showed up again to Gladys' great relief, and they continued to prepare for their long-awaited escape. It took two more years for that to happen, but finally they were reunited with their children. After Spain, next they emigrated to the United States, arriving destitute but joyful to be together and to have the opportunity to begin a new life in freedom.

The Cuban people had not been as lucky. Cuba had merely exchanged one dictatorship for another.

21

The Appeal of Conch Shells

1995

Me at the Bottom of the Sea

There is a house of glass at the bottom of the sea
Facing an avenue of stony white coral.
At five, a great golden fish comes to greet me,
bringing a red bouquet of coral flowers.
I sleep on a bed somewhat bluer than the sea.
Through the crystal an octopus winks at me;
In the green forest surrounding me –ding dong–ding dong
The sea-green mother-of-pearl sirens rock and sing,
and over my head, in the twilight,
the bristling crests of the sea are aflame.

-Alfonsina Storni,
Complete Poems

HE SWAM LAZILY, with the current as it pulled him away from the beach. The warm water and the sun's caress lulled him, and strokes came automatically. Momentarily free of mundane concerns, he could focus fully on his thoughts and involuntarily, his mind returned to images of his life at the office and the characters that had swarmed around him.

It had been quite a while since work stimulated him. His life at the office had become a routine he wished to escape. Colleagues and friends celebrated him as a brilliant executive, and at a different stage of his life, their awe would have been vital to him. His enemies - several of whom he wished to forget - hated him furiously. Rumor had it that their hatred was well deserved given his selfishness and lack of scruples, but Abel attributed it to their envy. His business deals made him wealthy if often at the expense of others. His portfolio had grown over the years, and had taken on a life of its own that required barely any effort from him. That's how it used to be, but it was different now.

As the current swept Abel along, Martha's cute little face suddenly appeared on his radar. He hadn't seen his spouse in nearly three weeks, and in fact few of his peers would say that they lived at the same address. Abel reminded himself that Martha's life was complicated as well - a frenzy of social obligations and activities related to her involvement with a string of committees and her long list of charities. She was frequently off on vacations to the most exotic, far-off corners of the world with her girlfriends, and Abel cheerfully paid for all their expenses - including hairdresser appointments, swimming classes, and pampering pleasures quite removed from his own world. At times it seemed like they lived on different planets although Abel didn't blame Martha.

Years ago, newlyweds still hoping to have children, they thought they had much in common. In those days Martha was so attentive to him. Abel could still remember how much in love he'd been for years following their wedding. Early on, business had not been as good, they led a simpler life, but it might have been the only time they were that happy.

With professional success, life became more complicated for the couple. Abel grew busy with urgent matters that took priority over his personal life with Martha. The couple's nightly encounters, once eagerly anticipated, became a routine subjected to by mutual agreement, a burden on a dying relationship.

As the scenes of his married life darkened, Abel's consciousness came to focus on Lucia. His perfect secretary had become an important part of his professional life, and soon came to occupy his personal life as well. For a while he sought other interests as well - a string of women who occupied his nights. But Lucia wore him down. He was flattered that she pursued him tirelessly, though Lucia couldn't help but notice his sexual vigor flickered like a dying candle. Yet it didn't diminish her loving attention.

"Honey, one must separate material things from spiritual concerns; pure love is more important than an orgasm, don't you think?" she would remind him.

Though he couldn't quite put a finger on it, Lucia's enthusiasm for the purity of her feelings seemed less than sincere to Abel, and Martha surely wasn't born yesterday. She was no fool. Finally it became clear to Abel that he had to choose. He could never decide if he had chosen well or not.

It was different with Mary Jo. The truth was that this girl wasn't like the ones who hovered for his money. Yes, he said to himself, he had the looks, wealth and he could convincingly fake feelings when he needed to. But in private moments, Abel admitted to himself that he was an inveterate hypocrite who spoke the truth only when it cost him nothing.

Initially loured perhaps by his valiant effort to appear younger, Mary Jo fell madly in love with him - at least with an image of a vigorous man - a man who loudly proclaimed his ideals and affirmed that he sought a new life.

Abel's fervent posturing had convinced even himself, and he considered options he'd not contemplated before, such as leaving Martha. But Abel wasn't successful in continuing to fool Mary Jo, and before long the reality of their tepid intimacy destroyed her image of him. Faced with yet another disappointment, young Mary Jo's frustration with him proved the final blow.

After reviewing his personal failures, Abel shifted and began to accept his new financial reality. Heretofore, he had denied his economic disaster as if it hadn't happened - as if it was a nightmare from which he would surely awake.

As he floated along, his gloomy reminisces were interrupted by a series of curious, sharp clicks. He realized that a pod of dolphins had located him with their sonar, and he'd become the object of their attention. They were all around him, at his sides, behind and in front of him. They seemed to be having an animated discussion as if trying to communicate with him.

Dolphins playfully leapt in the air near Abel. But in the distance past them he could see the unmistakable fins of sharks following at a distance. He had the feeling that the dolphins were protecting him, and he recalled having read that sharks avoided encounters with dolphins because, especially when there were many dolphins, the sharks frequently were the losers. Unable to decipher their cheerful clacks, the novelty of their presence wore off quickly. Under different circumstances he might have enjoyed trying to interpret their puzzling message, delivered in a mysterious language. Finally, under the gentle sun, Abel's eyes began to flutter shut and he grew sleepy.

In a dream Abel drifted back to an evening when he had arrived home after a horrible day, despairing over a loss of control over his life. The market had collapsed, and a review of his assets led him to conclude that he owed much more than he had. He was poor again.

As if fast forwarding through a film, scenes displayed the string of his personal relationships. Martha had lost hope in him long ago, so much so that Abel had felt their relationship was irreparable. But watching her now as she slept next to him, she looked so beautiful. He found himself wrapped in an embrace with renewed enthusiasm. Martha appeared to be pleased to find she'd recovered what she thought had been lost forever. Her surprise was greater, though not pleasant, when he told her of the catastrophic state of their finances.

As his dream carried on, Abel saw himself talking with Martha over breakfast. She confessed she'd been thinking of moving out, but said she was willing to give their relationship another chance. She would fight at his side as she had at the beginning. Abel was pleased, and the couple began making plans for their future.

He recalled that although he'd had lost his fortune, he had miraculously recovered his sexual vigor. He'd found the love of his wife once again, and filled with joy, he kept telling himself that he was still young and could rebuild his finances.

The film rolling in his mind shifted scenes to a *tête à tête* with Lucia. Surprised that he'd called her unexpectedly, she was nevertheless happy to see him again. Abel watched images of a wonderful evening with her, and found her more attractive than ever as he explored every inch of her body. Lucia responded fervently to Abel's great satisfaction. After their sexual catharsis came the moment of truth. Abel confessed his stumbles with the stock market, but though penniless, he vowed he would work to recover everything he had lost.

While Lucia did not find the images of his poverty appealing, Abel reminded her that they were still young and that together they could recover his fortune. "Most importantly," said Abel, "we love each other, and though I'm poor I will make you happy." Lucia's angelic face lit up. She had rediscovered her lost love.

The kaleidoscope of images whirling through Abel's brain now led him to Mary Jo who also was charmed to hear from him. Abel confessed his misfortunes, but explained that he was a new man who'd been thinking a great deal about their future. He proved himself in bed with her, demonstrating that although poor, he had recovered his vigor. Chatting in the morning over coffee, Mary Jo confessed that she had fallen in love with him originally before really knowing him. Now, learning of the changes in his life, she was not afraid to be poor and would trust him once again.

Waking from his dreams, Abel opened his eyes. He faced the reality that in fact nothing had changed. He noticed he was sailing along quickly on the back of a dolphin that was approaching the beach as its companions frolicked happily around them. Suddenly, his transportation submerged and left him floating. The dolphin twirled a couple of times, emitted sharp clacks of farewell and rejoined the group which swam away, having fulfilled their mission.

Abel realized that his feet could now easily touch bottom, although he glanced repeatedly at the coast behind him. It seemed to beckon for his return. Though he could walk out of the ocean to the shore, he could also allow the current carry him back out.

After only moments, Abel turned back to the sea, took a few strokes, and let himself flow with the current away from the shore.

22

The Bubble

2010

Society is a masked ball
where everyone hides his real character,
then reveals it in secret.

-Ralph Waldo Emerson,
Conduct of Life

AT FIRST IT WAS A tiny pink bubble, microscopic in size. I barely noticed it as it quickly flew by my eyes.

The guests' masks displayed grotesque grimaces, monstrous mouths revealing sharp teeth ready to attack, and flat painted laughter that lacked spontaneity.

The bubble expanded as the hours passed and became increasingly visible. Unnoticed by anyone except me in my spectator's seat, the bubble gradually enlarged to the point where it enveloped the guests in a microscopic chamber where the untitled comedy would be performed.

The bubble was both the stage and part of the plot. The tall, portly lead actor, costumed as Jesus Christ, wore a bearded mask and imitated the Creator's benevolence and wisdom when he spoke. He held a paintbrush and the expectant congregation watched as He painted the inside of the bubble with broad strokes of pink-dominated tones. His intent was to instill hope, the ingredient the congregation sorely needed, and the Lord's entourage consisted of angelic-looking beings who rhythmically nodded their head in approval.

Everything suggested an inconceivable harmony. Songs and praise to the Lord were heard all around. As the play continued, the Lord's philosophy was revealed as He sang His truth in a most authentic Gregorian style. The brotherhood followed enthusiastically singing the chorus with great devotion.

Not only were the characters in costume, but the language was cryptic, so spectators had to endure perpetual uncertainty unless they managed to interpret the mysterious language. Breaking the code was difficult because the action on stage was dominated by secrecy, and the reward for anyone outside of the inner circle who succeeded would be the Siberian cold for all eternity.

Each keyword had the opposite meaning while a careful reading of the script revealed important repetitions which transmitted precise information as in the genetic code. For example, the code's degeneracy meant that words as apparently different as quality, teaching, excellence, learning, and merit were synonymous with money. Mountains of numbers and terabytes of information conveniently obscured the truth.

When on rare occasions some reprobate hinted at having doubts or proposed an idea that departed from the dogma, the Lord gazed upon him with compassion, smiling ever so sweetly. As if having received a tacit signal, his avenging angels launched into dizzying flight around the black sheep, flooding the bubble in unison with censoring disapproval that smothered the culprit with shame. The Illuminati's experience set the tone, so the congregation remained respectfully silent during discussions of the most ardent topics, while heavenly music was heard with the angels providing an appropriate choral background.

The Lord and His celestial choir successfully created an oppressively homogeneous atmosphere free of dissent for the guests at the feast. There were more than twelve in the choir and each innocently trusted the wisdom of the Creator, unaware that Judas might be among them.

The dialog was strenuous, sometimes solemn, occasionally tragic, and almost always oppressive and monotonous. It was perhaps the script for a tragicomedy, sounding familiar to many who knew it well. The unique thing about the play was that the spectators were at the same time the actors and were therefore exhausted by the final curtain.

I myself had become numb in my seat, and I required a supreme effort to free myself from the masqueraded crowd, from the hypocrisy and reigning confusion. I needed urgently to breathe clean mountain air.

My feet dragged as I trudged up the hillside with the mountain quiet broken only by the joyful burbling of spring water flowing over stones. At last I stood at the door to the sanctuary.

I had not, up to that moment, been able to guess the fate awaiting me in my dream. Without my touching it, the door opened as if by magic, and the clear day transformed to a mystical gloom. Like a robot I marched to the altar as the door mysteriously closed behind me.

A lovely red rose perfumed the sanctuary, and an impulse prompted me to strip and stand before the altar. I recall being mesmerized by a twinkling white light and hearing an amazing strumming from invisible strings. The slow strum of the zither sounded vaguely oriental with melancholic tunes, but I was sure I had never heard such music before. I sensed an external *force* that I could not see ordering me to surrender, and I did without resisting. The rose's perfume penetrated my pores, but I could no longer see the rose. My thoughts drifted as I fell into a semi-conscious state of sleep.

I dreamed that firm but gentle hands clasped one of my feet in as the music continued in the background. Magic fingers slid voluptuously across my flesh, then trapped my other foot, which went up in flames. My hands came alive as an irresistible *force* suddenly lifted me like a feather and gently placed me on the altar. My blood boiled in my veins and my skin was electric in its wake. The twinkling white spot had disappeared, and the *force* bid me to close my eyes. Darkness came and was absolute as the zither tirelessly played its monotonous, numbing melody.

I had the impression that my spine was a piano keyboard played by tiny fairy feet that danced happily on my vertebrae. Their magic surrounded my neck, and I felt a firm pressure that gradually increased to the point of pain. I enjoyed it greatly and wished the moment could last forever. The pressure gradually subsided but did not completely disappear - as if the ecstasy of its *force* had been suspended in space.

I can't be sure how much time passed before the music stopped. The sense of contact vanished, and the silence became thick, almost solid. The only thing still connecting me to the *force* was the penetrating perfume of the rose.

Almost awake now, I sat up and opened my eyes. I felt ethereal, my body was as soft as cotton as I dressed with deliberate slowness, then the door opened.

Outside the sanctuary, the sun had set, and the bubble-enclosed mountain blended into the night. The dreamy experience had renewed my strength and thus invigorated, I awoke in my seat as the performance was ending.

The bubble's pinkness faded, and it grew huge until it finally exploded bringing the Divine's comedy to an end. The actors and the angels in the Lord's entourage applauded wildly, while in His dressing room the Lord took off His divine mask, returning to the stage with his troupe to reap the applause. Barren of His costume, the Lord exhibited His corrupt features, revealing a Machiavellian grimace, the unequivocal confirmation of His success. The actors had been transformed into a flock of uniform sheep, bleating endlessly, nodding their heads in an affirmation dominated by an uncontrollable, unending twitch. The choir angels were clearly ecstatic as they took off their masks. The comedy had been a resounding success.

The fake evangelists chatted tirelessly, interpreting the messianic message according to the Lord's Bible, the lie disguised as truth that the flock had received with great pleasure during the mind-boggling comedy that had played within the bubble.

As for me, I could only rescue my dream and the lingering perfume of the rose.

23

Board Meeting

1998

While I was unknown to the world,

all who knew me loved me

and I had no enemies;

but as soon as I revealed myself,

not a single friend remained.

-Jean-Jacques Rousseau,
Confessions

A CURIOUS THING HAPPENED last week. After working hard for several years, the company at long last recognized my merits, and I was appointed to the board of directors. It was the culmination of my career. Since my mantra is to always do my best even when undertaking the most insignificant tasks, my attitude did not change with my promotion, although I admit I was elated.

The board meeting at which I would have my baptism by fire was scheduled for the following day, and I spent long hours studying each director's background to anticipate their pet topics.

I was confident that I could effectively handle any subject that arose during the meeting, and I felt well prepared. I would be seated midway down the table between Ciro Cuadrado, a career economist, and Magdalena Camacho, a stone-hard administrator without the slightest sense of humor. I had never seen this blunt, stiff, inscrutable woman smile.

One of the company's dinosaurs, a heavyweight in every sense of the word, would be seated directly across from me at the elegant, carved oak board table. Weighing almost 400 lbs., the enormous Antonio Vargas with his aggressive demeanor inspired holy fear. Unless one was the recipient of his ire, Vargas was a spectacle worthy of a front-row seat. It was fascinating to watch him rant in his stentorian voice, slamming a fist on the table and making the furniture, lamps, and everyone around him tremble. Vargas' favorite topic was almost an obsession; he had become fixated on professional ethics and had disqualified many aspiring candidates, preventing them from moving up in the company.

I was feverishly studying statistical treatises, management manuals, business administration texts, the fundamentals of public relations and codes of professional ethics when the phone rang.

"Serrano?" I recognized the Chairman's loud voice. Without waiting for me to reply, he said, "We're having a visit tomorrow from Aurelio Marquez, an executive from IGT. I want you to take good care of him and update him on every detail of the work our two companies have in common. You will report to us at the board meeting. Got it?"

"I understand, sir," I answered as the Chairman hung up without another word. The Chairman's assignment was not complicated for me. I knew all the details of the IGT negotiation perfectly and could handle Marquez easily during his official visit.

I didn't sleep well the night before the meeting. After tossing for several hours, I finally dozed and dreamt about the board meeting imagining the Chairman nodding approvingly at my presentation. Even Magdalena Camacho and Mr. Cuadrado exchanged unlikely smiles. My immediate horizon was dominated by Vargas' enormous humanity, snorting like a walrus as he rhythmically nodded his imposing head in approval. I awoke as the Chairman was congratulating me; then I faced reality.

I dressed with great care that morning, determined to make a good impression on my distinguished visitor and my colleagues at the meeting. My experience with the company had taught me that dressing well was crucial to success.

After a long, hot shower to help me relax, I splashed on plenty of 4711, the cologne that Petra had chosen for me. I carefully combed my hair, arranging the scarce strands forward and fixing them in placc with spray. I chosc an clcgant, starched, blue shirt with narrow stripes that matched my burgundy tie, and the herringbone three-piece suit I picked to wear for the first time for the occasion.

Petra, being of good German stock, was the utmost perfectionist. She had laundered and ironed my clothes herself, for nobody could do it better, and had matched the colors, chosen, the cologne, and shined my shoes so I would look like a king. Fifi, Petra's spoiled cat, lay sprawled on the floor in front of my mirror blocking my access, so I moved her aside with my foot for a final look at my attire, much to Fifi's displeasure. Petra's watchful eye hadn't missed a detail, and after a careful inspection, she gave her approval and kissed me goodbye.

It was a cool, dry morning, and the delicious aromatic blend of jasmine and wisteria enveloped me as I walked through the garden. On the way my car was immediately overwhelmed by the scent of the 4711 I had so generously applied. Arriving at work, I spoke with my secretary Mirta to fine-tune the details for our visitor's arrival, and then sat at my desk to review the documents while I awaited Aurelio Marquez.

Almost immediately I noticed a strange smell stronger than the subtle aroma of the 4711. I couldn't identify it at first, but after sniffing around I came to an inescapable realization: I was surrounded by the unmistakable stink of piss. But where did it come from?

I began to sniff: the desk, armchairs, bookshelves and every inch of every corner of the room, hunting like a well-trained dog. But the smell of urine followed me everywhere. To my horror, I deduced that the smell was coming from me. *From me!*

How could this happen? Childhood memories raced to mind. As a child, I had peed my bed until I started school. The doctor had diagnosed nocturnal enuresis, but it turned out to be a psychological issue that resolved itself without aftereffects. I never again had even a slight episode of incontinence. The evidence, however, was overwhelming. I must have pissed myself!

I considered myself a young man full of life. Nobody would guess I was almost 60. True, sometimes I forgot things I should know perfectly well. Was it a sign of early senility? Alzheimer's? I had a dark flashback and remembered Anselmo, an uncle on my mother's side, who shortly after turning 50, began having animated conversations with imaginary radio announcers. At the time we thought it was quite funny. However, at the moment the memory wasn't at all humorous. The image of his pants bulging with adult diapers ran a shiver down my spine. On top of that, my guest was expected at any moment, and at noon I would be attending my first board meeting.

A quick glance at my wristwatch showed it was 9:30. There was no way I had time to go home and change. I took a deep breath and rushed into my private bathroom, locked the door, and quickly pulled off my pants and boxers. I took the presumably offending garment and scrubbed my shorts frantically with hot water and soap. After rinsing it, I hung it on a peg in a corner. I washed my privates with soap and water, dried myself well, and finally breathing easier, I put my pants back on, leaving my underpants to slowly dry on the peg. As I finished dressing, I was startled by tentative taps on the door. It was Mirta, my secretary, announcing the arrival of Mr. Marquez.

"Please ask him to wait a moment," I said. As soon as she left, I set the fan from the office in the bathroom, aimed it at the shorts, and set it to the maximum speed. I finished dressing and asked Mirta to show Marquez in.

I still perceived the odor but told myself my sense of smell had been overly stimulated. I'd dealt with my underwear later and I assumed the problem was solved though I felt quite naked without underwear. But nobody would know, so I went to welcome Mr. Marquez, and we shared a warm embrace.

"My esteemed Serrano, what a huge pleasure to see you again," he said to me, suddenly stepping away, his face twisted in a grimace. He added, "I hope our meeting will be productive. And brief."

"Yes, of course," I replied, somewhat concerned by his curious reaction. "We've finished the necessary paperwork for a successful transfer, and I will set you up with Mr. Fermin who heads the negotiation."

We traded previously prepared documents, and I asked my secretary to contact Fermin as I walked with Marquez to his next meeting. As we proceeded along the hallways, I noticed that Marquez kept a prudent distance, pretending to rearrange his paperwork. I didn't try to chat with him but walked quickly, hoping to outrun the infernal cloud of stink surrounding me.

Fermin was waiting for us when we arrived at his office, so I said goodbye to Marquez who had no choice but to approach and shake my hand. The IGT man's words were cordial, but the expression on his face reminded me of someone seeking to avoid a leper. As we stepped away from each other, we both breathed sighs of relief.

I was bathed in sweat by the time I got back to my own office. As I stepped in, I saw Mirta coming out of my private bathroom, looking infinitely perplexed. She looked at me and didn't say a word, but I knew what she was thinking. I sat at my desk as if there was nothing going on, casually reviewing some papers, waiting for Mirta to leave me mercifully alone. She finally left, and I felt suffocated and persecuted, surrounded by the smell of urine. My underwear was still damp, and saw that it was five minutes to 12 - time for the board meeting.

I took a deep breath and finally said to Mirta, "I've had a small mishap that I can't go into right now. Do you have any perfume you could lend me?"

"Yes, of course," she replied, smiling slyly. "However, I don't think you'll like it," adding, "it's too flowery for a man."

The fragrance was exactly as Mirta had described it, nauseatingly sweet and penetrating, but I thought it would cover up the pervasive smell of urine. Taking the bottle of scent I prayed would save me, I once again stepped into the bathroom, dropped my pants, and sprayed a large area of my body with abundant quantities of Mirta's perfume. I then headed to my first board meeting feeling like a pig led to slaughter, hearing the sharp squeals of his terrified pen-mates ahead.

The board members were sitting around the table when I entered and I took my place among them. There was an atmosphere of professional sobriety in the room, and everyone was paying close attention to the Chairman's remarks as he began to cover the agenda. Nobody seemed to notice my entrance.

I made a conscious effort to calm down, and was reviewing the notes I had prepared for my presentation, when to my left I heard the scraping of a chair being hastily moved aside. I glanced over and saw that Magdalena Camacho, looking more disgusted than usual, had put a greater distance between our two chairs.

While I was looking at Camacho, I heard a similar sound from my right. With dismay I saw that Ciro Cuadrado had also moved away, all the while inscrutably working with endless calculations on his handheld device. Meanwhile, the mix of urine and Mirta's overly sweet perfume had enveloped me in a suffocating mist reminiscent of a skunk.

With a few introductory words concisely summarizing my performance in the company, the Chairman welcomed me as the newest member of the board. The two colleagues on either side of me, now seated a substantial distance away, looked at me with disgust. The Chairman finally indicated that I should begin my report on the current state of negotiations with IGT.

I stood up, focused on the report and wiped my sweaty forehead with a handkerchief. I looked straight at the Chairman as I spoke, and heard an uncommonly loud, scratching noise from across the table, as if someone were pushing a desk across the floor. I continued my presentation, undaunted, but noticed that everyone's eyes, including the Chairman's, were focused on Antonio Vargas who had noisily moved his chair away from the table and was covering his nose with a handkerchief. Tears streamed like waterfalls from his eyes. I wrapped up my report, grateful that there were no questions, and a few minutes later the Chairman called the meeting to a close.

Looking neither left nor right, I exited the board room as quickly as possible and headed straight for my office. Fortunately, Mirta was on her lunch hour, and my underwear was dry. I left her a note saying I wasn't feeling well and was going home early and left the building as if chased by demons.

The smell of piss inside the car was unbearable, and I left the windows down all the way. Were anyone to ask me which route I took getting home, I'd be unable to say because I drove like a dazed automaton.

When I arrived home, Petra took one look at my face and before I could say a word, exclaimed, "What a horrible skunk smell. It's like a mixture of urine and cheap perfume!" She added, "What kind of woman have you been with?"

Not bothering to reply I rushed to the bedroom, yanked off my tie, and began frantically to unbutton my shirt. The smell of urine nearly bowled me over, and for the first time I suspiciously considered the shirt itself. Sniffing it all over I found an almost imperceptible tiny dark stain near the collar on a blue stripe where the skunk smell was concentrated and was practically lethal. Nauseated, I walked to the laundry room where Petra had stacked freshly ironed clothes ready to be worn.

I tossed the shirt into the dirty clothes hamper, and as I was leaving the room in search of clean air to breathe, I tripped noisily over Fifi, Petra's spoiled cat. I heard Petra's muffled laughter as she methodically inspected the shirt collar.

24

The Magic Ring

"Identity is memory;
when memory disappears,
the self dissolves and love with it".

John Lahr,
"Joy Ride: Lives of Theatricals"

I -A VINEYARD IN TUSCANY

THE VINEYARDS IN GAIOLE were still asleep in early spring and at five in the morning it was still night. The sky, full of dark clouds, threatened to storm, The rain had fallen torrentially until dawn on Giussepe's vineyard.

The winemaker rose at dawn to tenderly care for his vineyard. As usual and with great care, he worked his land, furrow by furrow, manicuring the vineyard in his wake, carefully pruning the superfluous branches and leaving the vines free of weeds.

As Giuseppe climbed to the top of the vineyard he spotted an unexpected sight. A car, apparently empty, was parked at the crest. As he approached, he noticed that the wet, rain-soaked earth smelled of gasoline. He opened the trunk and was shocked to discover a naked man in the fetal position, tightly bound with rope, unconscious and possibly dead. He quickly freed him from ropes that bound him like a stuffed flank steak and pulled him from the trunk. His helpless body and head covered with blood clots bore witness to physical abuse. Although the man showed few signs of life, Giuseppe noticed he was still breathing and had a heartbeat.

Though the man in the trunk was tall, with some difficulty Giuseppe lifted him to his shoulders and carried him home where his wife helped wash the wounds. An ambulance was called, and the man was rushed to a regional hospital where he was hydrated and treated for injuries.

X-rays showed a skull fractured in several places and a huge subdural hematoma that was surgically drained. After being comatose and between life and death for several days, he opened his eyes.

The doctor asked, "What is your name?"

Silence.

"Where are you from?"

No answer.

The poor devil seemed to pay attention, but was very confused. His brow wrinkled as if he was thinking as a cryptic grin spread across his lips.

Despite his efforts to respond to the doctors, he could not answer their many questions. The physician on duty thought at first that the patient might be a foreigner who was unfamiliar with the language, but the doctor soon realized that not only could the patient not articulate words, but his brain clearly was not functioning normally.

The police quickly took over, but they were unable to learn much about the injured subject. They discovered that the car had been stolen in Rome, but they found no digital prints. They couldn't identify the patient because his fingertips on both hands had been sliced off, and they found no documents at the scene of the crime.

After a few days, the patient began to regain some of his physical strength, but he grew increasingly violent; his mental state deteriorated to the point that he needed a straitjacket and he had to be transferred from the hospital to a psychiatric institution.

In time he began to heal from his head injuries. However, the physicians were not optimistic about his future mental health. Discussing the case during rounds, they noted that while his cerebral edema had subsided, several injuries caused brain damage that might be permanent. They mentioned lesions in the hippocampus, the organ of memory visible on an MRI and abnormalities in his EEG. Understandably their medical expectations were reserved. The patient's condition raised concern that amnesia and perhaps dementia were likely to result.

Given the circumstances, as the patient was considered potentially dangerous, he was transferred again this time to an insane asylum. Reports noted that he had fits of fury and agitation in addition to having lost his memory and much of his mental capacity.

As his general condition improved, he was often seen wandering through the gardens of the asylum, moving his mouth without sound, apparently having lively conversations with invisible interlocutors, or sucking on the stumps of his severed fingers with delight. He had become incontinent and was sometimes seen walking aimlessly, his pants wet with urine, in the patio where the asylum's residents received visitors.

For a reason neurologists could not understand, the patient developed the power to move his ears in the fashion of dogs and cats, focusing them in desired directions to better hear messages, presumably from beyond the grave, that were inaudible to the rest of mortals.

II -THE INSANE MAN COMES BACK TO LIFE

Chirp, chirp, chirp ... I was awakened by the crickets that never abandon me. It was still night, but I could clearly see thousands of phosphorescent dots glued to the walls and ceiling of my room as they disappeared little by little. The crickets kept up their racket continuously, and I felt them inside of me as if they'd settled in my ears. I made superhuman efforts to brush them away, but my arms were held by an invisible force, and I felt a stabbing pain in my hands.

A faint light appeared bit by bit on my narrow horizon and though the cricket sounds grew less intense, they still never stop singing. I began to see spirits, perhaps ghosts from other worlds. Their faces were riddled with dozens of little holes like smallpox that changed positions when they or I moved.

One idiot who I could not see because he spoke from outside my reduced field of vision kept asking relentlessly with the regularity of medieval torture, "Who are you? What's your name?"

How could I know since I have no past, and I know less than he does of my present. My memory is a total void, blank, and thinking about its emptiness gives me the chills. I don't have the least idea who I am, but judging from the questions I get, I wonder why they are so interested. But I don't remember. It's possible I was a human like them. In any event, even if I had known who I was, it was obvious I could not articulate a single word they could understand.

Despite receiving no answers from me, my interrogators would repeat the same questions with the insistence of a broken record. It made me angry enough to want to strike them if I could. During their inquiries, I would twist my back in the chair and flail my arms hoping to scare away the crickets that were driving me crazy. When I did my interrogators secured me with a straitjacket and tied my arms with ropes to bind me tighter, but it made it easier for the crickets to torture me.

Sometimes when I thrashed they give me injections, and after a while I don't hear the crickets and I fall asleep. But then I'm tormented by nightmares. When I awoke, although I was less agitated, I was horribly frustrated because although I searched the depths of my soul, I was unable to find even a hint of my past.

Occasionally my torturers leave me alone, and then the crickets accompany me everywhere. I have time to ponder my life, but my past remains a mystery. I pass the hours searching, and never lose hope that I will remember some fact, no matter how small, that will help me recall who I was. But I find nothing, nothing, nothing, except the wall that blocks me from accessing my previous life. I despair and crash against the wall and, at the height of frustration, I ask myself, "What are we without memory? Nothing."

Yet, though I never learn from my experience, each time hope is irrationally reborn. I lose control of my thoughts and the cycle of the endless search for my roots repeats and repeats.

The earliest memory of my stay at the hospital is that I slept most of the time only to be constantly shaken by turbulent dreams. A particular nightmare repeats, with variations, and frequently torments me. I am the central character in my dream, yet I don't see any of the features I see when I look in the mirror. I don't know why, but I am certain the person in the dream is me. In my dream it is always night, and suddenly I find myself surrounded by a group of women without recognizable facial features. The faceless women dance frantically about me on a platform of dark clouds into which they plunge, one by one, screaming in terror as they are swallowed by the darkness of the night. When the last spectral ballerina sinks into the void and disappears, I awake bathed in sweat. An oppressive feeling lingers that I had something I was supposed to do - probably nothing good - and it involves the faceless women.

Somehow I acquired an awareness of time. I sensed that I was living in a world in which, for reasons unknown to me, my vision was fuzzy - out of focus. I didn't have the slightest sense of the rules of the strange community I found myself in, nor could I identify any of the people I encountered. I discovered, much to my immense irritation, that although I retained the mechanics of their language, despite all my efforts, I could not utter a word.

Someone they call 'doctor' comes to see me every day, and stupidly asks how I am, awaiting an answer while patting my back. I resent that he treats me like a fool every time, and I cannot control myself and piss in the chair. The 'doctor' then delivers a stern lecture which has no effect whatsoever because I still urinate every time he visits. Despite all my efforts, I have not been able to get rid of him.

When leaving my room, the doctor told someone that I was getting better. I also think I've improved because my bones hurt less, and my hands don't bother me as much as they did.

I overhear them saying that I'm behaving better, and it has been several days since I've been allowed out of my straitjacket, although they continue to give me tranquilizers in the morning. I held them in my mouth and spit them out when they aren't looking. Unfortunately, after a while they discovered what I was doing, and they no longer give me pills. Instead, I get an injection three times a day. Right after the injection I feel soft as jelly and for a time the crickets leave me alone until they come back to attack more fiercely than ever.

Another big change in my life is that I'm allowed to leave my room, and I share the dining room with the other inmates. Now that I see the fingers of the inmates that I dine with, I understand why my hands did hurt so much. Mine are different. Instead of longer fingers like theirs, mine are short stubs. The tips of my fingers lack nails but have scars with scabs that I peel off. I suspect something bad happened to my fingers. Although they no longer hurt, I feel a compulsion to suck them one by one. It calms me and puts me to sleep.

Though I cannot participate in the conversations during meals, I really enjoy listening to the inmates. Sometimes I try to communicate with them by sign since I can't speak, and they think I'm one of the brotherhood. Some in the group at my table don't speak at all. Others speak continuously to themselves or make agitated speeches to an audience I've never seen.

One of my companions seems different and less troubled. He greets me politely and doesn't ask questions because he knows I can't talk. He comments on the food and chats with caregivers and the nurses. He told me that his profession was considered essential to national security. He said that his case was under review because he had trouble making his payments to the asylum, and that he had petitioned Woodrow Wilson to support him for the rest of his life. I suspect his request was denied because one day he disappeared, and I never saw him again. Anyway, the forced exodus of my partner made me wonder why I was here, and how I had managed to stay in the asylum without being ousted as he was.

I have no doubt now. This is a psychiatric hospital. I don't think I'm crazy, but a familiar, inner voice tells me that very few of my fellow inmates think they are crazy. I believe I'm here because the hospital staff thinks I'm crazy. I'm also sure that I have lived another life, but I can't remember anything about it, perhaps because I'm not young and I might be old. My previous life is a dark night, and since I can only make guttural sounds, I am isolated from the outside world. I know almost nothing about what's out there.

I have tried to convince the doctor that I'm not crazy, but without success. My gestures and loud grunts just annoy him, and when I chase him like a blowfly to get his attention, he shoves me away and says, "Get away, you lunatic!" That gets me agitated, and he puts me in the straitjacket again. So I have abandoned my attempts to convince him.

III -THE ADVENTURES OF THE DEMENTED MAN

I don't know how I got the idea of escaping to have a look at the outside world. After everything that has happened to me, it seems that it was a crazy idea. But I decided I really wanted to have a look beyond the walls that confined me.

To succeed in my plan, it thought it was essential that I behave well for a time to inspire confidence in my keepers. I became a model inmate with a great fondness for walking through the corridors and patios of the asylum. The path I always took brought me near the only front gate, but there was always a guard, a big man with a menacing look. I thought without knowing why that in my past I had also been held in a country governed by a dictator, in a building like this one with only one exit door that was heavily guarded by a soldier.

The wardens got used to seeing me around, so my presence aroused no suspicions. I decided it would be easier to attempt my escape during the noon hour when visitor traffic was heavy. I got close to the front gate often, but I did not dare to leave. Then, on one of my passes, I noticed that the guard was busy giving directions to some visitors. I followed my impulse with little thought and changed my direction. In an instant I found myself out on the sidewalk walking calmly, enjoying freedom for the first time in my memory.

I noticed that some passersby looked at me like I was a freak, but they didn't stop me so I continued on my merry way. I realized, too late in my escape, that my light gray cotton coat was attracting the attention of people familiar with the uniform of the asylum inmates.

When I reached the corner, a passerby crossing the street stopped and stared at me. But I kept walking undeterred, enjoying the caress of the sun and thinking how nice it was to be free. Suddenly I was startled by the sound of a car screeching to a stop just inches from my legs. The driver who had to slam on his brakes to avoid hitting me, leaned out his window and screamed, "You moron!!" I realized the man was very upset, and for a moment it further occurred to me that I had heard that insult before.

Someone else looking from the curb shouted, "He's an inmate escaped from the asylum!"

I started running, dashing through a group of boys who had just left school. They followed me, shouting in a chorus, "Lunatic! Lunatic!" The person on the sidewalk curb who had sounded the first alarm screamed, "Stop him, he's escaped from the asylum!"

The episode ended when a swarm of patrol cars with a concert of sirens surrounded me. The police were everywhere. I soon found myself back in a straitjacket, and that concluded my fleeting wanderings through the free world.

Often an odd character who lived near my room came in and with great fanfare would talk in a strange gibberish that I couldn't understand. "*Probably another crazy person*," I thought. Initially, I believed that the man who appeared in a worn frock coat with a tattered, high collar knew that my condition rendered me unable to speak. I assumed that was why he didn't expect an answer. But when I saw him in the dining room and in the hallways talking to other inmates. I realized that he harangued them also, babbling on endlessly without waiting for an answer despite that they had no difficulty speaking.

In time I began to decipher his gibberish. His favorite subject was sin, and he repeatedly urged me, "Ask the Lord to forgive your sins and receive you into the kingdom of heaven! Don't let your sins lead you to the eternal fire of hell!"

Although the madman in the frock coat may not have suspected it, his words didn't fall on deaf ears. Rather, they awakened a lot of questions in me. "Who is this Lord of whom he speaks, and where is this kingdom of heaven?"

I surmised that the Lord might be the owner of a chain of psychiatric hospitals and that the kingdom of heaven was a luxury hospital where only the chosen ones get to go. I wondered how the Lord picks among the insane who aspire to go to his kingdom of heaven.

I thought repeatedly about sin and wondered, from my limited perspective, what was sin and what was it all about. From the madman's pathetic tone, sin must be terrible, and one who sins ought to be embarrassed. I thought it likely that the madman was referring to my escape attempt. I found it unlikely that the owner of the asylum chain would easily forget my recent escapade and that he wouldn't allow my entrance into heaven, his special accommodations for those who rank the highest. Perhaps I had committed a cardinal sin. In any case, I did not remember having sinned before or after my brief venture beyond the asylum walls.

But I kept wondering about my previous life although remembering nothing about it. How can I ask forgiveness for sins that I don't remember? I suppose many try to forget their sins, and then they don't have to confess them. But it seems to me that God must keep a record of all sins and cannot be fooled easily. And this hell he spoke of? Whatever hell is, it horrified me and made me worry about hell's eternal fire. Was hell as bad as the madman painted it?

Eventually my loneliness became almost absolute, a horrible torture on the long sleepless nights in the winter. Sometimes I felt a warm sensation between my legs, and my diapers would flood with a slimy ooze while the name of Villagra appeared in my consciousness. I didn't know what it meant. Maybe it was the name of an old friend that I can no longer remember.

IV - A HINT OF THE PAST THROUGH A MAGIC SMOKE RING

Today I had several visitors but no one that I knew. They entered my room in a group while I was busy trying to get rid of the crickets. One of the group said nothing the whole time but just stood in a dark corner. Another waited in the threshold of the door looking like a frightened chick. The third visitor looked like a snake or perhaps like a woman. I'm not entirely sure.

I don't know why I think it was a woman because I don't remember ever seeing a woman before. It is one of the many things I think I know, but I don't know how I know it. But I think it was a woman even though she evoked an image of a rattlesnake. When she came into my room the crickets abruptly changed tone, and their singing became sharp. I imagined I heard the sound that a rattlesnake's tail would make when wagging in the vicinity of its prey.

She approached slowly with her head up and her gleaming eyes fixed on me. Her mouth, open slightly, exposed her pointed tongue and sharp fangs poised to attack. She stared at me for a long time, perhaps marveling that I did not drop dead on the spot under the influence of her poison. I felt a little sorry for the snake since she was surely used to obtaining instant success. Little did she know that miraculously I was vaccinated against her poison.

She called me a strange name, "Lázaro?" in a voice that sounded like a moan from beyond the grave. It was a name I don't remember hearing before, but she said it with the anxious look of someone who does not want an answer. I didn't know who she was talking about, and I tried not to look at her. Hearing no response, the serpent slowly backed away with her charge of poison intact. When she reached the door she quickly turned around and left, fluttering the rattle of her tail. The other two visitors instantly disappeared behind her. The crickets, relived at their departure, celebrated and began to replay their old tune.

Sometimes I'm visited by a very attractive middle-aged woman who comes with one or two young girls. They are almost always different girls, but they closely resemble each other. It was as if the mother had an inexhaustible supply of girls all made from the same mold. They looked at me with curiosity and talked nonsense the way one would if talking to a nursing child.

It puzzles me that sometimes this woman also calls me Lázaro. The only Lázaro I ever knew, and I don't know how, is the biblical leper thought to have been resurrected by Jesus. But when she calls me Lázaro, I don't know who she is talking about.

I still remember the last time they came to visit. They were waiting for me when I returned to my room from my walk. The woman the girls call 'mom' was accompanied by a young lady who I suspect was the oldest of her daughters. The mother sat by my side, and the girl lit a cigarette. Although the act of smoking was one of the many things I had no memory of, for some reason I instantly knew all about it. I smiled, pleasantly surprised, when I smelled tobacco. The two women looked startled by my reaction, but as if by mutual agreement and without a word, the mother took out a cigarette and put it in my mouth while the girl gave me fire.

As if I'd always known how to smoke, I took a deep breath with relish, and I was amazed when beautiful smoke rings of a bluish-gray tint came out from my mouth. If I'd been asked how to blow smoke rings, I couldn't explain it. But apparently I knew how to make them quite well. That's when something quite mysterious happened and I can't explain it either.

Through my voluptuous smoke ring, I clearly saw a lovely young girl with black braids and big eyes. She was having coffee with a handsome young man, looking at him with affection. I suppose they were in love because it was obvious that both youngsters were happy and enjoying each other.

I remember feeling transfigured by the thought that the young man I saw through the ring could have been me in my previous life. For a fleeting moment I was sure I had seen the young girl before, and I had the impression that she had been important in my life. The long, pointed fingers of the dapper young man were unlike my stubby fingers without nails, but I was excited watching his fingers play with hers and hearing his fluent, baritone voice - so melodic to my ears. It seemed that I was reliving an episode of my own life in the past. As a smoke ring lingered, for a brief moment I had the impression that as it hung, delightfully suspended in time; it's magic was illuminating a dark and forgotten period of my life.

But I guess this may not have been the case because the ring's edges suddenly blurred, and in my smoke-filled room all I could see now was a beautiful, mature woman and a grouchy, young girl. Despite every effort, I have not been able to place them in my past. The girl, irritated, yanked the cigarette from my lips and said, “Enough mom!” It broke the spell. She stubbed out the cigarette in the ashtray and led her mom out by the arm. I could not say how long their visit lasted, but when they left, the ashtray was full of ash and cigarette butts.

As the last ring dissipated, the enchanted moment died. A bluish haze gave my room a spectral look, though the silhouettes of the two women who left without looking back remained imprinted in my memory.

More than once I have tried to place them in hopes of learning more about my previous life, but I have concluded they mean nothing to me, that I imagined their visit, and I never saw them again.

Often I fall asleep sucking the stumps of my fingers and I dream about the enchanted smoke ring. Looking through it in my dream, I see the fresh face of the lovely young girl with black braids and large eyes. She looks at me with affection as if she were in love. But sadly, the vision is always fleeting, the ring soon dissipates and as it fades, the fleeting image which is possibly a glimpse of my past life is extinguished.

Another's visit also repeats with the regularly of a circadian rhythm. It is that of a man with chubby cheeks who snorts as he walks, and each time he visits, the routine is the same. He enters my room looking tired, stops next to me and putting his heavy hand on my shoulder asks, "How are you, Lázaro?"

After reviewing these scenes repeatedly, the visits of the mother with her daughters, the viper and the snorting man, I think my name may have been Lázaro. I've repeated the name a thousand times, but it does not bring a memory.

Knowing that I am unable to answer him, the man with the chubby cheeks continues with the rest of his routine. He pulls the covers off the bed to verify that the sheets are not soiled, and he opens the closet to inspect my clothes on the hangers. He runs his finger over the furniture to confirm that they are not covered with dust, he thoroughly examines the bathroom, and he calls the doctor, and the two leave my room talking.

When they leave, I feel comforted, certain that my world is stable, and that I have nothing to be afraid of. This is absolute bliss.

One day my internal clock alerted me that the regular visit of the man with the chubby cheeks had not occurred. Although I did not know why, I felt unpleasantly dispossessed. Soon afterwards, out of sync, a new character appeared in my small world - a tall, thin young man with sharp features and incisive gaze arrived.

Upon entering my room, he greeted me with a heavy hand on my shoulder, "How are you Lázaro?" Without waiting for an answer, he stripped the bed and opened the closet wide open to inspect my clothes on the hangers. He verified that the furniture was clean, and that the bathroom was immaculate before calling for the doctor.

I was surprised that the routine of my young visitor was an exact repetition of that of the man with the chubby cheeks, and when he left with the doctor I detected a ring with an enormous, brilliant stone on his left little finger that seemed familiar to me.

V -CUPID'S ARROW AND THE AWAKENING OF A SLEEPING LOVE

The last time we saw him, María José and I visited him a week before returning to Buenos Aires. When we arrived at the asylum, Lázaro was wandering the corridors, and we sat in his room to await his return. He came in suddenly, walking with a stealthy, feline gait that did not reflect the hardships he'd suffered. He looked at us with curiosity, not recognizing us, then sat down, apparently very interested in listening to us.

"Mom," said María José, "it makes me nervous to see how daddy moves his ears when we talk to him. It's as if he's making an effort to understand what we are saying. He moves his ears like a cat, and have you noticed he walks like a cat also?"

María José smoked a cigarette while I sat close to Lázaro who seemed fascinated by our visit. Surprisingly, and with a bleak look on his face, Lázaro stretched out his hands, displaying the stumps of his mutilated fingers. He watched entranced as María José smoked. On impulse, I put a cigarette in his lips and María José lit it. Lázaro's withered face brightened, smiling ear to ear as he began to smoke.

I was fascinated by how easily Lázaro blew smoke rings. One ring after another created a window in time that triggered my memory. The rings seemed to touch some mysterious region of Lázaro's brain and mine like a magic wand. As if enchanted by his smoke rings, I forgot for a moment Lázaro's omnipresent selfishness which had such an impact on our lives. The memories inspired by the enchanted rings made me recall how I had been madly in love with his warm, baritone voice, his radiant and contagious smile, and the kinky hair that fell on his forehead.

I had been running out of my English class with my notepad and book under my arm, hurrying to catch the elevator when it stopped at my floor. I tried to enter as the door was closing, but was dismayed to see it was full. I stopped, but a man in the front made a place for me, and, smiling gratefully, I slid my body in against his. In my rush to enter, my fingers fortuitously brushed against his, perhaps for a fraction of a second longer than should happen accidentally. As the elevator started to descend, I sensed that my benefactor was watching me. I looked up, and for an instant we stared into each other's eyes.

When we reached the ground floor, I rushed out as the group dispersed, and as I did I heard a deep baritone voice asking=, "Marisa, are you Argentinian?"

I knew who had asked the question and without feigned surprise, I answered, “Yes, and how do you know my name?"

“On the cover of your notebook you have written in large letters, ‘Marisa Laverne.’ The Argentinian thing was a hunch. Why don't we talk about it over coffee?”

“All right,” I agreed. “And your name?”

“Lázaro.”

Suddenly I wasn’t in a hurry anymore. Lázaro was a very attractive, handsome young man. His hair was loose and kinky, and he had a wide forehead and the dreamy eyes of an enchanting lover.

“How do you happen to be in Los Angeles?” he asked with a charming smile.

“I came in a student exchange program after finishing high school. I spent three months in the home of an American family, and then I stayed, working during the summer as a kitchen helper in a company. And what are you doing in Los Angeles?” I said.

“I’ve done almost nothing since I arrived from Buenos Aires last year. Or rather, I work as a dishwasher in a nightclub to survive until I get something matching the profession I studied for. I graduated with a degree in economics which sounds impressive, but it’s not. I haven’t worked at all until recently. I’ve been taken care of like a mama’s baby.”

“Yes, I know very well how things go over there. Where did you live in Buenos Aires?”

“In Olivos,” said Lázaro, “next to the tennis club in Borges square.

And you?”

“By the Quesada street,” I said. “Or perhaps I should call it a river.”

“Quesada is in Belgrano, right? Why call it a river?”

Laughing I replied, "Because when it rains more than a few drops, Quesada street floods and you almost have to be a swimmer to cross it."

"What plans do you have after this summer, Marisa?" he asked.

"I'm not exactly sure, Lázaro. Next week I'm returning to Buenos Aires to take the entrance exams to study medicine," I said.

Two hours passed as if in an instant and we were still sitting over coffee. As we spoke about subjects that became more and more intimate, I began to smoke. I didn't even know why. I was a rookie when it came to that vice, but I marveled at the smoke rings that Lázaro had learned to blow in the Buenos Aires coffee shops.

I started to leave several times but without success because I didn't really want to go. I remember that, with the meager experience of my nineteen years, I tried to see beyond Lázaro the nightclub dishwasher and to imagine what Lázaro the young economist could be in the future. As I did, I began to fall in love with the object of my imagination. Finally we said goodbye with a promise to meet again next day.

As days passed, our relationship quickly deepened as if we'd both enrolled in an accelerated lovemaking course. On the day of my departure for Buenos Aires, Lázaro proposed, and I promised to return soon.

VI -THE PRICE OF SUCCESS

After finishing his studies in economics, Lázaro Agüero, had emigrated to the United States from his hometown in Buenos Aires. When he arrived, Lázaro had nothing but his youth, his charismatic personality and his knowledge of business administration which he put to work with great success. After working in Los Angeles for more than 20 years, it was common knowledge that Lázaro had amassed a substantial fortune.

Marisa was a beautiful, intelligent woman who had dedicated her life to her daughters and her husband. Lázaro was a tireless worker with a huge ego and an equally large weakness for blondes and brunettes alike - and sometimes a beautiful redhead - provided that they were well-endowed by mother nature and ever younger as the years went by. Lázaro's hunger for the opposite sex that had pursued him as a student, continued during and after his marriage.

Lázaro and Marisa had 9 daughters during those years but all was not blissful in the marriage, and they went through a stormy divorce. It was obvious that Lázaro easily got past the chaotic period following their divorce since it didn't prevent him from making a lot more money and leading life as a *bon vivant.*

Friends knew that Lázaro was an inveterate womanizer, and they delighted in listening to him talk about his romantic entanglements. Though frequently immersed in some new love affair, Lázaro did his best to hide it from his wife and daughters. But he could not fool Marisa. For years she had tried to confront Lázaro about his infidelity but without success. The magic of their love crush had long since vanished.

A day came when Marisa lost all patience, and she found a good lawyer who filed for her divorce. Both Marisa and Lázaro believed they had loved each other dearly, but Marisa was sick of Lázaro's infidelities.

As usual, Lázaro negotiated with her, promising he would change. He tried wheeling and dealing, imploring her and even swearing at her - trying every trick he knew, but in vain. Marisa, who had been disappointed too often, did not believe him this time. Her uncompromising stance surprised Lázaro who loved his daughters, was comfortable with the status quo, and did not want a divorce. But Marisa revealed herself to be much tougher than even the business competitors Lázaro also cheated.

Early on in the marriage, as Marisa was busy raising their 9 young girls, she had believed in Lázaro's sincerity. But in time she came to know him better. He was the epitome of selfishness, a man who loved himself above all others. He was dedicated to his work, but that didn't keep him from finding time for frequent escapades, a peppering of business with extramarital pleasures.

When the day came that Marisa, completely disillusioned with Lázaro, decided she'd had enough, she found a skilled lawyer who accumulated reliable evidence of Lázaro's multiple infidelities. Marisa confronted her husband with facts he could not deny, and then easily obtained a divorce and the custody of her daughters. She erased Lázaro from her life.

VII -LÁZARO'S LONELINESS

Though the divorce was finalized, Lázaro, continued to live at home. He felt ungrounded after the collapse of his family life and unsure of his prospects for the future.

The judge ruled that the mansion where the couple had lived for over 15 years now belonged exclusively to Marisa, a verdict Lázaro conveniently ignored.

One night upon returning from work to the manor he considered his home, Lázaro found a long row of suitcases and trunks with his clothes and other personal items stacked outside the front door. His surprise turned to disgust when his door key didn't work. Furious, he banged on the door and loudly demanded that it be opened, just as he felt a heavy hand on his shoulder. A police officer politely informed him that this was no longer his home, and that he must remove his belongings immediately as they were blocking the way.

Shocked, Lázaro stammered in protest, but the officer interrupted him and advised that loitering at someone else's property was a crime subject to penalties.

Livid and speechless, Lázaro returned to his car. Half an hour later a moving truck arrived at the door of Marisa's house, and two men loaded up his belongings.

After living in a hotel for almost a month, Lázaro bought a spacious apartment, but he discovered shopping for furniture and other home accessories was struggle. He'd never had to think about such things before. Marisa always handled them, and he discovered that it wasn't easy to choose the color of the rugs so that they wouldn't clash with the furniture, lamps, pictures and the decor that would surround him daily.

After work, Lázaro would arrive at his new apartment, lonely and upset, since it was painful to accept life without a family. He would lie awake at night for hours feeling isolated and unattached, longing for the warm family life he'd known before. He missed having Marisa greet him with a kiss and also missed his girls hugging him and squealing joyfully. He longed for his family dinner, surrounded by his wife and the little girls that Marisa had raised with such a perfect mixture of sweetness and firmness.

He remembered the nights when, after the children slept, Marisa was eager to share her day with him until she realized that while he pretended to be listening, clearly he wasn't. She would fall silent, and he would ask, "What's wrong?"

"Nothing... nothing," she would answer.

Despite the fact that their nine girls were testimony that a lot had gone on in their double bed, the fire of love had long ago extinguished. Evidently Marisa had lost the race with the numerous sexually attractive women who had captured Lázaro's attentions over the years. The couple's nightly relations became automatic, an aseptic routine without charm that both believed was required. But that was all behind him now, and Lázaro wanted to forget.

A psychiatrist said that he was depressed and prescribed an antidepressant to boost his spirits. It would help him, the psychiatrist advised, to accept that although he had not been much of a role model, he still had a right to enjoy life. The psychiatrist talked about the importance of the ego, and Lázaro would nod without answering.

After several sessions, Lázaro concluded that what the psychiatrist was saying was that he was important and had a right to a fulfilling life. He tried to consider the psychiatrist's existential advice, "You must think first of yourself, second of yourself and thirdly of yourself if you hope to realize an authentic existence."

"The psychiatrist couldn't know that his advice had always been my mantra," thought Lázaro, "although I doubt that it had much to do with the collapse of my family life."

Still, Lázaro was consumed with guilt and tormented by feelings of worthlessness, even as his ego struggled to adapt to his new life.

After much brooding and after feeling relaxed following several whiskeys, Lázaro was quite satisfied with the bright solution he'd arrived at.

He would remarry.

VIII -TÊTE À TÊTE WITH HIS CONSCIENCE

Lázaro was stimulated by the discovery of his ego, and he mediated on the significance of his existence. Then, after the divorce, he found himself with considerable time to think. That's when he discovered an inner voice that he could not control. The voice echoed repeatedly in what he called the microcosm of his soul. But the unexpected emergence of the involuntary thoughts that echoed in his consciousness created doubts and whispered objections to the decisions he was considering. This was new to Lázaro who had always acted on impulse.

"The world is full of beautiful, intelligent women, and I will surely find one who truly loves me," Lázaro thought. But he had to reluctantly admit, "It's not that Marisa didn't love me." And even as he hoped for a new love, his inner voice, perhaps his conscience, urged him to take a hard look at himself. So Lázaro stared in the mirror. "Hmmm!" he thought.

The image in the mirror reflected a cruel reality. The man he saw was prematurely bald, had a prominent belly, deep crow's feet, flabby muscles, and a red nose flanked by little blood vessels - perhaps belying his taste for whiskey.

"To think I once was a good-looking guy," he murmured. "Of course looks aren't everything. It's what's inside that's important. And I've discovered important virtues about myself, like my bank balance," he happily thought.

His inner voice countered, "What do the millions in your bank account have to do with love?"

"Hmm," Lázaro mumbled, remembering that the only time he believed he was in love was when he married Marisa, and at the time they were broke. They had been happy in those days, or at least living in a fantasy where they sipped at happiness.

Then came the financial success that they were not prepared for, and with it a string of temptations that lurked for Lázaro. His proverbial addiction to pretty women was driven by a selfish, weak nature that led to a whirlwind, libertine life. "But I can change," he thought, determined to start over with a fresh page.

"But, don't the pages you've already filled reflect the kind of man you are?" his inner voice prodded.

"I don't think so," Lázaro immediately replied. "I tore off the old pages and the new ones are blank."

"Not true," his conscience insisted, undeterred. "Your bald head, your fat belly, and your flabby muscles tell you a different story, don't they?"

"Yes, they say something, but my truth and yours are not the same. It's not that I lie, but what is truth, anyway? Absolute truth is a chimera, and my truth today is different from my truth in the past, and I'm sure it will change again in the future. But I'm in control now, and my friends tell me to get hair implants, maybe liposuction, take pills to lose weight and work out at a gym."

"That's easy to say, but difficult to actually do," whispered his inner voice and followed with a critical question, "Do you think your millions will help you find true love? How will you know if a women is attracted to your money or if she's fallen in love with Lázaro the man?"

After repeated attempts to get through to him, his inner voice quieted knowing that Lázaro was so consumed by his own ego, not to mention antidepressants and whiskey, that it was futile to pursue the argument further. Clearly he wasn't listening.

Even so, Lázaro was a man of action and determined to achieve his objectives. He decided that all he needed was to return to the life he'd known before the divorce. He'd been happy then, and he had only to go back to his old ways and he would be happy once again. So Lázaro began behaving the way he always had. His business continued to thrive and as before women fluttered around him. He shared good times with some of his old lovers and frequently initiated new relationships with beautiful women who made him feel young and who pleased him without making demands.

Lázaro would not let himself be overwhelmed by his youthful frenzy, so his nighttime encounters became a *ménage à trois* joined also by Lázaro's newfound friend – who he jokingly called "Villagra" – the silent participant in his nocturnal adventures.

He routinely discarded lovers as useless objects, followed them with new dalliances. But clearly something was lacking. Perhaps a new marriage would be the answer. As time passed and his list of affairs grew, he finally realized it would be easier to be married than divorced and single. But were he to consider marriage, it would be difficult to determine whether a woman loved him or his money. And despite the effort to ignore his conscience's key question, Lázaro was painfully aware that his inner voice had offered more than a kernel of truth.

IX -LÁZARO FINDS A GEM

For many moons Lázaro toyed at relationships with no greater enjoyment than sex, and while that was no small thing, it wasn't enough to fulfill him. That's when a new star appeared on his horizon.

Lucrecia Piedrabuena had arrived in town three months earlier, and all he knew about her was that she had lived in Chicago for more than ten years and had studied at the University of Chicago. A prominent employment firm had wholeheartedly recommended Lucrecia to one of his best clients, one Lázaro visited frequently.

Lucrecia was a pretty woman with generous curves that drew Lázaro's attention like a magnet when he visited his client's offices. She was less than half his age, smart, an effective executive secretary, stingy with smiles and carefully reserved. Her strict professional demeanor left little opportunity for a casual exchange - the opposite of the demeanor Lázaro usually experienced with women. They flocked to him – poor innocents – and communicated in languages expressed in wireless messages sent from their eyes, gestures, or hips.

Lucrecia was different – or so it seemed. She made no apparent effort to notice him, and though Lázaro didn't know it, Lucrecia's antennae had perked up when he visited his client's office. She knew very well who Lázaro Agüero was, and what's more, given her position, she was fully aware of his financial situation.

Lázaro's visits became unnecessarily frequent. One day, as Lázaro was taking the elevator up to his client's floor, Lucrecia got on at an intermediate floor. She was weighted down under a mountain of paperwork and with her hair down and her chin holding down the stack of papers, she looked irresistible to Lázaro. He wasn't about to miss an opportunity, "Good day, Lucrecia. Please let me help you," he offered eagerly.

"No, thank you, I've got it," Lucrecia replied briskly with a barely professional smile. Her smile evaporated instantly and she quickly stepped out as the elevator door opened. Lázaro followed and asked her to hold a moment.

"Yes?" Lucrecia asked.

"If I can't assist with your stack of papers, perhaps I could invite you to have lunch with me?" said Lazaro all smiles.

No innocent, Lucrecia replied with an equally charming smile, "Thank you Mr. Agüero, how kind of you. But as you can see, I am swamped and have no time."

Not used to rejection, Lázaro was stunned and felt as confused as an inexperienced adolescent.

As one would guess, Lázaro, his self-esteem injured, would not give up despite his initial stumble. After several attempts he overcame Lucrecia's reluctance. They went out for coffee and after several such meetings, dinner followed at a popular restaurant. More dates followed. They went dancing, frquently laughed together and clearly enjoyed each other's company. Lucrecia no longer feigned disinterest, but when Lázaro decided the plum was ripe and ready to pick, he got a second surprise.

"To your apartment? I couldn't possibly. I like being with you, Lázaro. We have lots of fun. But I have no intention of becoming another of your hobbies. Not a chance. It's best if you forget about me."

Lucrecia's performance was pitch perfect. Lázaro was sure he had fallen in love for the second time in his life.

X - A NEW LIFE AFTER THE HONEYMOON

Lucrecia and Lázaro had been married for several months, and to the surprise of everyone, Lázaro had become a faithful spouse. At every opportunity he would show off his young wife to friends who remarked that he looked happier and younger. Lázaro delighted in taking her to social events, and Lucrecia loved to dress in the latest fashions and wear impressive jewelry, as she arrived arm-in-arm with him.

Occasionally, though not often, Lázaro would once again hear whispers from his inner voice which never failed to remind him that it was an interesting curiosity that a young woman half his age would marry an older man. This was especially noteworthy when the wife was smart and full of wit.

"So tread cautiously," warned his inner voice, "and keep your eyes open." Lázaro, dazzled by the sparkling gem of a woman he'd acquired, ignored its advice.

He would routinely awake at dawn to go for a jog, then enjoy a long, restorative time in the sauna, followed by a massage to loosen up sore muscles. Despite his persistent physical training, nights with Lucrecia were a source of pleasure but also anxiety. Lucrecia's fire was unquenchable, and it was clear Lázaro wasn't giving all that she demanded. Supported by his trusty companion, "Villagra," he made superhuman efforts to stoke her flames but with inconsistent results. Even so, though not fully satisfied, Lucrecia appeared happy and an ideal mate. For his part, Lázaro was more than satisfied with his marriage partner.

Their life became a whirlwind of activity. Lucrecia usually accompanied Lázaro on his business trips, and then there were holidays ... to Bermuda, Hawaii, and the Côte d'Azur.

As winter's end drew near, an exceptional business opportunity presented Lázaro with the need to travel to Italy. Lucrecia advised she wouldn't accompany him saying she wasn't feeling well. So, though disappointed, Lázaro traveled to Europe alone.

Lázaro traveled to Rome on a non-stop flight from Chicago, then planned to wrap up his business deals before resting for a few days in his villa in Liguria. Next he planned a short stop in Bern, Switzerland to attend to some banking transactions before returning to Los Angeles.

He was a capable businessman and at his first stop, Rome, he met with a lawyer named Gambino whom his friend and lawyer Anthony Miller had recommended. The meeting was a simple matter of quickly providing his personal touch to finalize an important deal.

Lázaro's friend, Anthony Miller, was a prominent lawyer from Los Angeles and an affable man of impressive girth and rosy cheeks. A good, personal friend, Lázaro had given Miller a valuable ring, a large gemstone that sparkled as Miller walked.

Having finished his business in Rome, Lázaro drove his rental car North to Portofino, and there he wrote his beloved wife a letter.

Portofino, March 14

Dearest Lucrecia:

I miss you terribly. I finished my current business in Rome and will take a few days at our villa in

Portofino until I feel rested. I so wish you were with me. Without you, my days are long and boring, but we'll have plenty of time in the future.

I read the will our lawyer Miller had revised before I'd left Los Angeles, but I didn't sign it in Miller's office because I felt rushed and wanted time to look it over. It's a good thing that I didn't because there are some important details I wasn't in agreement with. I changed them to provide you with greater security should anything happen to me. Gambino, my lawyer in Rome, updated the document which I signed. Miller had recommended Gambino, and the man did an effective and speedy job. The document is in my briefcase and I'll drop it off in Miller's office as soon as I arrive in Los Angeles.

But before I leave, I plan to head South again tomorrow to buy us a few cases of a good Brunello. You recall that excellent wine we've enjoyed - which is exclusive to Montalcino. I can't wait for us to savor it again together.

I hope you're feeling better.

All my love, my dearest,

Lázaro

XI -FATAL ACCIDENT IN THE ALPS

The luxurious car that Lázaro rented for his business trip sped along northern Italy's Alpine highway. The driver was deep in thought, focused on the required banking operations he'd have to handle in the morning in Bern before his flight back to LA. He hardly noticed the comfortable ride of the expensive Mercedes, or the beauty of the surrounding scenery. His goal was to get to his destination as soon as possible and then return quickly home to his waiting lover. So far his business in Italy had gone smoothly, and everything suggested his plan would proceed as expected.

The luggage included two suitcases. The first had cash to be deposited in a bank account he intended to open in Bern. The second case contained expensive jewelry he planned to leave in the bank's safety deposit box.

In the distance the driver saw a line of headlights proceeding down the mountain but his thoughts were about the happiness that awaited him with Lucrecia. He was momentarily distracted by the bright lights of a train that passed by his side and seemed to cling to the mountainside as it roared by. But as he turned his attention back to the road, he was blinded by two bright headlights racing towards him and in the confusion he lost control. It all happened in an instant and the poor devil had no time to react before a violent, headlong crash flung the Mercedes into the air and it tumbled to the bottom of a ravine. There was a tremendous detonation as the gas tank exploded. The truck pulled over and stopped at the side of the road several hundred feet from the accident. The truck driver was the first to approach the burned wreckage followed later by the highway police. But the ravine's steep walls made access difficult and nothing could be done for hours to put out the flames until finally firefighters got them under control. All that remained of Lázaro's rental car was a twisted mass of smoking, charred metal. The wind scattered ashes leaving a white film on the rocks surrounding the destroyed vehicle. Lights from police cars illuminated the grim scene which looked from a distance like a huge, white candle flickering in the black of night.

"He must have been drunk," stated the truck driver. "He was going too fast and came straight at me until he swerved at the last second. There was no room for him to pass on the narrow road, and it was too late to avoid him. I was a blink away from ending up in the ravine myself."

Initially the police investigation could only recover unrecognizable, twisted metal shapes, and their search was made more difficult by the rain and mix of mud and rocks surrounding the smoldering wreckage. Though the license plate wasn't found, a detailed examination of the charred vehicle revealed the plate number. Human remains were found inside the car, but they were so terribly damaged that DNA testing was inconclusive. The luggage inside the vehicle had been destroyed except for some gems that survived the fire.

In Milan, where the investigation was based, it was determined that the automobile had been rented in Rome by one Lázaro Agüero, an Argentine billionaire who had arrived there three weeks earlier on business. It was determined that his wife was expecting him in LA on the following day. The investigators confirmed that Mr. Agüero had left his villa in Portofino two days before the accident. Italian authorities informed the Argentine consul about the accident, for although he had been living in the United States for a long time, Lázaro still traveled with an Argentine passport.

The scant human remains, cremated in the fire and turned completely to ashes, were gathered in a small urn and delivered to the consulate. A judge notified the widow of the death of her spouse and that gems had been recovered in the remains of the car and were left in storage. The judge declared the truck driver blameless, and the case was closed.

XII -THE TERRIBLE NEWS

Like aftershocks that follow an earthquake, the news of the accident in the Alps rippled through Los Angeles. The phone in Agüero's house rang and the answering machine picked up the call:

"This is Julio Corvalán, from the Argentine Consulate in Los Angeles. I need to speak with Mrs. Agüero regarding an urgent matter."

Lucrecia had been listening to the incoming message, and lifted the receiver. "This is Mrs. Agüero."

"I'm calling on behalf of the Consulate. I'm terribly sorry, Mrs. Agüero, but it's my duty to inform you. I have bad news."

"Bad news? About what? Has something happened to Lázaro?"

"Yes, ma'am, unfortunately that is the case. Your husband had a terrible accident while driving in the mountains in northern Italy on route to Switzerland."

"But… how is Lázaro? Is he hurt?"

"Ma'am, it was a terrible accident."

"But how is he? Can I speak to him?"

"I'm so sorry Mrs. Agüero. But your husband was killed instantly."

"This can not be. You must have made a mistake," Lucrecia said, weeping bitterly.

"I'm terribly sorry, ma'am."

There was a long silence at Lucrecia's end. After an appropriate pause she spoke.

"Please, tell me. His remains. Where are they? I want to collect them immediately."

"It won't be necessary for you to travel to Italy. There is nothing to see. The car went up in flames and the driver, we assume Mr. Agüero, was trapped inside and died in the fire."

"Oh my God," said Lucrecia.

"I'm terribly sorry. You have my condolences. Only ashes remain. They have been recovered and will be arriving from Milan tomorrow, Mrs. Agüero. I will call you later with flight details. Oh, and some jewelry was also found in the vehicle's frame. It's being held at the Varese Highway Patrol headquarters." Corvalán heard the widow's grief-stricken sobs over the telephone.

Lucrecia mumbled, "Thank you, Mr. Corvalán," and hung up.

Had Corvalán been able to see the woman on the other end of the call, he would have been surprised. Lucrecia's eyes were dry and her face expressionless.

A few hours after Corvalán's phone call, Lucrecia received a letter by express mail.

Rome, March 16

Lucrecia;

Just a short note to tell you that we had a lot of fun. The fishing trip was a complete success. The biggest prize was a fabulous trout that took the bait, and I assure you this trout will not be released back into the water.

Everything went perfectly. I'll tell you all about it as soon as I see you in Los Angeles.

Love,

Eduardo

Lucrecia's face lit up as she read Eduardo's short note. When she finished reading, she tossed it in the air and let herself dance crazily for several seconds as the paper floated to the floor. After calming down, she picked up the phone and dialed a number.

“Marisa? This is Lucrecia. I'm terribly sorry, but I have sad news and I want to be the one to tell you."

"Yes Lucrecia. I just read the terrible news in the newspaper,” replied Marisa sadly. "I can't believe he's dead."

"Then you know. Lázaro died in an accident in Italy!” exclaimed Lucrecia in a heavy, pain-filled voice. “Apparently his car crashed as he was crossing the Alps on route to Bern.”

“I read the details, but Lucrecia, please let me know the details of the funeral. I’m sorry for your loss.”

Despite their traumatic divorce, Marisa did not hate Lázaro, and still had some feelings for the father of her daughters. After all, Marisa had married for love and she was saddened when she read of his death.

“His remains will be arriving tomorrow, and the funeral will be held the following day,” Lucrecia told her. “I will keep you posted.”

XIII -LÁZARO'S WILL

As soon as she finished speaking to Marisa, Lucrecia had a long telephone conversation with Anthony Miller, the lawyer who handled Lázaro’s legal affairs. Miller was a prominent lawyer and Lázaro had dealt with him for twenty years.

“Have your read about my husband’s terrible accident in Italy? Did you see the newspaper?"

“Yes, Lucrecia. I’m so sorry. You know that Lázaro was both a client and a friend.”

“Mr. Miller, I would like you to send me a copy of Lázaro’s latest will. He told me he was going to sign it in your office before leaving for Europe.”

“I wish I could send it to you Lucrecia, but I’m afraid that isn’t possible. We finished the revisions and added the clauses you suggested that dealt with the bulk of his fortune and his intention to leave it to you. But before leaving for the airport, Lázaro stopped at my office and said he was running late and that he didn't have time to read it through carefully. So he took the will with him without signing it. He asked for the name of a good lawyer in Rome, and I recommended Tony Gambino, a man I know well and trust completely. I suggest you call attorney Gambino, and I'm sure that he can tell you the status of Lázaro's will."

After hanging up, Lucrecia dropped into a chair and heaved a lengthy sigh. Her eyes reflected both anxiety and determination as she dialed a telephone number in Rome.

"This is Mrs. Lázaro Agüero, and I'd like to speak to Mr. Gambino."

After a short pause, Gambino came to the phone. "This is attorney Gambino speaking. How can I help you?"

"Hello Mr. Gambino," said Lucrecia. "I am Lucrecia Agüero, Lázaros wife, and I've been informed by my lawyer, Anthony Miller, that my husband met with you regarding changes in his will. Are you familiar with that?"

"Yes, of course Mrs. Agüero. Nice to talk to you. Last week, we worked for several hours on the document Anthony Miller prepared for your husband. I believe Mr. Agüero was quite happy with the changes, and he left with the document signed and notarized. It should be in perfect order when he arrives in Los Angeles."

"So you haven't heard then. Unfortunately, my husband was killed in an terrible car accident, and I need you to send me signed copies of the document."

"I had not heard about the accident, and I am deeply sorry for your loss, Mrs. Agüero."

"Thank you, Mr. Gambino," said Lucrecia.

"But I'm afraid I can't send you the will. You see Mr. Agüero insisted on taking the signed original and all the copies with him. He said he planned to file them through Miller's office on his return. I recall he put the documents in a leather briefcase, so they must still be there."

"But my husband's car was completely destroyed."

"If your husband had them with him, perhaps the case it is in the possession of the highway police. You might try to contact them, Mrs. Agüero."

"I spoke with Julio Corvalán of the Argentine Consulate who informed me almost everything including the rental car was completely destroyed in the fiery crash that took my poor husband's life," said Lucrecia. "So I must have those copies," Lucrecia demanded.

"I'm sorry Mrs. Agüero. I want to accommodate you but I can not. It's not possible."

"Well you're no help at all, Mr. Gambino," Lucrecia slammed the phone down, wavering between disbelief and hysteria. Stumbling to the kitchen, she placed a couple of ice cubes in a glass and filled it with whiskey. She sat, slowly taking comfort in the drink as she sipped, wondering what to do next. It had all happened so fast! After calming somewhat, Lucrecia decided to call Miller again.

"Lucrecia, how are you…? Forgive me," apologized Miller. "of course, you're distraught."

"I don't know how I feel," replied Lucrecia, "but I'm a little confused. Attorney Gambino told me that Lázaro took the original and the copies of the new will with him, and that he does not have a signed copy. I also spoke with a person from Milan who said that anything recovered from the crash site is stored in a police warehouse in Varese, a short distance from the accident scene. What am I supposed to do? What if the briefcase can't be found?"

Miller, at a loss for words, paused, then finally spoke. "In that case the previous will that Lázaro signed over three years ago would be valid, and as you doubtless remember, the beneficiaries of that will are his ex-wife Marisa, and his daughters. That document is filed at our office."

"That can't be right. You know that's not what Lázaro intended," argued Lucrecia.

"I wish there was something I could do, but of course Marisa has a copy of the signed document," said Miller.

"But...but..." Lucricia protested.

After a brief pause, Miller changed the subject. "When is the funeral?"

"The day after tomorrow. It will be a brief ceremony. I'll let you know the details."

"Very well, I'll see you then," said Miller.

XIV -A WIDOW'S PAIN

The group that assembled for Lázaro's funeral included Marisa, her nine daughters, Miller, his son and partner, and a group of the deceased's friends and business associates who surrounded the widow to offer their condolences. The unadorned urn arrived from Milan and was placed on a small platform in front of the church altar. Lucrecia, looking drawn but composed, spoke quietly with the people gathered for the funeral.

As the guests chatted, a young man approached Lucrecia. She smiled as he came to her, and they moved aside to exchange a few words in private. Their brief conversation clearly deeply affected Lucrecia who could no longer hold back her tears. She trembled, weeping as she placed her hand on the urn and caressed its marble top.

The family's priest spoke briefly mentioning the few positive things he could come up with about Lázaro. Doing so required the priest to embellish his eulogy with fantasy. As he spoke, he split his gaze between Lucrecia, still weeping copiously, and Marisa and her daughters who were also moved by Lázaro's memorial.

Marisa couldn't stop staring at Lucrecia whose eyes flooded with tears that bathed her cheeks in torrents. Her spontaneous, and apparently genuine sadness surprised Marisa and the small circle of family at the funeral. Most of them, like Marisa and her family, had been convinced until then that Lucrecia married Lázaro for his money; that there had been nothing between them one would call love.

Lucrecia is either a first-rate actress or we were all wrong about her, though Marisa.

Attorney Miller, never easily surprised by anything, stood thoughtfully in front of the urn, his gaze unfocused.

A few days later, Marisa asked to see Miller, whom she had known well while married to Lázaro. "Do you know whether Lázaro had a new will drawn up after the one you prepared for him three years ago?" she asked.

"Since your ex-husband is dead and I am no longer bound by attorney-client privilege, I can tell you that I did draw up a new will for him. It named Lucrecia as his beneficiary, and reduced the portion assigned to you and your daughters to the lawful minimum."

Unsurprised, Marisa looked at him and asked, "Do you have a copy?"

"No, Lázaro took the original and the copies with him to Italy, and if I did have it, I could not show it to you without Lucrecia's authorization. Aguero was unhappy with a few of the provisions which he planned to modify during his stay in Italy. I'd recommended the services of a lawyer in Rome, Tony Gambino, who I've worked with in the past."

As if déjà vu, Miller listened as Marisa asked him the very same question Lucrecia had recently asked. "I suppose if the new will is not found, the previous one remains valid?"

"Of course," replied Miller with a stiff smile.

Marisa requested Attorney Gambino's phone number and left Miller's office looking pensive. She phoned the Italian lawyer upon arriving home.

"Attorney Gambino, this is Marisa Laverne calling from Los Angeles. Attorney Miller says you did some work for my ex-husband, Lázaro Agüero, who as you know was recently killed in a car accident. I believe you helped Lázaro revise his will during his recent trip to Rome."

"I did, Mrs. Laverne. Your ex-husband took the original and all copies with him," said Gambino.

"Would you be able to tell me what changes Lázaro made to the will?"

"I don't recall the specific wording Mrs. Laverne, but the effect of the changes to the will was to reduce the amount you and your daughters would receive, in favor of his new wife. I can't be more specific because we don't have copy in our files, and if we did, I could not provide it without authorization from Mrs. Agüero."

Marisa thanked Gambino and ended the call. As if paralyzed, she stood deep in thought, breathing deeply for a few minutes with the phone still pressed to her ear. She could not get the image out of her head of Lucrecia at the funeral; how heartbroken she appeared, weeping so heavily with her hand on the urn, and her tears that seemed real.

XV - LUCRECIA SEARCHES ALONG THE ROAD OF DEATH

After the funeral, Lucrecia took the first available flight to Milan. She had asked Eduardo Ramirez, an old friend who had come to Lázaro's memorial, to join her on the trip. They rented a car in Milan and headed north to the Alps intending to first go to the Varese highway police warehouse and examine items recovered from the accident. Lucrecia hoped to search the remnants for some trace of the lost will.

The highway police politely led them to the warehouse. The huge building held the remnants of recent highway accidents, each wreckage taking up only a few square feet of space. An officer led them to a spot that held the twisted metal skeleton – all that remained of the expensive rental car.

They found two open, badly dented metal cases but both were full of an ashy dust. Carefully searching the debris from the accident, they saw an unrecognizable heap of metal - all that was left of the engine, piles of scorched nuts, bolts, fragments of charred papers, and a mountain of crumbled glass that appeared to be from wine bottles. They did not found the briefcase which according to Gambino might contain the document Lucrecia needed urgently. She asked about the recovered gems and was told they were being held for her at the police station.

"Thank you, I'll pick them up on my return trip," she said, deeply disappointed at not finding the will. They again drove out towards Lucerne and soon arrived at the spot the highway the police described as accident scene.

They parked the car nearby at a lookout on the side of the road where a young couple, holding hands, was admiring the view. Eduardo and Lucrecia walked along the side of the highway to a spot where the guardrail had been recently repaired. Below they saw broken and charred tree trunks in the ravine, and the location matched the police description of the accident scene. Carefully, they made their way along the hazardous terrain to the spot where the damage was greatest. Melting snow and spring rains had softened the soil and turned the ravine into a mud hole. Shivering with cold, their muddy clothing soiled and disheveled, they scoured every inch of the area in their hunt for the golden fleece.

For over two hours they searched the area without success when Lucrecia tripped and sunk in mud almost to up her knees. Attempting to grab anything to break her fall, her fingers latched on an object. With tremendous effort she recovered her balance and lifted the object from the dirt. Grasping what might be a handle, she held up the mud-covered object and shouted excitedly to Eduardo.

"Eduardo, I think I may have found it!"

They climbed the slope, struggling to get back to the edge of the road where they carefully examined the precious find. Wiping mud off the case, Lucrecia thought that it was in fact the remains of Lázaro's leather briefcase. She attempted to pry it open, but the clasp had been ruined by the fire.

"Damn it!" exclaimed a frustrated Lucrecia. But before she could say anything more, a deep voice spoke from behind them.

"You are under arrest!"

XVI -A SKILLFUL INTERROGATION

Lucrecia turned and saw the young couple whom she and Eduardo had seen holding hands when they arrived at the accident scene. The stern voice was that of Inspector Travaglini from the Investigation Division of the Milan police, and the woman with him, whom they had assumed was his girlfriend, was in reality his assistant. Clearly the police had been waiting for them.

Lucrecia and Eduardo were caught off guard, covered in mud and stiff from the cold. The unexpected interruption by the police imbued the moment with threatening overtones.

"Under arrest? Are you accusing us of a crime? I demand to know what's going on," asked Lucrecia.

"You have not been formally accused of anything at the moment," the inspector replied courteously. "We are simply following a lead, and both of you will be detained until our investigation is complete. We want to ask a few questions, though of course you have the right not to respond. But I hope you will cooperate."

Inspector Travaglini made a phone call, and a patrol car promptly arrived at the scene and took the reluctant suspects to the Milan police station. Upon their arrival, Inspector Travaglini looked at their passports, then sat them at a table and asked Lucrecia to place the charred briefcase in front of them.

"We have the right to request our attorney before answering any questions," said Lucrecia.

"You do, madam," Travaglini replied offhandedly. "You could hire an attorney in Milan or have yours flown in from Los Angeles. But until you do, we have a court order to keep you here for your inquiries."

"Under protest but for the sake of expediency I will cooperate. What exactly do you want to know?" Lucrecia demanded.

"What are you looking for in the briefcase?" asked the inspector.

"It's the briefcase my husband always carried and should contain his personal letters and documents. I want to recover them. There can't be anything wrong with that, Inspector."

"That's perfectly understandable, madam. Then would you please open it," said the inspector.

Hands shaking and after quite a bit of struggling, Lucrecia freed the battered, metal clasp. Inside the briefcase was a shapeless mass of charred papers which the police spread across the table while Lucrecia looked on. The documents were obviously ruined and undecipherable.

"We have the contents of the briefcase, then. But now the truth, please. What were you expecting to find?"

All this time Eduardo sat white as a sheet of paper.

"I've already explained what I hoped to find, and I'm upset that the documents are unrecognizable," replied Lucrecia. "Haven't you caused me enough discomfort detaining us here after I lost my beloved husband? You expect me to provide reasons for trying to recover his personal documents?"

"I apologize, madam. It is surely not our desire to torment you, but there are details about the accident that we don't understand and would like to clear up," said Travaglini. "The investigation was closed by the district judge, but was reopened at our request. For when we gathered the remains of the vehicle to place them in the warehouse, we found a ring which didn't make sense to us, given what we thought we knew about the occupant."

"You would detain a widow and put us through all this because you found a stupid ring?"said Lucrecia.

"It's not my wish to inconvenience you. However, there are things about this 'stupid ring' we cannot decipher," explained Inspector Travaglini. Pausing, he took the charred ring from his pocket and placed it on the table in front of Lucrecia and Eduardo. "Does this ring look familiar?" he demanded.

"No!" Lucrecia and Eduardo answered together.

"I've never seen it," added Lucrecia immediately.

"Can you make out the initials engraved on the ring?" inquired the inspector.

Lucrecia studied the ring for a long time, and though trembling inside, her face appeared calm. She stated firmly, "I can see an "M" and a "P".

"And that is precisely what we don't understand. Your husband's initials were "L" and "A" were they not?"

"Yes," agreed Lucrecia.

"You might be interested to know that the ring was found inside the wrecked car."

"Lázaro did not wear a ring, not even a wedding ring," said Lucrecia. "Rings irritated his fingers. So, what is puzzling about finding a ring like this among the jewelry Lázaro carried in his luggage?" asked Lucrecia.

"It would not be of interest at all were that the case. However the jewelry Lázaro carried was inside one of the suitcases. This ring was not," explained the inspector.

"So you're saying the ring was found on one of his fingers?" Lucrecia asked.

"Not exactly," replied Travaglini. "The remains no longer had fingers. The ring was found among the ashes we sent to Los Angeles."

"I still don't understand. Lázaro could have had a ring and who knows how many other things in his pockets for reasons I can't imagine," Lucrecia stated confidently.

The inspector continued in the same professional tone. "Let me help you, Mrs. Agüero. A man named Mariano Peña was on the same Rome-to-Chicago flight as your husband. Do you recognize the name?"

"I don't recall anyone with that name. No," said Lucrecia.

"Mr. Eduardo Ramirez was also on that same flight. That's your companion's name according to his passport," the inspector added impassively. "You obviously recognize the man you are with, right?"

"Yes." Looking like a frightened child, rare for Lucrecia, she looked to Eduardo who sat listening, pale and scared as the inspector continued his skillful interrogation. She replied quietly with her head down, "Just a coincidence, so what?" she stumbled.

"After finding the ring, we went over the passenger list for the flight that Mr. Agüero took to Rome. Then we got in touch with the travel agent who issued the tickets for both Mariano Peña and Eduardo Ramirez. The travel agent informed us that they had been paid for with a credit card in your name," the inspector calmly stated. "Do you remember that?"

"Yes. Yes, I do," sobbed Lucrecia.

"Then, help me understand, Mrs. Agüero. What does it mean that Mariano Peña's ring was found among the remains of the driver of the car that your husband rented?"

After a long silence, Lucrecia whispered, her voice barely loud enough to be heard, "It's possible that the person who died in the accident might not have been my husband. Maybe it was the man - Mariano Peña - who you mentioned."

"I know what you were looking for in the charred briefcase, madam. But I'm interested in something else. If, as the ring with the MP initials suggests, the ashes we sent to you in Los Angeles were the remains of Mariano Peña, then what happened to Mr. Agüero?" the inspector demanded.

"I don't know. I swear it," a shaky Lucrecia replied.

For the first time, Travaglini turned towards Eduardo and asked him directly, "Where is Lázaro Agüero?"

XVII -TUSCAN ROULADE

Inspector Travaglini stood over Eduardo coolly continuing his interrogation. "So where is Agüero, Mr. Ramirez? Tell me exactly what happened?"

Trembling due to Travaglini's intimidating interrogation and suspecting the inspector knew more than he was saying, Eduardo replied, "If I cooperate, will it go better for me?"

"If you don't cooperate, it may go badly for you," said the inspector leaning into Eduardo's face.

"Well..."

"I mean it Eduardo."

"Well, Agüero was speeding as if he was familiar with the road," said Eduardo. "It wasn't easy keeping up with him in the Fiat that Mariano had stolen in Rome. We didn't want to rent a car to avoid revealing our names."

"Go on," Inspector Travaglini demanded.

"We followed Mr. Agüero to his villa in Portofino," said Eduardo, "where he stayed a few days while we kept watch nearby. We had to move the car frequently to avoid suspicion while we waited around.

"We expected him to head north since we believed his destination was Bern, but he surprised us by going south towards Tuscany. We followed him where he headed southeast to Siena and then turned onto a narrow road heading south."

"And then?" prompted Travaglini.

"We figured that for some unknown reason, Agüero was returning to Rome which would ruin our plan. But about thirty kilometers south of Siena, he turned onto a narrow road that passed by hills and vineyards, arriving finally, at a small town called Montalcino where he had lunch, bought a few cases of wine, and by mid-afternoon he returned and headed back north.

"He drove past Siena and through the heart of Tuscany. Unexpectedly, he stopped at the top of a hill covered with vines. We assumed Agüero was getting out to enjoy the spectacular view although it was getting dark and cloudy.

"Mariano thought this was our chance and we parked our car next to his Mercedes. Agüero must have thought we had the same idea, and said, 'What an extraordinary landscape! It's enchanting, don't you agree?'"

"We exchanged small talk until at one point he turned to speak to me." Eduardo fell silent a moment.

"And then?" the inspector demanded.

"Well that's when Mariano hit him as hard as he could with a blackjack and Agüero dropped to the ground like a stone.

"We bound Agüero with ropes in a fetal position, then stuffed him in the Fiat's trunk, He looked like a roulade. Mariano cut the tips of Agüero's fingers off with a wire-cutter so nobody could identify his remains, then Mariano hit him with the blackjack two more times. 'So he won't suffer,' said Mariano as he slammed the trunk shut.

"We drenched the Fiat in gas and laid a long fuse to give us time to be far enough away before the car exploded. Mariano stopped to light it, and we sped away.

I returned to Rome on a scooter that we brought in the Fiat, while Mariano continued on to Switzerland in the Mercedes. Mariano told me he was supposed to deposit the jewels and the money in a safety deposit box before returning to Los Angeles. That's it. That's what happened, sir."

Travaglini asked, "Did you actually see the car catch fire?"

Eduardo shrugged his shoulders and mumbled, "We did not see the fire or hear the explosion, and I don't think we would have since the fuse was so long and we'd sped away. If the car didn't explode, I have no idea what happened to Agüero."

Eduardo was exhausted after his confession and he turned pale and looked terrified as he sunk deep in his chair. Lucrecia listened to it all with her eyes shut tight.

"Well," said Travaglini, "now we know more, but we still don't know what happened to Agüero."

XVIII -A VISIT TO THE ASYLUM

After Eduardo's confession, the Milan police sent out a bulletin with a description of Agüero asking for information about a man missing somewhere in Tuscany. Inspector Travaglini had just received a report that a vineyard owner found a person badly beaten but still alive, left in an abandoned car. It occurred to the inspector that the person found in Gaiole at Giuseppe's vineyard could possibly be Lázaro.

The man from the vineyard remained unidentified and the police were also informed that the victim in Gaiole had been transferred to an insane asylum. Inspector Travaglini took Lucrecia and Eduardo with him to the asylum in hopes of determining if the patient was Lázaro.

When the inspector, Lucrecia and Eduardo arrived at the patient's room, it was immediately clear to Lucrecia that the man in a straitjacket was indeed Lázaro. Lucrecia shuddered when she saw his gaunt face, expressionless eyes, and his stiff, oily, uncombed hair He was sitting up in a wide chair, held firmly to its back by wide leather straps. .

Travaglini observed it all with an almost scientific curiosity, and stood in a corner of the room to observe the encounter. Lucrecia approached Lázaro slowly and stood near without touching him. Though her face was emotionless, Travaglini had the impression she was fearful that Lázaro would recognize her. It was obvious she didn't know what to expect of her husband in this condition. Since he hadn't died, she probably hoped that at the very least, he'd lost all memory.

Travaglini noticed a change in Lucrecia's breathing, and it became obvious after a few minutes of silence that the patient did not seem to recognize either Lucrecia or Eduardo. She moved in closer, placing her face in front of Lázaro's and staring into his eyes. Lázaro didn't seem to notice her but stared ahead as if contemplating an imaginary scene. It was as if he was looking right through her. Lucrecia stepped back slowly, perhaps fearful she might break the spell.

For his part, Eduardo, who got no further than the doorway. might as well have turned to stone. When Travaglini realized that the meeting would offer nothing more for the investigation, he left the room, followed by a much relieved Lucrecia and Eduardo.

The inspector sat the two detainees in different rooms so he could question them separately. He spoke to the attending physician for a long time about Lázaro's mental state and his prospects for recovery.

XIX -THE DEAD DON'T SPEAK

For a moment Lucrecia considered denying she had recognized the patient, but soon realized Inspector Travaglini could probably determine Lázaro's identity. They had no options and after further interrogation by the inspector, both admitted the man was definitely Lázaro Agüero. Only then was Inspector Travaglini satisfied, and he planned to leave any remaining action to the Italian judiciary.

It had been revealed during the investigation that Lucrecia and Mariano Peña had lived together in Chicago for five years prior to her moving to Los Angeles. Counsel for the defense underlined Mariano's role as the main perpetrator in the attempted murder of Lázaro, chiefly responsible for the harm he suffered. Eduardo's defense focused on his testimony that Mariano had hired him to do a "job" in Italy, and that although he accompanied Mariano on the trip, he took no active role in the car theft or the assault on Lázaro, though he was present at the scene.

The defense relied on heavily on the truism that the dead don't speak in his arguments on behalf of his two clients. But the judge was not swayed by the argument that the "job" had been exclusively performed by Mariano. Eduardo was still sentenced to fifteen years in prison as Mariano's main accomplice.

When it came to Lucrecia, the prosecution argued that she was primarily responsible for the plot to murder her husband.

Marisa attended the trial in Italy, and finally understood the reason for Lucrecia's copious tears during the funeral. Lucrecia had been weeping for Mariano's death, and not for Lázaro's.

Most damming as proof of Lucrecia's intent was that she had used her credit card to pay for her friends' airline tickets. But the prosecution could offer no legal proof that she had hired them to murder Lázaro because Eduardo would not testify against Lucrecia and denied any knowledge of her participation in planning the "job." He claimed to be surprised by the evidence proving that Lucrecia had paid for his ticket and pointed out that Mariano had handled the trip details. He testified that he wasn't at all surprised that Lucrecia had endeavored to recover the will which benefited her. Wasn't that to be expected?

At that point the trial took an unexpected turn. Lucrecia could not be found guilty of murder since Lázaro, as if risen from the dead, was found alive in the asylum. For his part, Lázaro was mentally incompetent and remembered nothing. The court ruled that although Lucrecia was still legally married to Lázaro, she was guilty of planning the crime and her participation disqualified her from inheriting her husband's assets. Those assets, in accord with the original will, would go to Marisa and her daughters.

A good lawyer recommended by Miller and ironically paid for with Lázaro's funds was able to obtain a relatively light sentence for Lucrecia that allowed her to remain under probation after a few years in jail. Miller invoked professional ethics as the reason for not taking on Lucrecia's defense but, at the judge's request, he accepted the role of administrator of Lázaro's assets until they were transfered to Marisa.

Despite everything that had happened, Marisa, occasionally accompanied by one or another of her daughters, would visit Lázaro. His only other regular visitor was Miller who faithfully fulfilled his responsibilities as administrator and oversaw the quality of care the patient received per the judge's orders.

It was difficult for attorney Miller, who had participated in and witnessed the entire trial, to determine if justice had been adequately served. Mariano was dead. Eduardo was jailed, which pleased the attorney. But Miller was ambivalent about whether or not Lucrecia had been adequately sentenced for the attempt to kill her husband.

Years later after Lucrecia was released, she received a heavy package, delivered together with a brief note:

> I'm sending you the ashes, over which you wept so profusely. I feel no bitterness towards you.
>
> Marisa

XX -THE FINAL JUDGMENT

I don't know how many moons have passed. I'm finally alone with the crickets which fall silent for hours after the injections. The crickets abandon me momentarily, but in the end, they came back...only to leave again. Like the crickets, things around me vanish gradually, wrapping me in a fog that is increasingly thick, and I am alone. Forever.

When my isolation from the rest of the world was complete, and it occurred I might be dead, I heard a firm, high-pitched voice calling me, "Lázaro." That was the name my visitors used, and I recognized that it was the voice of a woman.

"Lázaro," she said, "your passage through the world has ended, and you must face the final judgment now. I have reviewed your earthly record, and it is obvious that you have done a lot of harm to yourself and to many others. You have been the architect of your own fate, and you have not paid for your cardinal sin."

"It's true that I tried to run away from the asylum and that I enjoyed walking free along the street. But my freedom did not last long," replied Lázaro, "and I confess that I am not sorry about that."

"No, Lázaro. That small breach of the rules is unimportant. There is, however, something significant in your record that you don't even remember, but I have it underscored on my list. Your cardinal sin is your selfishness and your macho arrogance.

"Marisa and your children loved you, as did many of the women you abused for your selfish pleasure. You've shown contempt for women and treated them as objects all your earthly life. You lived as if women existed solely to serve you and as if you were the center of the universe. That, Lázaro is your cardinal sin."

Her words surprised me, for although I had always known I would face some form of reckoning in my final hours, I had expected to hear a man's, deep baritone voice. I never imagined God could be a woman.

I was alarmed by God's gender, but I thought being a male would not count against me given the divine's equanimity. According to her verdict and from vague memories of my life in the asylum, but mostly from what I could glimpse through the magic rings of smoke, I slowly began to realize the truth and what the voice was telling me; that for centuries man had made the rules solely for his own benefit, and I had contributed to this abuse by treating women as inferior.

In my defense, I reminded the divine that as an inmate in the asylum, I had little recollection of my past egotism or of a chauvinistic attitude, and I did not recall any sins.

The divine responded that forgetfulness is not a valid excuse, and that I was of sound judgment during all the time I sinned. I thought of my own pleasure only without considering the consequences of my actions on human beings whose feelings for me were genuine.

Knowing my thoughts as only God can, the voice continued, "In recognition of your earthly suffering and allowing your recent condition as a mitigating factor, I grant a reduction in your punishment. Consider it an act of divine grace you may enjoy for all eternity."

I pleaded with her to be lenient saying that I was not the first chauvinist who considered himself the center of the universe.

The divine voice responded, "This is true Lázaro, but every guilty person must be punished, and I assure you there is a day of reckoning for each of them. They've all been punished and today is your turn.

"I grant you complete freedom to travel through all my celestial realms where you will find no one around to disturb you as you contemplate the man you are. The punishment for your terrestrial selfishness is an eternal boredom - that you will be able to see only yourself, and not anything or anyone else...for all eternity."

The divine verdict was unfair, and I thought her sentence was excessive for crimes that I could not remember even when I tried to recall them through the magic rings of smoke. Looking into the rings I was shocked to encounter my recurrent nightmare and to see again the faceless women, undoubtedly those I'd abused, dancing frantically around me and then, in a moment of agonizing pain, they faded one by one into the shadows of the night.

That's when I was struck by dreadful realization - that there would be no appealing God's word.

Lázaro, Lázaro, Lázaro, Lázaro ... its echo persisted for a few moments until it was lost in an eternal nighttime. Then there was only silence...and me, me, only me...

About the Author

Félix Fernández Madrid was born in Chivilcoy, Buenos Aires province, Argentina, and has lived in the United States since 1960. Fernández Madrid obtained his medical degree at the University of Buenos Aires, and did an internship and internal medicine residency at the University Hospital, "Hospital de Clínicas José de San Martín in Buenos Aires.

Post-graduate studies in molecular biology at the University of Miami, Florida led to a PhD in Physiology, Cellular and Molecular Biology. Subsequently he became Chief of Rheumatology at Wayne State University School of Medicine in Detroit, Michigan where he is a professor of internal medicine.

In addition to clinical activity, his academic activity centers on teaching internal medicine and rheumatology, and doing basic research on the relationship between autoimmunity and breast carcinogenesis.

Fernández Madrid has published numerous scientific papers and books for the layman, "Treating Arthritis", *Medicine, Myth and Magic*. In addition, his writing includes various works of a non-scientific nature including G*ray and Pink Tales*, a collection of short stories, *Calidoscopio*, a collection of poems in Spanish, and *Che Guevara and the Incurable Disease*, the latter published in English.

Books by the Author

Calidoscopio. Ebook Bakery, 2018, is a collection of poems and allegorical paintings with symbolism. "*Calidoscopio* is a hymn to the art of poetry and the poetry of art, a song to life and death that faithfully reveals the intimacy of human nature."

"This is a perspective with constant twists that allows appreciation of the spectrum extending between sublime beauty and ultimate human misery, like an exotic Middle Eastern bazaar that we visit to enjoy shapes, colors, aromas, and sounds, at once common and strange." Sylvia Pellizari.

* * *

Che Guevara and the Incurable Disease, Dorrance Publishing Co., Pittsburg 1997. Félix and Che Guevara played rugby together on the same standby team for San Isidro Club in Argentina where Félix was the team captain of the Reserve Division, and years later they were classmates at the Buenos Aires School of Medicine, where they both obtained their medical degrees on the same day of 1953.

Fernández Madrid offers a perspective of Che's deeds, based on speculation and historical facts, introducing the concept of the incurable disease as the source that is largely responsible for the oppression and wretchedness afflicting the world today. In Félix's opinion, the incurable disease is fear, paranoia, and loss of mobility experienced by a society essentially motivated by money and blind to the hardships and economic oppression of a huge segment of the world's population.

* * *

Treating Arthritis, Medicine, Myth and Magic, Plenum Press, New York 1989.

In the words of one of the luminaries in the science of rheumatology, Daniel J. McCarthy, "If you are one of over 40 million people seeking relief from arthritis, you will be fascinated by the information provided by Dr. Fernández Madrid, a leading rheumatology expert. In this comprehensive study of unusual or unorthodox primitive, mythical, and contemporary treatments, we find that many of these cures for arthritis sought by the public have clearly been practiced for centuries.

Unique in its approach, *Treating Arthritis: Medicine, Myth and Magic* will arouse vital interest in people suffering from arthritis who seek that long-awaited cure among ancient treatments and what modern medicine offers."

J. McCarty, Jr., M.D., Professor of Medicine at the University of Chicago.

Cuentos Grises y Rosados (Gray and Pink Tales). Ediciones La Lámpara Errante, Buenos Aires 1999. A collection of short stories now out of print. Some of these stories have been included in *The Magic Ring and Other Stories.*

www.ingramcontent.com/pod-product-compliance
Lightning Source LLC
LaVergne TN
LVHW010054110826
845155LV00028B/328

* 9 7 8 1 9 5 3 0 8 0 4 1 7 *